WITHDRAWN

the truth and lies
of ella black

the
truth
and
lies
of
ella
black

emily barr

PHILOMEL BOOKS

PHILOMEL BOOKS
an imprint of Penguin Random House LLC
375 Hudson Street
New York, NY 10014

Library of Congress Cataloging-in-Publication Data
Names: Barr, Emily, author.
Title: The truth and lies of Ella Black / Emily Barr.
Description: New York, NY : Philomel Books, [2019] | "Published in Great Britain by
Penguin Children's in 2018." | Summary: Ella, seventeen, has a very dark side—Bad
Ella, or Bella—but when she is whisked away to Brazil and learns she is adopted,
she questions everything she thought she knew about herself. | Identifiers: LCCN
2018007948 | ISBN 9780399547041 (hardcover) | ISBN 9780399547065 (e-book)
Subjects: | CYAC: Identity—Fiction. | Mental illness—Fiction. | Runaways—Fiction.
| Adoption—Fiction. | Love—Fiction. | Family life—England—Fiction. | Brazil—
Fiction. | England—Fiction. | Classification: LCC PZ7.1.B3726 Tru 2019
| DDC [Fic]—dc23 | LC record available at https://lccn.loc.gov/2018007948
Printed in the United States of America.

ISBN 9780399547041
1 3 5 7 9 10 8 6 4 2
Design by Ellice M. Lee.
Text set in Stone Serif ITC TT.

FOR CRAIG

CHAPTER ONE

I AM HUDDLED on a bench, shivering, but I don't care about being a bit cold, because I'm busy. I have a pencil and a sketchpad balanced on my knees, and I'm sitting in a park in front of a view that has the Houses of Parliament in it, leaning on Jack, who is reading a book. I'm totally focused on my drawing. I'm not actually drawing the view in front of me; I do have a few pages of Big Bens in my sketchbook, but it's just not the thing that seems to be appearing on the page.

"Are you nearly done?" says Jack. "I mean, you have to take as long as it takes, but it's going to rain and . . ."

He leans over and looks at my drawing.

"Oh," he says. "Oh, right—a metaphorical interpretation of the view?"

"Yep."

"Ella Black has made me shiver on a bench for an hour so that she could draw a picture of . . . Ella Black."

"It's not Ella Black."

"Sorry to break this to you, sweetie, but I think it really is."

I look at it. She looks like me but she isn't me. She has the same newly dyed purple hair, the same pale face, but there's something in

1

the eyes . . . I wish Jack could see that, though I don't know how I could possibly expect him to. I have never told him and I never will. I laugh a bit, from nerves, and he does too.

"How's your book?" I say.

"Brilliant, actually. The apocalypse is well under way. Hey. You know, you're right. This doesn't look quite like you. It's like you with psychotic eyes, isn't it? It's you thinking about something you really, really hate."

I look at him. I steady my breathing. "Yes," I say. "Yes, actually. It really is."

"You're not thinking about me, are you?"

I look at Jack: blond, unexceptional-looking and one of my two best friends in the world. One of my only two friends in the world. I love his face. I love the way we know each other's secrets. Actually, I know his big secret, but he doesn't know all of mine.

"Of course I'm not thinking about you, you dick," I say, and a raindrop falls right onto my drawing and blurs its face. I close the sketchpad, and Jack puts away his apocalyptic thriller, and we run to a big tree and stand underneath it. We look at the rain and the people putting up umbrellas and hoods and walking fast to unimaginable places. We wait for it to ease up enough for us to walk to Trafalgar Square and catch a train home to Kent.

We ran away to London because it was half term. We spent the morning going to free galleries and looking at art, and then we bought some books and went to sit in the park. I tried to draw the lovely view, but I ended up drawing myself with psychotic eyes instead. I know why I did, though, and I'm glad I did.

By the time we get to Charing Cross, rush hour has started. It's later than we realized, even though I was literally looking at one of the most famous clocks in the world for quite a lot of the afternoon.

"Massive miscalculation," says Jack.

"I know, right?"

We stand and look at the people on the concourse. It is much busier than it ought to be, not just with commuters (though mainly with them) but also with half-term people like Jack and me, people who have come to London to look at the sights and then forgotten that you need to get a train home either earlier or later than this. If we get the right train, it will take only forty minutes, but it might be an uncomfortable ride. We live in a commuter town, and people are going home by the thousands. It infuriates me. It makes me particularly angry because we have to make our way through it if we want to get home. All of a sudden, I long to yell at them to get out of my way.

The journey is horrible, and although I try hard to fight it off, by the time we are halfway back, my head is ringing. I'm standing up, separated from Jack by two businessmen types who got on at London Bridge and are pretending they're still at work. One is pressing right up against me, reading some boring financial thing on his iPad. The other is hanging on to a pole as desperately as if he were a stripper, and making a very important phone call about a shareholders' meeting. My head is ringing, I tell myself, because I'm standing, and tired, and fed up. I haven't got my phone for distraction, because I lost it yesterday. I can't talk to Jack because he's too far away. I have to live in the moment, and everything is blurred around the edges because

I am standing and tired and fed up. I mutter to myself to try to keep it together. No one cares. No one notices.

By the time we're walking back to my house, though, I know things are going wrong. I should not have drawn that picture. My ears are ringing with a high-pitched sound even though we're out in the open air, hand in hand, looking normal. Sometimes grabbing Jack's hand can ground me, and he never minds me doing that. I try to make this feeling stop. I try to use Jack's energy to balance myself.

The ringing gets louder.

It

gets

louder and louder.

And although I am walking toward my house, and though I look normal, I know that I'm not a normal girl and that I have to get to the safe place; I have to get to my bedroom, with the door closed. I have to be on my own now.

I squeeze Jack's hand, and he squeezes back because he has no idea what is going on inside my head. The pavement is dark with recent rain, and the clouds are gathering again, but right now the sunset is making the sky look like a purple bruise, and everything looks like a painting.

Please go, I say internally. *Go now. You can come back later.*

She makes my vision go a bit blotchy around the edges, and that's her way of saying, NOT. LATER. NOW.

"Actually," I say to Jack, "I need to do some art homework." I'm trying to breathe evenly, to appear normal. He doesn't seem to have noticed anything different.

"I will not impose upon the artiste any longer," he says. He flings

4

a hand dramatically across his brow. "I need to paint! I live for my art! Is that you saying you want me to bugger off?"

"Would you mind? I mean it in a nice way." Bella is pressing on the inside of my head. I have to get him to go. I do wonder whether he can tell something is off, particularly after this afternoon, but doesn't ask because he knows I don't want him to. I wish I could tell him but I can't.

I can't because I'm not brave enough. The part of me the world sees is a bit of a pushover, easily bullied, easily ignored. That's the better version of me: I don't dare to try to be belligerent, particularly at a time like this, because anything could happen. The girl in my drawing might come pouring out and poison all of this. That would be the end of everything.

Jack knows I want him to go, but I can see in his eyes that he is sad.

"OK, fine. You can come in for a minute," I say, feeling Bella listening carefully to every word I say, "and then—well, then yes, you can bugger off. I've got, like, a whole painting to finish and you know I'm not very sociable when that happens. Only Humphrey can come anywhere near."

Jack laughs. "You spoil that cat."

Then it's raining again, so we run the last bit, hand in hand, up the hill to my house. We run past a woman with long tangled hair who's struggling to put up an umbrella, and a man pushing a bike with a toddler on the back. The toddler waves at us and shouts, "I gettin' wet!"

I wave back with my free hand and feel Bella in the other,

gripping Jack, trying to use her powers to electrocute him, wishing he would die because he is normal and happy and she doesn't think that's fair.

Jack is not really normal and happy, but he is, compared with Bella. I love him. Everyone thinks he's my boyfriend, but he's not: he's better than that. We have a thing that works for both of us.

I don't want a real boyfriend. I don't think I'll ever want a relationship. My school is a posh girls' school, but a lot of the sixth-formers live in a world in which they defer absolutely to boys. It's pathetic and it makes me mad, but I haven't been brave enough to say anything, because that would draw more unwelcome attention. Actually, if I tried to argue with them, Bella would jump out and smash the nearest simpering handmaiden with the closest fire extinguisher, so it's probably best that I bite it back.

Jack likes the best side of me, which is the only thing he sees. Hanging out with me has helped him in all sorts of ways, and for a while he raised my status so I was not a top-level target. But that didn't last long, and soon after, the girls at school started on me again. I don't really know why they do it, except that I've always known I don't fit in. I expect the girls who are mean to me don't feel they fit in either, and probably they're using me to make themselves feel better. I don't know. All I know is that I am not widely liked, and that feels like shit.

I've never told Jack about the things that happen to me at school. He would only get upset and mad, and nothing would change, apart from him being a little less happy. And I want Jack to be happy. Only Lily, my other best friend, knows what happens, and Lily protects me from it as much as she can.

When we burst in, Mum is standing in the hallway, pretending she just happens to be there, holding something in her hands and smiling in smug anticipation.

I look at it. "My phone!" I say, and she grins and holds it out to me.

"Someone handed it in," she says. "The police called and I picked it up. It restores your faith, doesn't it?"

Mum is just saying that because it's a cliché: she doesn't need her faith restored. She's not disillusioned or cynical about anything, though she does make sure to keep me as safe as she possibly can at all times, from dangers that don't actually exist. I take my phone from her and quickly check it; everything's exactly as it was when I last saw it yesterday morning, just before I lost it in town.

I don't think Mum has looked through it. I hope she hasn't.

Bella is inside my head, clearing her throat, demanding attention. I push her aside.

Mum doesn't look as if she's had a shocking insight into my school life. She is happy to see us, Jack and me. She lives for us. She stands around in the hall waiting for me to come home because I am her life. It's weird. Obviously it's nice, but I do feel bad for her, because her life must be boring. Sometimes I try to imagine my way into her head, and I just can't. I don't think she has a dark side at all.

She would be so upset if she knew the truth about me. That's why I can never tell her. Right now Bella is knocking on the inside of my skull, and I need to get away.

As soon as we are through the door, Mum clicks all the locks shut behind us. No house is quite as secure as ours.

For as long as I can remember, keeping me safe has pretty much been Mum's career. She is compelled to make sure I am always safe—always, always safe, all the time. It's almost funny that she relaxes when I'm tucked away in my bedroom, considering the fact that it's actually the danger zone.

Jack is grinning back at her.

"How are you, Mrs. Black?" he says in his polite way. "You're looking lovely."

She loves that. Mum adores Jack. She wants us to get married and give her lots of grandchildren. Again, she has no idea that that can never happen, which is sweet. I say nothing, because Bella is in my head and I can't talk very well at the moment.

"Cookie?" she says. "I've just made some. Still warm from the oven."

I'm not going to stop to have a cookie, but I'll save some for Bella because she might like them later. Unless they're the spelt-and-sweet-potato ones Mum made last week, too, in which case no one will ever, ever want one.

"No, thanks," I say.

"Yes, please," says Jack at the same time. He's hoping for the chocolate chip cookies, I know it.

While he follows her into the kitchen, I walk straight ahead and go into the bathroom and close the door and lock it and lean against it and try to breathe. I have to get rid of them both. I have to make Jack go home in the next few minutes. My head tightens. Black spots dance across my vision.

He is sitting at the table, flirting with Mum. They both do that. I think Jack finds it funny. God only knows what Mum is up to. She grins at him and looks coquettish and reminisces about her youth, and he laughs in all the right places and says the right things back to her. Neither of them particularly cares whether I'm bothered when they do this, and although it's gross, I just roll my eyes and look away.

I hear Mum say the cookies are ginger and sultana. That's just about acceptable, so I do my best to clear my head. I unlock the bathroom door and try to act normal, taking three cookies and wrapping them in a paper towel.

"Sorry, Jack," I say, and under Mum's approving eye I walk over and kiss the top of his head. "Got to do some painting. See you tomorrow."

He laughs. "Sure. See you tomorrow, Ells. I won't hang around."

"You're welcome to—" Mum starts to say, but I silence her with a glare and leave the room, gasping for breath, taking the stairs two at a time.

I close my bedroom door and try to breathe. My head is ringing so loudly, I wouldn't be able to hear anything else, not even a fire alarm or a nuclear siren if it went off. Maybe one of those things is happening right now. But I don't care if it is. I roll up my sleeves and look at the tiny lines on the insides of my arms. I'm ashamed of them. I'm never going to let that happen again. They are so small that only I know they're there.

Be nice, I say to Bella.

BE NICE, she replies, imitating me. *BE NICE. ALWAYS BE NICE.*

Oh, please stop.

PLEASE STOP. PLEASE STOP. PLEASE STOP.

Leave me alone.

LEAVE ME ALONE.

Leave

me

alone.

LEAVE.

I don't know what is me and what is her.

I put my hands to the sides of my face and scream silently like the painting. All I want is to be normal.

I draw in a shuddery breath and press the palms of my hands on the carpet, feeling the floor, being here in this moment, myself in my room. One thing I have learned over the years is how to pretend, and when this door is closed, I don't have to pretend anymore. It can all come out.

I pull the pictures out from under the bed. They are meticulous explosions of horror. They are filled with death and maiming and nightmares. Bella drew them, and she likes to look at them. Perhaps I can assuage her with them.

I call her Bella because she is the dark side of me. It's Ella but not. It's Bad Ella. Bella. I gave her a name a few years ago and that made it a bit better, because before that I called it the Monster. Anything is a tiny bit better when it has a name. Bella is better than the Monster. I didn't know then that *Bella* means "beautiful": my Bella isn't beautiful at all. She is the opposite. But she's still Bella.

Bella is desperate to own the whole of me: as Ella, I am alert and battling all the time. Sometimes I have to let Bella out before everything explodes. That's when she draws these pictures. It's scary, but after that happens, I feel calm and peaceful and, I think, kind of happy. Everything is balanced for a while. I look at the drawings now. They are done in black ink—huge sheets of tiny detail like Hieronymus Bosch, but with modern bits in them. Children are decapitated here. Body parts are everywhere. There is blood and murder. These pictures take us ages and I hope no one ever finds them, but they're definitely the best art I've ever done.

But today is different.

She doesn't want to look at them now. *LATER,* she says.

It's hard to breathe. The ringing grows louder. I push my hands down on the carpet and try harder. Humphrey is waiting, I see. Humphrey always turns up when Bella's here.

"Have a cookie," I say desperately, and I unfold the paper towel and let them all fall across the carpet. I grab one and shove it into my mouth, but Bella spits it out because she sees something much better than a cookie.

Humphrey has carried a terrified bird into my bedroom, somehow getting it past Mum, who would have screamed and shooed him away if she'd seen it. The bird is tiny. It looks like a baby. I wonder if Humphrey pulled it out of its nest, whether its mother is missing it.

The bird is flapping its little wings and trying to fly away, even though its body has been punctured by Humphrey's teeth.

He does this often, my cat. He's very much on Team Bella rather than Team Ella. He knows.

I crawl over to it. I can't even hear the ringing anymore: it's just a white noise that blocks out the mundane world. I feel all traces of Ella leaving and then I am fully Bella and Ella has gone and that's good because she is pathetic. I can hardly breathe as I reach for the hammer that Ella keeps under the bed. It's a little hammer that looks ladylike and inoffensive: when Mum found it, Ella said it was part of her sculpting kit for art, and she totally believed her. But I know the truth. She keeps it there for me.

I pick the tiny thing up by a feather and place it on top of a history essay, which is on top of a textbook on the floor. I straighten it, stroking it with a finger. Ella would hate this. She loves animals. But I am not Ella.

"Hello," I whisper, and I am Bella through and through.

Humphrey gives me a look. He is excited. He is a bad cat, and he never pretends to be anything different.

My breathing quickens as I stare at the little bird.

I can't hear anything. I can't see anything but the bird.

And I know what I'm going to do. I wouldn't have arranged the creature and gotten out the hammer if I didn't. I know what I'm going to do because it is what I live for.

The world is dark around the edges like a spooky photo. Everything else has faded away. Bird, book, cat, hammer.

Bella.

I feel sick, but not in a normal way. Nothing about this is normal for anyone but me.

I can see the bird trying to fly away, and I know it will never fly again. I am Bella, and I can do anything. I have the power of life and death.

I pick up the hammer, wait for a moment with it raised just high enough, savoring every second, and smash it down on top of the creature.

I

feel

it

crunch.

I

watch

it

shatter.

I stare at the remains. I love doing this.

"Thanks," I breathe to the cat, and he tilts his head toward me in a you're-welcome sort of way. A we're-in-this-together way.

This is what it's all about. I love it when I get to take over. I want to be Bella forever; I want her to stop being Ella Black and let me stay here, in her body. I could do anything.

The white noise starts to fade. Bella does too. I try to hang on to her.

I hate doing this, says Ella's pathetic voice.

GO AWAY, I tell her.

I'm scared, she says.

NO YOU'RE NOT.

"Ella?"

The voice slices through everything, and Bella shrinks further away.

The ringing is back, but it's quieter. I am mostly Ella now, cross-legged beside my bed, on the other side of the room from the door. It takes me several seconds to force down these feelings, to know that I need to be Ella again and not Bella, and when I do, I push the hammer under the bed and jump to my feet. My legs wobble. My heart pounds so hard, they must be able to hear it downstairs.

Lily has opened my bedroom door and is standing in the doorway.

I look around, gasping for breath, drawing in great lungfuls of air and trying to use them to force the ringing away.

I am in my bedroom. The walls are pink and blue, with anime posters and my sketches of Rio de Janeiro. My clothes are on the floor, my books on the table. There is a photo collage of me and Lily and Jack, laughing, doing ironic duck-faced pouts, posing with our arms around one another. Everything looks normal.

Everything

looks

normal.

But I know nothing is normal.

I don't know what Lily's seen. I don't know if she saw Bella lift the hammer and kill the bird. Bella is not here. She is not. Lily cannot see her. She cannot see this. She cannot. I push the darkness away, away, away.

In my head I say the words that bring me back to myself. They work only after Bella has done her thing and is nearly gone.

The universe the universe the universe, I say.

The universe.

The universe.

The

whole

universe.

The only thing that fully chases Bella away is that cosmic perspective. If I think of the entire universe and how tiny I am, everything feels manageable, because nothing I do matters. Nothing at all matters. Ella doesn't matter and neither does Bella. Unfortunately, this really only works when she's on her way out. It doesn't stop her from arriving.

I discovered the universe thing by mistake. I was in the downstairs bathroom, about eleven years old, battling a demon I understood even less than I do now. I had my back against the locked door, and I was pulling the wallpaper off the wall because I couldn't control myself and I had to destroy something. As I did it, Bella started to fade, and I read a line in a poem that is still hanging up on our downstairs bathroom wall.

> *Whether or not it is clear to you,*
> *no doubt the universe is unfolding as it should.*

No doubt the universe is unfolding as it should.

The universe is unfolding.

It made Bella leave me alone. Now just the words *the universe* work. I say them over and over again.

The ringing is fainter still, and then it just about stops. The edges of the world are sharp again.

Bella is gone.

My lips move, but I don't think any sound comes out.

I must be nice.

Be nice.

Be normal.

I

have

to

be

normal.

Smile.

You

must

smile.

"Oh, hey, Lily," I say. My voice trembles, but the words are kind of right. "Um. Don't come in!"

My voice snaps on the last bit as she steps into the room. She stops. I wobble to my feet, then sit on the bed because my legs give out. Bella has zapped me of my energy.

"Oh, Ella." Lily is lovely. She is confused by my snapping at her because I never do that. "Are you OK? Your mum said I could come up. I just came by because you haven't got your phone and I wanted to—" I see her look at my bed. I see her notice my phone. "Oh, you got it back?"

"Yes. Back. Um."

Be normal.

"Sorry," I say. I form the word carefully. I am Ella. "The cat brought in a bird. It's really grim. It's made me sick. Sorry. Really, don't come in. I had to put it out of its misery. I . . . had . . . to . . ."

It's so difficult to come back to myself. It's harder every time. One day I won't make it. One day I will be stuck as Bella. I know she wants that. I would hate it. It can never happen.

"Oh, shit," says Lily. Lily could never understand, and I would never tell her, because if I did, she might not be my friend anymore, and I need her. I need her. Her friendship pulls me back, often, and always without her knowing. "Oh, Ella. You poor thing. I've got a tissue. Hang on."

She is walking toward me. Humphrey crouches, then runs, streaking past her legs and out of the room and down the stairs.

I pull her down to sit next to me on the bed and take her face in my hands. I cannot let her look at what I did. Her springy hair on my fingers grounds me. I am with Lily now.

"Seriously," I say, my face right in front of hers. "Don't look. I'll clean it up. Could you maybe run down and get a plastic bag from my mum?"

I am hiccupping. It is all too much. I've always managed Bella better than this. I've always kept Lily away from her. Lately it has been getting worse.

"Sure. Shit, Ella. You poor, poor thing." She puts an arm around me, and just for a moment I lean in and bury my face in her shoulder.

Her hair is loose. It tickles my face. I cling on, and then I force myself to let go.

When she has gone downstairs, I put my head in my hands. This is awful: I can't keep it up. Lily actually walked into a room and found Bella in it. Next time it could be worse and then everyone will know. I can't get my thoughts straight or stop shaking, but I have to clean this up. I can't let Lily know, and I can't let Jack know either.

They cannot know.

No one

can

know.

I leave the poor smashed bird where it is and fold the history essay around it. I am shaking, and a feather falls out of the package. I kick the textbook out of the way and try to pick up the stray feathers, though I really need to vacuum to get the carpet clean.

Mum will be pleased to see me spontaneously using the vacuum cleaner. At least that will make her happy for a bit.

When Lily comes back with the bag, I drop in the bird in its essay coffin and drop most of the feathers in too.

"I'll just wash my hands."

Lily ties the handles of the bag and takes it downstairs while I lock myself in the bathroom and try to breathe without it catching, without gasping or taking such shallow breaths that I feel dizzy. I wash my hands with lots of soap. I splash my face with cold water and soap, and take off my old makeup. I put on some moisturizer to make my skin soft and smooth. I breathe in and out. In. Out. In, deeply. Out, deeply. I close my eyes. I remember smashing the bird. It made Bella happy, and Bella is part of me.

I do not want that to make me happy.

I do not want to be part Bella.

I do not want it to build up inside me like this.

I do not want to be someone who smashes birds with a hammer.

I do not want to be this girl.

I do not want to be bad.

CHAPTER TWO

"ELLA!" SHE SHOUTS up the stairs. I notice that Lily is keeping away from my room today, after what happened on Wednesday. I grab my bag and run down, smiling, ready to be relentlessly nice all day long.

"Hello!" I say, super enthusiastically.

She grins. "You look gorgeous."

I don't, but it's nice of her to say it.

"*You* do," I tell her. She's wearing skinny jeans and a big white shirt. "You really do. Classic and beautiful." I immediately feel messy beside her, in my leggings and long-sleeved T-shirt. I feel like a child, but that doesn't matter.

Lily and I have been best friends for nearly ten years: that's more than half our lives. We became real friends when we were eight, when we were put together for a school nature walk and were let loose in the forest with a sheet of paper and a list of random things to collect. We went farther and farther from the base. I wanted to get lost to see what would happen (Bella was young then too, and her plans tended to be haphazard), and Lily was happy with that plan because she likes an adventure.

It didn't go brilliantly, but we ended up friends.

19

. . .

As we walk into the kitchen to say good-bye to Mum and Dad, they stop talking and plaster on fake smiles. I wish they'd just argue properly: lately they are always breaking off a whispered fight as I walk into a room.

"Hello, girls!" says Mum.

Dad looks up from his paper, as if he had been absorbed in it. He might as well be holding it upside down, because he definitely wasn't reading.

"How's everything?" he says. Mum is clattering about, cooking. I wish that sometimes she would read the paper while he cooked, but no. They just don't do it like that. I'd like her to have a break sometimes. Dad does occasionally offer but she insists on doing it all herself: at the most she'll let us set the table or take the compost out to the worm bin.

Yes. My mother seriously has a worm bin. It's like three hundred pets that eat all our kitchen waste and poo out the compost. I love them. Sometimes I take the lid off and stare at them. Once Bella tried to make me pour boiling water onto them, and I had to run all the way to my room and slash one of my own paintings to pieces with a craft knife just to save them.

Mum continues cooking. She's tall just like I am, and blond just like I used to be, and she beams at us. "Would you like some soup, girls?"

Lily says, "That's really kind of you, but we're just off to Mollie's."

"It smells great, though," I say, even though it really doesn't.

Mum's lentil soup is so thick that you literally can use it as wallpaper paste. Once I stuck a sketch to the wall with it, a picture of Humphrey stalking a mouse, just to see if it worked. Mum was out and I was messing around with Jack. I bet him that it would stay up, and it did. We laughed so much that we cried. It's stayed up for weeks now, on the wall to the left of the window.

Dad and Mum both continue to pretend we haven't walked in on another argument, so that feels insanely awkward. Dad smiles at me and at Lily and turns a page of his paper. Generally Dad is much easier to live with than Mum is, because he does his thing and gives me all the space I need, which is a lot. I can talk to Dad about things and he'll engage with me. The other day he said abstract art wasn't really art, and I told him why he was wrong and he totally got it and changed his mind.

"Watching movies?" he says now.

"Yep," I say.

"It's *Psycho* today," says Lily.

"The Bates Motel," says Dad. I don't answer. Lily humors him for us both by singing a version of the shower music, and Dad does a stabbing motion, which I notice he aims at Mum.

After we say good-bye, we get on our bikes and cycle off. I love cycling. It feels like the wind is in your hair even when you're wearing a helmet. I like the way your legs hurt and you feel as if you've done something good. Sometimes I have even managed to cycle Bella away from me.

As I follow Lily, her hair springing out from under her helmet,

21

I think about the fact that Mum and Dad were unusually happy to see me leave the house today, and I know it's so they can continue their secret arguing. I was always glad my parents weren't divorced like most people's, because I'd rather live with Dad, but, judging by what happens to many people, I'd probably have to live with Mum. Now I wish they'd just do it already. I'm seventeen, so I could live wherever I wanted. I have no idea what is going on or why, and I certainly don't want to think about one of them having an affair, so I guess I'll just leave them to it.

I don't think Lily noticed the awkwardness between my parents, but I'm not surprised. She hasn't seen her dad since she was eight, though she still gets money from him. That must be horrible, but she says it's just what she knows and so it's perfectly fine. She is, indeed, one of the happiest people I know.

A little while later we are in Mollie's massive living room almost at the exciting part of *Psycho*. I can't relax here because I don't belong: these girls don't like me, because I'm nervous and scared and awkward. I look like one of them (or I did before I dyed my hair), but I'm not one of them. I'm only here because I'm with Lily. She and Mollie and the twins are all A-list, and I'm a hanger-on. I often say the wrong thing, or I say nothing at all, and generally they just act as if I'm not there. They don't actively hate me, though, so that's something.

I sit quietly on the squashy sofa with Lily, our legs pressed together, and that comforts me a bit, though I can't say so out loud.

Mollie's dad puts down a bowl of Maltesers in front of us, and a minute later, they're already half gone; I've taken most of them out of nerves. Mollie will be angry if she sees that I have taken all the Maltesers. Fortunately, everyone's staring at the screen, so they don't even notice. I will bike home extra hard later to make up for it.

Mollie is applying to film studies courses at university, and she's trying very hard to watch every important film ever made so she'll be able to talk about them at interviews and get offers from every place she applies. We are all watching them with her (or rather, she invited Lily and the twins to watch them with her, and Lily brought me along) because we will be off to college next year too, and they all like the idea of being seen as cool and stylish film buffs. I do too, obviously, but mainly I just enjoy switching off and watching the movies. When I'm absorbed in someone else's traumas, my own can fade into the background. It's the same with books. It's why I love reading and why I love art, too.

The idea of going away from here is exciting. Unlike Mollie, I don't know what I want to do or who I want to be. I only want to apply to art school, but you can't exactly have a career as an artist (not according to the career advisers at school, anyway). Whatever it turns out to be, I can't wait to leave this town because I have only Lily and Jack here, and no one else really cares about me. Maybe if I went away, I might be OK. Maybe, just maybe, I might finally manage to fight Bella and kill her off forever. I could be Ella all the time. I could be someone good.

I take a deep breath. Perhaps I should apply for film studies too. I'm enjoying this film. But I wish the rest of them would stop talking and go back to watching the movie so I could concentrate, though of course I can't ask them to.

Unfortunately, Lily is telling them about the bird. She didn't tell them right after it happened, but she's telling them now.

"God, Ella," says Mollie, looking as if she's actually a bit scared of me, and perhaps she should be, in fact. "That is so fucked. I mean— here's a bird in distress." She laughs. "Let's, like, get *Ella Black* to put it out of its misery."

She and the twins burst out laughing. I look at Lily. She mouths "Sorry."

"But," says Nisha, "that is seriously so gross. I literally couldn't have done it." She looks at me as if I might be a monster, as if this is a story that might travel like a brushfire around the room if she were to tell even one more person, as if it is something that could make my life just that much worse, and I know that it is.

I try to give her a bright smile, though I think it comes out all wrong.

"I just did what I had to do," I say. "That poor thing."

I think those are the right words. I have to measure my words all the time when I'm with the alpha girls. The slightest misstep and they become vicious. Everything is reported to everyone.

I imagine for a second what might happen if I told them that it wasn't actually me who killed the bird, that it was my other self, Bella. My inner monster, who takes me over from time to time, who is scaring me by getting more brazen each time.

It would be the beginning of the end of everything.

I try to refocus my thoughts on the woman in the film who has just gotten into the shower; I know this means the famous scene is about to happen. Everyone seems to have lost interest in me, and we all stare at the screen as the classic *Psycho* music starts and Janet Leigh is murdered.

"Ella, I'm so sorry," Lily whispers, right into my ear. "I didn't mean for them to—"

"It's OK," I say, cutting her off. "Truly." And it is. I could be annoyed with her for telling them about the bird, but I'm not. She said it to make them sympathize with me, and it's not her fault it didn't work.

She takes my hand. "Love you."

I spend the rest of the day as the hanger-on, being as nice as I possibly can. I always try to do that. Because I'm getting more and more scared of the bad thing that lives inside me, and because Lily walked in when I was under Bella's control, I work on being normal more than I have ever done before. I concentrate all my efforts on being kind and helpful, not that anyone but Lily cares what I do. After the movie is over, I sit with Mollie and talk her through the essay on *Sons and Lovers* that I've done and she hasn't, and she accepts my help and says "Thank you."

That feels like a breakthrough.

"Why *did* you do that to your hair?" she asks, picking up a strand of it in her fingers as we work side by side and looking at it with distaste.

I shrug. "I just wanted a change."

It's the biggest lie ever.

My hair used to be long and blond like Mollie's, but now it's lopsided (much longer on one side than the other) and purple. The lopsidedness came after a horrible incident at school with this girl Tessa, whose hobby is making my life, and the lives of everyone else who doesn't quite fit in, as difficult as she can. It was part of a complicated accommodation I made with Bella to stop her from attacking Tessa with her own knife, and it meant me cutting half my hair off instead. The purple was just for fun. But actually I like the color. I'm different from everyone else, so I might as well look different.

"Right." Mollie is smirking. She doesn't believe me.

Suddenly I can't wait to get away from here.

CHAPTER THREE

"LILY?" SAYS MRS. Browning. "Perhaps you'd like to answer."

I look at Lily. She is fiddling with her fingernails, staring down at her desk. She hasn't got a clue what to say. I know that she didn't hear the question because she was drawing a picture of herself as a manga character in her notebook under the table. She has colored her skin light brown and her hair pink with colored pencils. Her eyes are huge. Underneath it she has written "Lilichan."

We are supposed to be sensible now that we're in our last year of school. We're meant to be adults now. We should be taking these subjects because we are committed to them. We are not meant to yawn and mess around and draw cartoons under our desks, and yet of course we do, because they treat us like children, so that's the way we behave.

"Sorry," says Lily.

There is a muffled snicker from the rest of the group. It's raining outside. Drops are rolling down the windowpanes.

"Lily—answer my question about the text. This is advanced English. If you don't want to answer a very basic question, you should not have picked this class."

27

Mrs. Browning is a good teacher and I like her. No one else does. I don't like it, however, when she picks on Lily, who daydreams her way through advanced English because she didn't know what to do for her third subject and picked it only because I was doing it. Lily's heart is not in English, and although she is the most focused person I know, when she's in an English lesson, that focus is never on the book. She's generally thinking about music and drama instead.

Lily shifts in her chair, pulls her skirt straight, and stares at the book in front of her. I take the drawing from her under her desk, just in case Mrs. Browning asks to see what she is doing. The rain has turned to hail and the stones are battering at the window. A year from now we will be out of here, and Mrs. Browning will still be behind her desk, trying to get people whose minds are elsewhere to talk about books they haven't read. I wish I could communicate that thought to Lily right now.

I know *Sons and Lovers* and I like it. I heard the question. I clear my throat and talk quickly before I can decide not to.

"Mrs. Morel's jealous of Paul's relationship with Miriam," I say quickly. "And that's . . ."

"No, Ella. I asked Lily, thank you. I know *you* know."

The silence is tangible. It is a thick thing, a fog, heavy in the air. There are only ten of us in this class, and when I look around, I see that I am the only one who is not staring down at a piece of paper, desperate not to be called on.

My head starts to ring, and I start a frantic internal bargaining with Bella. She cannot take over at school. She cannot.

. . .

CAKE, says Bella.

No, I reply.

ANOTHER HAIR COLOR.

No. Later. We'll do something later.

HURT THE TEACHER. SHE'S BEING MEAN TO LILY.

I can't hurt the teacher.

Mrs. Browning, unaware of the danger she's in, is staring at Lily, who is hunched in on herself, looking at her lap. *No one* gets to make my best friend feel like this. Lily is an angel.

This cannot happen at school. It can't. It did once before, and I only just got through it by locking myself in the bathroom and taking it out on myself until Bella went away. That's why I have the tiny scars on my arms. Not now; not in class. No.

But Bella won't listen to me, and she won't back down either. The edges of my vision black out. I look around frantically at the edge of everything to make it come back into focus.

It doesn't work. Bella is coming.

"Your hair looks nice today, miss," Bella says to Mrs. Browning, using my mouth. I am horrified. I only ever speak in class to give an answer. I never do anything like this.

Mrs. Browning touches her hair, which is as flat and scraggly as it always is.

"Well, I wish I could say the same for *you*, Ella," she says, her lips tight.

"Yeah, but it does. Where do you get it done?"

Everyone is staring at me, wide eyed.

"Lily. Answer the question."

"The question?" Lily says, very quietly.

I close my eyes and take some deep, deliberate breaths, because I cannot let Bella do anything more than this. But being rude to Mrs. Browning was not enough for her. I can feel it happening. She's rising inside me. I can't look at everything quickly enough to stop it from blurring. I am becoming Bella. I want to fly at Mrs. Browning. I want to shout. I need to hurt her.

I

am

Bella.

PULL HER HAIR.

I can't, Ella replies.

THROW HER BAG OUT THE WINDOW.

I can't.

PUNCH HER.

No.

<u>HELP LILY. LILY IS THE PERSON YOU LOVE THE MOST. YOU CAN DO THAT.</u>

About that, my two selves are in tentative agreement. The line between them blurs and the ringing returns. Bella is getting weaker.

The universe the universe the universe.

I pull my notebook down under the table and start scribbling, breathing deeply, pushing away the ringing and the blurring. I focus only on the words, and when it's done, I push it toward Lily, who reads it quickly, then says, "Mrs. Morel is jealous of Paul's relationships with Miriam and Clara, which has a damaging effect on Paul. So even though she dies, I would argue that she has still won."

Mrs. Browning rolls her eyes. I can see that she is on the brink of walking out, even though there are still twenty minutes until break. I hope she does. I will her to. That would end this.

But she doesn't.

"*You* would argue that, would you, Lily?" she says.

"Yes, miss."

"Ella, you are doing Lily no favors whatsoever," she says. "Yes, I know *you* can do it. I know you've read the book and can produce a considered argument. You won't be able to pass Lily the answer in her exams, will you? She needs to do the work herself, or else drop the class. If she can't be bothered to read a novel that is not at all difficult—or even to read the stupid CliffsNotes about it—then this class is not the place for her. And as for your rudeness, Ella, we'll be discussing that later."

"Lily's going to get an A," I say. I reach for her hand under the table and squeeze it. She squeezes back, clinging on.

The universe the universe the universe.

- I chase away what remains of Bella with the words. I hang on to Lily's hand.

My breathing comes more easily. The ringing subsides and I can hear properly; I can see properly too. It is the biggest relief, the best thing. I close my eyes and appreciate having my head to myself.

The lesson staggers on for fifteen more minutes that manage to be both dull and tense, and when it is over, I take Lily's hand in mine and we walk out of the room together. Mollie walks on Lily's other side (though I don't know where she was before, when Lily needed backup), and none of us look back. We go straight to the student lounge.

Lily blinks back tears and tries to laugh. I want to look after her like she looks after me.

"Oh, fuck," she says. "She's kind of right. I know. I was going to read the book. I just . . . didn't."

"Read it," I say quietly, "and you'll be fine. You *will* get an A and then we'll be out of here. All the teachers have to stay until they die."

Lily smiles at that.

"Coffee?" says Mollie, to both of us.

"Sure."

I am still shaky, but I don't think anyone is looking at me. I reached a compromise with Bella and it was just about OK. It was a horribly close call. If I'd done what she wanted and punched a teacher, I'd have been arrested by now. It doesn't bear thinking about.

Nothing like this can happen again.

The problem is I don't know how to stop it. It's getting worse, and I don't know how to make it stop. Lately, Bella wants to come out almost every day. I use almost all my energy pushing her back down. It's beginning to feel impossible.

I watch Mollie from across the room as she tips the stale coffee out of the bottom of the carafe and refills the filter. The student lounge is big, with sofas and beanbags, and a coffee station with a kettle and coffee machine. The room as a whole smells of coffee and perfumed deodorant. It is always filled with teenage girls making a big point of relaxing, or desperately trying to finish overdue homework before it slips out of control, or going through crises and breakdowns, alone, together, collectively. I know I'm not the only one with struggles. I imagine I am the only one with a demon, though.

.   .   .

I enjoy being with Lily, but I don't want to be here. I have a list of places I would rather be on my bedside table. Only Jack has seen it, because he made his own at the same time. We didn't make the tragic "bucket lists" terminally ill kids make: we just wrote down some places we would rather be. I added the last two items when I was alone:

Ella's Wish List

1. Go to Rio—particularly Copacabana beach. Draw it from life, not from a photo.
2. Visit a tropical island anywhere in the world, with sand and palm trees. Find a beach that is the opposite of where we went last year, in Cornwall.
3. Live in a huge exciting city, e.g., New York.
4. Find a job and earn money doing something fulfilling and interesting, independent from my parents.
5. Be away from my life in Kent. JUST BE ANYWHERE AWAY FROM STUPID ENGLAND AND MY FRUSTRATING LIFE.
6. Be someone different from this Ella Black.
7. Learn to live with my dark side.

Jack and I had fun writing them. His is full of shocking ideas, and I bet he added some extras when I wasn't there, too.

I have written my list several times, and this is its current incarnation. Each time I try to make it measured, but somehow I just can't.

I'm going to apply to universities and art colleges in cool places, but not as cool as Rio or New York, because there's no way Mum and Dad would ever let me go that far. Still, I'll probably get into more than one of them and be able to choose. I do well at school, and this summer I'll have qualifications in English, art, and history.

I'm not totally sure what I'll be able to do with an art degree, but I do know I don't want to work hard just to get some dull job like my dad and work all the time. No one here thinks I'm adventurous, but I am, in secret. I long to be free from everything I currently know. I don't belong in this school. I want to run from everything, from being seen as pathetic, from Bella, from my mother's constant locking of the door once I am safely inside.

I want to be free.

"Thanks, Mollie," I say, taking the stained mug of black coffee she's holding out to me. It is a big thing, Mollie making me a coffee. I smile broadly at her and take a sip: it's hot, and pretty much nasty, but it's what we drink.

"Well, Ella," says Mollie. "You were epic." She is staring at me with something like awe. "Seriously." She turns to the twins, who don't take English. "Browning was giving Lily a hard time. And then Ella just goes, 'Your hair looks nice, miss.'"

"Ella?" Anusha gasps.

"I know, right?"

Everyone within earshot bursts out laughing. I try to smile along with it. The moment is reported again and again, to people who didn't hear the first time. I shrink into my seat and look at Lily.

"You OK?" I say quietly.

"Yeah," she says. "I'm fine. But where the hell did that come from? 'Your hair looks nice, miss'?" She giggles, and I giggle too, and then we are both laughing. We don't notice that there's a teacher in the room, heading in our direction, until she's almost beside us.

No one really takes any notice when teachers come into our lounge. They try to be cool when they do. They make a show of "treating you like adults." They do this by saying, "Hi, girls!" and "Enjoy yourselves." They try to slouch a bit, to show us that, impossible as it seems, they were young once too.

Today, though, it's our form tutor, Mrs. Phipps, and she is not trying to be *down wiv da kidz* at all. She is walking purposefully, looking only at me.

Mrs. Browning said we would talk about my rudeness, so this isn't totally unexpected. Even so, I am trembling. I never get into trouble. I hope I'm not heading for another Bella situation.

"Ella," says Phipps. "Ella, I need you to come with me, please. Bring your bag and your coat."

I widen my eyes at Lily and Mollie to hide the fact that I am cold all over. They are sending me home for being rude to a teacher? I pick up my bag and toss the long side of my hair and try to smile as I stand to leave.

Phipps is looking at me strangely. I don't like it. She normally approves of me. She usually says things like, "Thank goodness for you, at least, Ella," which makes the others hate me even more.

"Coat?" she says.

"Actually—I don't have one?" I say. I talk in the slow, slightly Australian way I've heard other girls do when they want to annoy the teachers. They hate a sentence to sound like a question. I don't know what else to do. My heart is pounding.

"Really?"

"Really."

She starts to say something but then stops. She's wearing a horrible dress, and Lily points at it behind her back and makes a face to the others, who snicker. I appreciate her support.

By now, everyone in the room is looking at me, and I'm glad to be leaving. I keep my head down and follow Phipps out of the room. I wish she would walk faster. Tessa the bully looks up and rolls her eyes at me as I walk past.

The ringing begins faintly, and I find myself going slightly out of my way to kick her bag.

Bella is stirring.

I am out of the lounge now and heading straight into trouble.

My mother is in the principal's office. She is sitting on a chair, and Mrs. Austen, the principal, is swigging, as ever, from the bottle that says "water" on it but that everyone knows really contains vodka. Neither of them looks happy.

This does seem over the top, considering. But I'm so nervous, I don't move from my spot in the doorway.

I imagine myself saying, "It wasn't me. It was Bella. She's a kind of demon who lives inside me. She's been there as long as I can remember, and she likes to come out when I'm particularly tired or angry. You thought I was just having tantrums, so when I was about seven, I realized I had to hide her." That would make it all kinds of worse. My parents would send me away to some upmarket asylum, and I'd be forced to sit quietly in group therapy until I could convince someone I was "better." Everyone back at school would talk of nothing else for weeks, like they do when someone goes away to have their anorexia treated, and I could never go back.

"Here she is," says Phipps, standing just behind me, a hand on my shoulder. I know it must be a keep-her-from-running-away grip, though it feels more like a don't-worry hand. I want to push it off, violently, but of course I can't. In fact, a part of me knows that Bella has already scoped out the trophy sitting on a shelf behind Mrs. Austen and wants to use it to smash everyone in the room, but she's just about under control at the moment. "Apparently the pounding hail outside is no reason for a sixth-former to bring a coat to school, but she's got her bag."

"Thanks, Sarah," says Mrs. Austen, and the door clicks shut and there are just the three of us there.

My mum is in the room. I was a bit rude to a teacher, which admittedly has never happened before, but it wasn't that bad. I was defending my friend, and all I actually said was "Your hair looks nice." They called my *mother*. They have no idea how much worse it could have been.

No

idea

at

all.

Mum is looking at me with the strangest expression. Her hair is plastered down with rain. She hasn't brought a coat with her either.

I wait for someone to say something, but they don't. I'm certainly not going to be the first to speak. I feel the moment stretch out. We are all suspended, waiting. The ringing gets a bit louder as the uncertainty builds. Something is about to happen, but if no one says anything, then it won't. I'm good at not speaking. This is easy for me. Bella's enjoying the tension, so she's happy just watching beneath the surface, for now.

"Ella," says Mum, cracking first. "Ella. Darling. We have to go. It's a bit sudden. I'm sorry, darling."

"I don't know what I even did," I say, straight at Mrs. Austen. My words tumble over one another. "It's not fair. I was a bit rude to Mrs. Browning but—"

I stop talking, because I can see from both their faces that they don't know what I am talking about. I have just confessed to something they had no idea I did.

"Were you?" Mrs. Austen says, inclining her head. She has helmet hair and looks like Angela Merkel. "That's not like you, Ella. But this has nothing to do with Mrs. Browning." There is a big question on her face, but she doesn't ask it.

I look at my mum. She sits there, silent.

"Your mother needs to take you away, my dear." Mrs. Austen tilts her head toward Mum.

"Yes. Darling. Ella. We need to go, right now. It's not in the least bit your fault. Of course it's not. Though you shouldn't be rude to teachers."

Her voice drifts away somewhere. I see that she is hugely stressed. I feel bad for her, but I have no idea what's going on.

"Where are we going?"

"I'll explain on the way. But we have to get going quickly or we won't make the . . ." She stops midsentence.

I stare at Mum. She doesn't meet my eye. I need her to finish the sentence, to tell me what we won't make. All my muscles tense. I don't know what is happening, but I am terrified that she might have found my drawings under the bed. They are dark, dark drawings. They are pictures of violence and horror, of the inside of my head.

If Mum found them, she would take me straight to some kind of psychiatrist. I know she would. This must be something big.

We have to get going quickly or we won't make the . . . appointment?

Everything is going to unravel. I work so hard to keep myself separate from Bella, and now they're going to pull my life to pieces. This is why I have tried so hard to keep it a secret since I was seven, when I realized how bad I was. I knew I wasn't normal. I knew I couldn't tell anyone.

I am trembling all over as the ringing in my head gets louder still, because I know Bella won't take this lying down either. It's only a matter of time.

"I don't understand," I say.

"We have to go right now, I'm afraid," Mum says, her lips tight. She is always dressed like a hippie, my mum, but today, I notice, she is trying to look fancy. She's wearing a floaty dress with flowers all over it and the seashell necklace she puts on to go to weddings and parents' evenings.

I try to gauge from her face whether she is scared of me. My parents have no idea what goes on in my head, and I need to keep it that way. I have worked hard to make them think that I'm awkward and shy (both of which are true) and absolutely nothing else.

She doesn't look scared, but she does look worried about me. She is treading carefully. I am terribly afraid that she is going to take me to some clinic.

I have always known Mum would do anything for me, within a carefully defined range of things. If I said I wanted to learn the oboe, for example, she would make it happen for me instantly. Ballet would be a yes (and it was, for years), but cheerleading would be a no. Too dangerous. If I wanted to see a counselor to talk about the monster in my head, I imagine she would work hard to convince me there was no need for that sort of thing at all.

Mum could have done things with her life because she's clever and lovely, but all she did was have one baby and then chain herself to a clean eating cookbook and a drawer of craft materials forevermore. She opted out of everything. I love her for devoting her entire life to me, even if it is sometimes annoying, but I feel bad for her too. She waits for Dad to come home from work, and puts nutritious food in front of him. She buys me the things I need for my art. She looks after us. She considers it her job. If I thank her for driving me somewhere, or anything at all, she says, "Oh, that's OK. It's my job."

She could have done anything, and she chose to look after me instead. I love her, but it's not a choice I'd be making if I were ever to have a child. We have talked about this, though we never argue. She says, "Part of feminism is having a choice, and I chose to stay at home." I tell her that is a bit of a cop-out because it's a choice you can make only if you have a spouse who can support you while you do it, but instead of arguing her point, she just says, "Yes, you're probably right, darling."

"Now, Ella," she says.

Hearing Mum say my name draws me out of my head.

She is already on her feet. "Let's go. We have to leave now. *Right now.*"

I don't know where to start. The ringing is getting louder. I fight it.

"But, Mum," I say. "I'm at school. It's education. I should really stay here, and I'll see you at four. OK?"

I wait for backup, but it doesn't come. I realize that the principal of my expensive school had me collected from the lounge for whatever this reason is.

They would do that only if it was an emergency. They wouldn't do it for no reason.

They would do it if someone was dead.

Mum is here.

"Is Dad OK?" I say, talking to my shoes.

"Yes," Mum says, though she doesn't sound surprised to be asked. "He's perfectly fine. He's meeting us here. Now."

"What, then?"

Mum is alive. Dad is alive. They wouldn't collect me from school if it was the cat. Still, I hope it's not Humphrey.

"I'll tell you on the way," says Mum, "like I said. Come on."

I look at Mrs. Austen.

"Off you go, Ella," she says. "We'll see you when we see you."

That fills me with horror. She should have said *tomorrow*. Clearly, she doesn't know when I'll be back. But I have studying to do. I need to be at *school*. I don't want to go to therapy.

She will see me when she sees me.

That opens up a chasm. I hold on to the edge of the principal's desk, trying to tether myself. The ringing grows.

Mrs. Austen looks calm, but she is holding a little piece of card and tearing it into tiny pieces, dropping the shreds into a pile. There was handwriting on it. I wonder what it said. When I look into her face, she looks away. I look at Mum, who is standing by the door now. I don't know what to do. I don't want to go. I hate it at school, but now I want to stay.

"*Why?*" I manage to say. "What's going on?" My voice is tiny.

"We'll talk in the car." Mum's not looking at me.

"Do I really have to go?" I say this to Mrs. Austen. My voice is trembling. The ringing is loud. Bella is feeding on the tension.

"Yes, Ella," the principal says. "You really have to go. Don't worry about school for now. We'll be here. You'll be all right. Off you go."

On the way out I text Lily and Jack.

Mum seems to be kidnapping me, I write.

"Put your phone away," says Mum.

A minute later Dad is parking in a space between teachers' cars. He is all right. I am surprised to find that I am so swamped with relief, my legs nearly give way. A part of me didn't believe Mum at all and thought she would tell me in the car that, actually, he was in a coma or something.

It is still raining, but it's mostly just a drizzle now. We all ignore it, though normally both of them would whip out an umbrella at the first sign of anything. Dad walks over to meet us, and I can't help hugging him. I whisper, "What the hell is going on with her?"

"So sorry, darling," he whispers back. "It's not Mum. I promise. We'll tell you in a minute. Let's just get away for now."

I swallow. "OK."

We get into Mum's car. Dad is apparently ready to leave his Audi behind without a backward glance. Parents aren't allowed to park in the teachers' lot. They're certainly not allowed to abandon their cars there.

Abandoning his car is very much not a thing my dad would do. He is very responsible. This is all a bit too strange.

I turn around in the backseat and watch the school disappearing through the rain-splattered rear window. I don't know when I'll be back.

I am utterly terrified.

I can feel Bella inside me, biding her time, waiting to see what this is before she makes herself known. I hope Dad really will tell me in a minute.

The car radio beeps the hour. Everyone in the lounge must be talking about me, and I am not there.

"The news headlines at eleven o'clock," says the radio. *"Nuclear tensions increase as the standoff continues. Amanda Hinchcliffe is released from jail after a third appeal. Two more cases of simian flu have been confirmed in the United Kingdom—"*

Mum jabs at the car radio and it goes off, flicks on again, then goes back off. They both inhale sharply. Mum's hand is shaking. Dad wobbles the steering wheel and almost runs over a longhaired woman who is standing at the end of the school drive, texting in the rain.

"What?" I say. "Tell me. What is it?"

"Let's just have some peace and quiet so we can talk," says Mum. "Sorry, darling. I know this is weird, but it's nothing to worry about. It's to do with Dad's work. We need to go away for a little while, but it will be fine. In fact, it'll be fun. You're going to enjoy it."

It turns out that this is all they are planning to say. This is the promised "explanation" in all its pathetic glory.

"Dad?" I say, my voice so quiet it barely comes out.

"Later," he says.

Mum passes me a Twix, and I put it in my pocket for later. Bella loves bad food, and I might need it to pacify her.

43

"Where are we going?" I ask. "You have to tell me that, at least."

"Heathrow," says Dad.

I text Jack and Lily the word *Heathrow* without looking at my phone. I don't know what word it actually sends.

"And after that we're going to Rio."

Dad and I sit in a coffee shop outside of security while Mum goes and sorts out some things. I am drinking "coffee" that is actually mildly flavored milk: although I hate milk, I'm drinking it because it gives me something to do with my hands. I can't fiddle with my phone because my parents have taken it from me and put it in Mum's handbag. That is more annoying than I could possibly say.

"Why are we going to Rio?"

Dad smiles. "Ellie, you've talked about Rio a lot. You did that huge painting of it that your mother and I thought was wonderful."

Only my dad calls me Ellie. I like it.

They know that everything about Rio enthralls me. The mountains, the sea, all of it. It seems wonderful and alive and full of samba and life and excitement. Before I stumbled on Rio while looking for a tropical setting to attempt to paint from photographs, I had no idea that there could be a place like that. I want to be someone who is at home in Rio de Janeiro, rather than a nervous schoolgirl in Kent who is just an easy target.

But I didn't want to go there like this. I would prefer to get myself there when I'm older and braver, rather than being escorted by weird shifty parents.

"But right now? I can't even express how weird this is."

"I know, Ellie, it's sudden," Dad says, and he looks exhausted.

There are big things they're not telling me; I wish he would just spill it, whatever it is. "But this thing came up for me, workwise, and we know how much you would love to visit. So we thought we could make a family trip out of it."

"Right." As if I believe that. As if.

"Aren't you a little bit pleased?"

I sigh. I take a sip of coffee and wipe the milk froth off my top lip with a napkin. I contemplate pretending to be delighted at being taken along on this "work trip." I imagine myself saying, "It's amazing! Thank you so much!" But I can't.

"It's just a little bit too weird," I say. "You like me going to school. If we were all going because of your work, then you would have arranged that and figured out the time off in advance. In no universe do you just decide on the spur of the moment and grab me from school and drive to the airport and then take my phone away. For fuck's sake. I'm not *that* stupid."

I just said "fuck" to my dad. That's never happened before. I look at him. He looks at me. His eyes crinkle. We both know I would never have said that if Mum were here.

I'M WATCHING, Bella says.

I know, I tell her.

"We thought you'd love the idea," he says.

"What about Humphrey? Who's looking after him?"

I can see from Dad's face that they forgot all about my cat. My poor Humphrey will be baffled. He will hate me when he realizes I've gone away, and if no one is there to feed him, he might die.

I hope he'll be OK; there are feral cats, and Humphrey is vicious enough to survive. I know that better than anyone. But still. When I get home, he'll be thin and tough, and he won't bring me presents anymore.

"I'm sure your mother's got that covered," Dad says after a while.

"And Jack," I say. "Jack's coming over tonight. I won't be there."

I know that Jack won't actually turn up, because I told him I was going to Heathrow. The rest will have been filled in for him by my peers: he will know that I've been swept off halfway through the morning and immediately after being rude to Mrs. Browning.

"Oh," says Dad. He is out of his league. This is actually scary. It feels as if we are running away, but we cannot possibly have anything to run from, because we are normal and boring and law abiding— or at least my parents are. We're running away from something they're not telling me about. This is spiraling into something very, very weird, but at least they're not dropping me off at an asylum, I suppose.

"Can I call him?" I say. "Can I at least tell Jack that I'm off on the 'trip of a lifetime' and will be back . . . when? Next week? How long are we going for?"

"Oh. I'm not sure. Look, you know you can't call him. We don't really want anyone to know that we're going to Rio."

"You've got some work stuff to do in Brazil and it's top secret?" I think of something. "Have we even packed? Oh my God, Dad. Where's my stuff?"

I look around the concourse purely as a dramatic move, but I'm glad I do, because someone is walking in our direction, and even from this distance I can see that it's Jack. I know his blond hair and his tall skinny body. I know the way he walks.

"It's complicated," says Dad. "Mum's packed some things. We'll buy the rest."

"Jesus." But I'm not looking at Dad. I'm looking at Jack, and I'm grinning. I hoped he would do this. Jack has a car, and we both use Find My iPhone.

Dad turns to follow my gaze and then closes his eyes and breathes deeply.

"Ellie," he says. "Oh, for God's sake."

But I am on my feet and running toward Jack. He sweeps me up in his arms.

"Thank you so much," I say. "Thank you for coming."

"What's going on?"

"No idea."

My dad is, of course, right next to us. He says, "Good to see you, Jack," in a tone that makes it clear that he means the opposite.

"Ella sent me a couple of texts," Jack says, seeing that he needs to explain, "and I had a free period and I had my car at school, so I just thought I'd come and say good-bye."

"Well, that's very romantic." Dad does not see what's right in front of him. He and Mum were both so pleased when I started hanging out with Jack—delighted that their little girl had a lovely boyfriend—that neither of them noticed that we're not actually boyfriend and girlfriend at all. That's fine by me and fine by Jack, though I found it hard to keep a straight face when Mum insisted on ceremoniously handing me a bag of condoms a few months ago.

"Dad," I say. "Can Jack and I just have a minute? I promise I won't talk about the thing you just said not to talk about."

He rolls his eyes.

"I'll get you a drink, Jack," he says. "What'll it be?"

"Flat white?" he says. "Thanks so much."

Those minutes with Jack are exactly what I need. We lean forward, resting our chins on our hands, and talk with our heads close.

"What's the thing you're not allowed to tell me?" he says as the airport bustles around us.

"That we're going to Rio. Don't tell anyone."

"Fucking Rio! Can I come?"

"I wish! I don't know what's happening."

"Enjoy it, babe. Whatever it is."

"Will you be OK?"

He sighs. "Yes. I'll miss you, though. I had a close call on Saturday. I went to the Admiral Duncan with Tony, and there was a teacher from my school there. Mr. Jones. He's quite new. Young. Fit. Anyway, he saw me and I saw him, and I knew he'd tell the other teachers, because why wouldn't he, and also he could see I was technically breaking the law by drinking. So I had to grab him at school this morning and beg him not to tell anyone. He said he won't. I hope he means it."

"I'm sure he does. He knows what's at stake. And you'll be out of there soon."

"I will."

"You'll be OK without your girlfriend for a while?"

"Yeah. Will you be OK without your boyfriend?"

"I have no idea."

There are tears in my eyes. I don't want to leave Jack. We met in Wetherspoon's one night, when I was tagging along with Lily's friends and he was pretending not to be on a date with a boy. Poor Jack. He was having a drink with someone and then half the girls' school walked in. I watched him leap in the air and walk away from his date. That was intriguing: I'm always on the lookout for other misfits. We started talking, and then I found I had a new best friend. When everyone started assuming we were going out, it worked for us both, so we kept up the pretense.

Obviously it's fine to be gay. Obviously it's not the 1950s anymore. Try telling that to Jack's parents and their church, though. He just needs to keep them from taking him to conversion therapy until he's done with high school and can leave home forever. I've never seen anyone fit into their environment quite as badly as Jack does. Not even me.

I reach out and ruffle his blond hair. He grabs my hand and squeezes it.

"I'll miss you," I say. "E-mail me. Keep in touch. I'm sure I'll be back soon."

He laughs. "Yeah. You'll probably be home in a couple of days and my dash to the airport will look ridiculous."

"It's the best thing anyone's ever done for me."

We hug and say good-bye.

When he's gone, Dad and I sit quietly. There are echoing announcements that I cannot quite hear, and there are people all over the place, none of them particularly looking as if they are traveling for fun.

I go over the day's events in my head: This morning Mum drove me to school and told me to have a lovely day. A few hours later she abducted me to take me to Brazil, and now she has confiscated my phone.

That doesn't happen.

"Going to the bathroom." I say it in an offhand way, hoping that this will make Dad casual too.

He shifts in his chair, runs his fingers through his hair.

"Can you wait for your mother to get back?"

"No. No, I can't. Am I not allowed to go to the *bathroom* anymore?"

I walk away before he can reply, aiming for a distant yellow-and-black sign with a woman in a sticking-out skirt on it. Dad actually gets up and walks beside me. I walk faster, but I know he's trailing close behind. I cannot begin to address how weird and embarrassing this is, so I pretend he's not there. I walk across the concourse and ignore my father, who is gaining on me all the way. When we get to the bathroom, I stand back and gesture to him to go into the ladies' room ahead of me.

"I'll just wait here," he mutters, and he stands there, a bathroom guard.

I sit and try to think. My parents are boring. They cannot have done anything they have to run away from.

I THINK THEY'VE DONE SOMETHING TERRIBLE, Bella says helpfully.

Like what?

STEALING. ARSON. DRUNK DRIVING. WHATEVER PEOPLE DO.

They must have done something; she's right, but what?

Dad works as a financial adviser. He does go away for work from time to time, so I could almost believe it, but he never actually has to drop everything and flee the country.

I flush the toilet and wash my hands, staring at myself in the mirror as I do. An Asian woman is washing her hands next to me. She looks at me in the mirror and grins, nodding at my hair. I smile back.

I still look like me. My hair still looks great. It looks very un-Ella. It looks more Bella than Ella.

I am, however, still wearing my school uniform. I will be flying to Brazil in a black school skirt and white blouse and green V-necked sweater. I hope Mum has done some halfway reasonable packing. I hope she has brought me some books, my pencils, my little sketchbook. If this wasn't all so strange, maybe I'd be able to enjoy the idea that, after having produced a massive painting of Rio as part of my art exams, I will soon have the opportunity to draw it from real life. For now, all I can think is that I have headphones, but they're useless without my phone. I need my things. I need all of them. If I don't have my world around me—my books, my music, my art, my phone—there will be too much blank space, and I know who will leap in to fill it. I have to have my stuff to keep my head filled with normal things, to ward off the badness.

Dad escorts me back to our table in the café, where we discover that no one has stolen or blown up our bags or taken away the dregs of our coffee. I stare at him over the top of my cup while he looks anywhere but at me. I wish I'd asked Jack to stay right up to the last minute. I wish he were here now.

Finally Mum comes back, but she looks different. Again. She is grinning, though I can see she has also been crying, and she is holding up boarding passes.

"Right. I've checked us all in and dropped off the bags. We can go through security now." She smiles with her mouth but not with her eyes. Her eyes look at me with huge, unnameable emotion. "Let's get you to Rio, darling."

It is quite nice to be locked in a metal structure that has been flung, by the power of burning fermented fossil, into the air. We are trapped, but no one cares. Everyone has chosen imprisonment. We are in a massive metal container, and it's slowly leaking fuel in a controlled way that means it lands in one piece when we get to Rio. And it's messing up the environment as it goes.

I am on my way to Rio. Although it's freaky and weird, it is also interesting. It is the very thing I wished for when I sat bored and ignored at school.

However, I have a bad, bad feeling about it.

I alternate between staring out the window at the clouds and staring at a film about a woman who is a surrogate mother and then doesn't want to give up the baby. I am not interested—I am barely even following—but it gives me moving shapes to look at. I have a book on my lap, and it's one I really want to read, that I bought at the airport, but I can't focus on that either. The people in front of me are talking loudly about their trip to Latin America.

"She'll meet us in Lima," says a woman, "if we get there before the twenty-fifth. If not, she says we can try to hook up in Cusco." It goes on and on, the discussion of complicated arrangements. The people behind are also talking nonstop, but I can't understand them at all. I put my headphones back on.

I won't understand anything anyone says in Brazil: I don't even speak Spanish a little bit, and I gave up French last year although I was actually good at it. French won't get me far in Rio anyway.

I imagine myself in Rio making new friends. Brazilian friends. They will be glamorous and beautiful with glossy black hair, and they will make everyone at home look dull and drab. I will fit in just fine with my asymmetrical purple hair: I will be the cool, quirky English girl.

I shake my head and bring myself back to reality. Flying to Brazil, for the three of us, can't be cheap. Is it from their savings? Is it embezzled? Stolen? Laundered?

If Dad had been embezzling, then he would be caught and arrested and taken home. There would be flashes from cameras, and everyone in the whole world would know that he stole money and we ran away to Rio. Everyone would be terrified of us as we were taken off the plane in handcuffs.

Dad could not have done a thing like that. He just couldn't. It can only be money they had in the bank.

My parents are too normal for this. That is a fact. Yet here we are.

On a plane that smells lightly of sweat. And of recirculated air. I have drunk a little bottle of white wine, and now Mum says I can have only soft drinks, because even though I am seventeen, they are acting as if I were five. I could have sat here and gotten drunk. It wouldn't have been exactly *fun*, but at least it would have distracted me. Besides, I'll be eighteen next month.

Both my parents keep looking at me, quickly and sneakily. Every time I look around, one of them is doing a surreptitious check. It's extremely unnerving. What aren't they telling me?

I take my headphones off.

"What is it really?" I say to Mum, who is pretending to read an in-flight magazine.

"What is what?"

"The thing we're running away from."

I look into her eyes for a while and cannot read what is in them, but the look still feels like the most honest conversation we have had since she showed up at school this morning. Mum's eyes are a grayish blue. Mine are light brown like Dad's. Hers would go better with my hair: they're almost purple.

"Let's just enjoy the time away," she says after a while. "I promise no one's in trouble. It's not like that."

"What is it like?"

We stare at each other some more. She wants to tell me. I hold my breath and will her to do it. There is a tidal wave of emotion in her eyes, but she doesn't say another word. Still, she's worried about me; I can see it. And I realize:

This is about me.

This is not about Dad's work, or Mum having a breakdown.

It

is

about

me.

They would whisk me away to the place at the top of my list only if they thought this was my only chance to go there.

If they knew something terrible was about to happen.

If they wanted me to have fun while I still could.

I need to stop thinking.

I put the headphones on and turn back to the film. After a while a woman appears beside Mum with a trolley of food, but although I ask for the chicken, as soon as it's in front of me, I don't want to eat it. I stare at it and smell its horrible smell and wonder why this chicken and I met right here, right now, in a sealed tin can thirty thousand feet up in the sky.

Someone farmed and killed that chicken. It probably grew up on a factory farm, too fat to be able to stand up on its legs. It never flew. It never even stretched out its wings. It was a crop, farmed like a cabbage, kept alive only because its life force was the thing that kept the meat fresh.

Then it was executed, sent off to a different sort of factory, and made into an airline dinner, nestled in with potatoes and slimy broccoli, covered in a gray gloopy sauce, sent up into the sky, warmed through, and presented to me.

The thought of it all makes me sick, but I give in and eat it quickly because I am starving. It is, oddly, delicious, and I smile at the way the world is set up for humans to do what the hell we like. Bella likes that too.

Later I wake with my face creased from the little pillow. I make my parents move so I can get in line for the bathroom. I have no idea what time it might be, but I suppose that it is night back at home.

I wonder who is thinking about me. Jack and Lily. Girls at school will talk about me for a bit and then move on to something else. Only Lily will actually miss me at school. Only Jack actually knows where I am.

I yawn and remember the first time I met Lily. She was the only mixed-race girl in the class, and I was in love with her bouncy hair from afar. When we were put together for the nature walk, I remember that my head was ringing, and I knew I had to do something naughty to make it stop, and I was glad I was going to do it with Lily.

"I think there's a whole pile of fir cones just over there," I said, and took her hand.

"Sure. Maybe some blackberries too," she suggested, and we walked together off the path. We climbed over branches and pushed our way through brambles and past nettles, and ended up in a clearing deep among the trees, where we sat down and talked. We hadn't really talked before. Lily told me that her dad had just left and her mum was taking her back to Ghana for the summer. I told her that I was getting a kitten next week and I was going to call him Humphrey.

We stayed away for ages. I loved being away from the rest of the class, who ignored me and laughed at me even then because sometimes I was quiet and shy, and at other times I lost control and had huge tantrums and they all thought I was crazy. I didn't really know Lily at all, but suddenly she felt like my only friend.

It took ages before they started shouting for us. We passed the time by talking about any old thing. I told her some stories I'd half stolen from books. I adapted tales about orphans and castles and forest adventures, realizing I could be myself with Lily. She had a beautiful singing voice and sang some songs to me very quietly. She taught me some words of Akan.

When we heard them shouting, I wasn't scared about being in trouble, because there were two of us, and the ringing had stopped and I was back in my own skin. We stayed tight, giggling.

Our dresses had been ripped by brambles, and our hair was all over the place.

After a while we went back to the others.

"It's OK," she whispered, squeezing my hand. And it really felt that way. Lily and I were friends now.

The teachers were frantic. All the other girls were standing at the edge of the forest, holding hands in pairs and looking scared. We ran toward them, and then I let go of Lily's hand and flung myself at Mrs. Barrett, throwing my arms around her waist and sobbing.

"We got lost," I said. "We went off the path because we saw a rabbit and then we couldn't find it again. We were so scared."

I could hear the teacher's heart pounding. She put a hand on my head.

"Well," she said. "You're safe now. But no going off the path again, girls. OK?"

I looked around Mrs. Barrett and saw Lily standing a little way away, crying and being fussed over by other girls who all wanted to look after her. Our eyes met, and we both smiled tiny little smiles.

"Here you go." My mother hands me my passport and a white form, snapping me out of the memory. "Your immigration form. I filled it in for you."

"That's nice, since I can't read or write."

She sighs. "Ella. You were asleep."

I look away and realize we're just about to land.

Soon we are off the plane and walking through the airport. We stand in a line of irritable travelers. All of them want to get out into

Rio, and I want it more than any of them. Lots of them are talking fast in languages I don't understand—or at least, in one language I don't understand. I let it drift past me. None of these travelers look as if they're being kidnapped by the people who are supposed to take care of them.

None of them looks as if there might be something wrong inside their bodies.

Actually, some of them do.

"Hello," says the immigration man, and he gives me a quick, bored smile. I pass over my passport and white form, and he stamps the passport and hands it back, part of the form still in it.

I say "Thanks" and join Mum and Dad, who are, of course, both right there, waiting for me. Mum extends a hand, and I give her back my passport and its form. She puts it in her handbag.

I am five years old.

We have one single suitcase among us, and not much hand luggage either. "We'll get the right sort of clothes when we get there," Mum said (God knows what she's packed), and so I am actually showing up in Rio in my school uniform. I'm trying to make it look as un-uniformish as I can by hiking up the skirt and rolling up the sleeves as far as possible, but if you're wearing a short black skirt, black tights, and a white top, and you're not at school, you look like a waitress. I twist the long side of my hair around my finger. I don't want to be wearing tights in Latin America. The air, even indoors, is humid and heavy. Everything feels strange.

Then we are getting into a taxi. A man grabs our suitcase and throws it in. I ignore both parents' attempts at conversation and climb into the front. I slam the door before either of them can tell me that I need to sit in the back with them.

It is dark outside, but I can still see trees with huge green leaves in strange shapes. There are lights twinkling all around. People live in this city: it is their world, and I know almost nothing at all about it.

The driver goes fast, using his horn often. It's totally amazing. He swerves around corners and through tunnels. I'm happy to be his passenger. I can sense both parents tensing behind me, nervous, scared of crashing, but I don't care. This is wild and exciting.

There are buses everywhere: they hurtle along, taking their unimaginable passengers to unimaginable destinations. They are awesome buses, the opposite of the stupid ones that hardly manage to speed up at all between stops at home. One veers toward us from the next lane, but our driver stops it with the liberal use of his horn. I hear Dad clear his throat from his seat behind the driver, and I know that he wants to ask him to slow down and drive like he does, all sensible, checking his mirror and indicating turns and following the rules of the road. I also know that he won't say anything, because he hasn't got the words, and even if he did, he would feel that it was too rude.

I am giddy with excitement. I knew this would be my place, and it is. Everything is different. Everything is wonderful and exciting and dreamlike, and none of it feels real. My head is not ringing. My vision has never been clearer. I feel alive. And entirely myself.

There are mountains silhouetted against the dark sky. I have been longing for the mountains. A light is shining on top of one of them, and the driver points to it and says something to me. I say, "*Que?*" and hope he understands.

"*Cristo Redentor,*" he says, turning toward me with his eyes off the road in a way that makes both parents gasp behind us.

"*Cristo Redentor*," I repeat, and he nods, pleased.

We keep driving until we are past the mountains and there are buildings all around. I cannot stop staring at them. When people say city centers are all the same, they are not talking about this city. There are no chain stores here; no H&M, no Uniqlo, no Zara. Shops flash by, all closed, and occasionally we pass restaurants and bars with people sitting outside, but I can't get a good look at anything because we're driving too fast for anything to come into focus.

I am a bit scared because I still don't know why we are really here, but I stamp that out because this is amazing. It's the place I have looked at every day on my bedroom wall, the place I painted for my art exam. I have always imagined myself here, and now it is happening. I'm here and it's real and better than it was in my head. I am absolutely longing to draw it all.

Soon we are outside a hotel with a shiny front, and a man in uniform opens my door. I am the first out of the car, the first to set foot on the Rio pavement, which is made not from normal paving stones, but from black and white mosaic tiles in swirling patterns. The air is hot. It smells exciting—like the sea and tropical plants and adventure.

I smile at the doorman. I watch my parents fumbling, thanking the driver, thanking the hotel doorman, and I know that they are wondering whether they ought to be tipping either one of them, and if so how much, and what Brazilian currency is all about anyway. I see them looking worried, and I know that they are trying to remember what they paid for the cab when they bought the voucher at the airport, and figuring out what the right percentage of it might be for a tip. While they're doing that, the cabbie drives off, without a tip, and the doorman carries our suitcase into the hotel. I follow him in from the warm damp outdoors to a sharply air-conditioned lobby that is all shiny with marble.

I stand in the cool. Mum and Dad scurry after me and walk up to the desk, where a friendly man welcomes us all in English, hands my parents some forms to fill out, and collects their credit card for check-in.

The three of us are sharing a room. I know it would be twice as expensive if we had two rooms, but I'm sure the reason they're making me sleep in the same room is so that they can watch me all the time, awake and asleep. I had my own room when we went to Cornwall a couple of months ago, but now I am demoted to theirs. I might as well still be a baby. I feel like an object that they have to remember not to lose.

It's a big and beautiful room, though, and I would be monstrous to complain about it. My single bed is quite far away from their double, even if they will still be able to sit up in bed and check on me whenever they want.

I sit on my bed, then lie on my back. The room has a high ceiling, a marble tiled floor, a minibar and a safe, and it's clean and shiny.

"What time is it?"

"Eleven thirty," says Dad. "But that's one thirty back home."

Mum ignores us both and fumbles in the suitcase. She has opened the wardrobe too. Her fussing around the room, trying to look casual, catches my attention, and I start to watch her closely while pretending to fiddle with my shoe. I see her take my phone plus a bundle of papers out of her handbag and open the little hotel safe: from the expression on her face I can tell they are important. I lean forward and try to see them, but all I can tell is that she has brought a handful of official-looking envelopes with her.

She looks around to see whether I'm watching, so I quickly turn away. Then she presses buttons carefully until they beep and the safe is locked. She looks at me again. I pretend I didn't notice a thing.

"Is this the Southern Hemisphere?"

"Of course it is," says Dad.

"We crossed the equator."

"We did," he says. "I believe it goes through the north of Brazil. It's nice to see you excited, Ellie, if I'm allowed to say that."

I smile at him. I am seized with an urge to jump up and down and sing. If, this morning, you had told me my day would end in Rio, I would, of course, have thought it was unimaginably amazing, as well as impossible. And it is. And I am here. I am in a magical place, the place of my dreams. For a moment I forget about all the questions and just love the fact that I'm here.

But I don't jump and sing. I just tell Dad that he *is* allowed to say it. I don't say that Mum wouldn't be: that's not fair but it's true.

I walk over to the window to look at Rio. The window looks out over a courtyard with other people's windows. There are lights on in two balconies that are crammed with flowerpots and bikes and laundry hanging out to dry. Those are not hotel balconies: they are actual Brazilian people's lives.

"Do you want a shower before bed?" Mum says. Her eyes are wild. She is hanging up clothes. She seems to have brought a couple of random outfits for each of us.

"We're not going to bed now," I say. I look at them and see that they both think we are. "Mum! Dad? Hello? You show up at school and pull me out in front of everyone and you say it's for Dad's job, but I bet Dad's not going to go to work tomorrow. You make me sit on a plane for hours without telling me anything that makes literally any sense at all—and now you're telling me to have a shower and go to bed? We're in *Rio de Janeiro* and I'm *not* going to bed. You saw it out there. It's amazing! I don't know what the hell is going on, but we're here, and it must mean something bad is about to happen. So take me out for a drink. Please."

My head is ringing a bit, but I am not having that, not here, not now. My eyes dart around the edges of things, trying to keep them clear. I feel Bella stumbling out of her cave, so I make my way over to my bed and sit on it. I take deep breaths. I tell her to go back. I might need her later. I don't need her now.

She actually does back off. That's unusual. The idea of going out in Rio must be enough for her right now. It makes me very happy.

Neither parent notices anything. Mum sighs and puts both hands to her temples, which is just completely annoying.

Dad shakes his head. "We can go out tomorrow, darling. Not now. It's one thirty in the morning, and we're in a foreign city. You have to be careful in Rio. You can't just wander around in the middle of the night. You're young and you have no idea how sheltered you've been."

Mum does a little huff when he says this. "We might as well write big signs saying, 'Mug me' and hold them above our heads."

"People wouldn't understand them, because they'd be written in a foreign language," I say.

My vision is perfectly clear now, even though I'm annoyed. I shift backward and lean on the wall. I am all Ella. "Besides, it's eleven thirty, not one thirty, and I'm old enough for you to stop sheltering me, if that's what you've been doing." I am cross, but it's a mild, normal sort of cross. I just want to go out in Rio. It's nothing bigger than that. It feels normal and amazing. "Let's ask at reception if it's safe for us to go out," I say, using the most reasonable voice I can produce. "Please. If there isn't somewhere right on this block, then we can come back and go to bed. I don't want alcohol or anything like that. I just want to sit out on one of those chairs on the street. Now that we're here."

They look at each other. They look at me, their daughter, smiling at them, happy to be here. They both start putting their shoes back on. I close my eyes, lean my head against the wall, and feel the gratitude flooding through me.

The man at reception laughs and says that of course it is absolutely fine to go out, and that there's a bar almost next door. Even though I'm still wearing my school uniform, I can't wait to go there.

We leave the hotel, and the bar is right where he said it would be. There is live music blasting out, and all I want to do is go inside and let the music go right through me and dance and dance and dance. People are standing up, listening to the band play. Some of them are, in an unshowy way, dancing in the street. I want to stay and dance in the street too, but obviously Mum and Dad don't, and anyway I don't want to dance with *them*. I look closely at the people as we pass them. These people are Brazilians. I am in their country. I am a foreigner now.

I am foreign.

I am a stranger.

I am an outsider.

It is thrilling and scary. I want to roll up the sleeves of my school sweater, but I don't because I'm scared of my tiny white scars, even though they are probably too small for anyone to notice.

When we get to the corner, I see the name of our street on a sign.

"*Nossa Senhora de Copacabana*?" I read. "Copacabana? Is that where we are?"

"Yes." Mum looks far less happy with this fact than I am. "Yes, darling. This is the area where lots of the hotels are."

"Copacabana?"

"Yes."

"We are standing in *Copacabana*? Actual Copacabana in Rio? Where's the beach? I want to paddle in the water right now! I want to look at the little mountains out in the sea! I spent ages painting them."

"In the morning." Dad sounds exhausted, and I know that, actually, I am pushing it now. "Absolutely not now. That beach is seriously dangerous after dark. It's a block or so away from here—I don't know in which direction—we'll find it in the daylight."

"Is it really dangerous? Or is that just something people think?"

"Really dangerous. I'm not comfortable as it is, leaving the hotel at night. We're doing it for you, Ellie, when both your mother and I want to go to bed. And if we don't see a decent-looking café in the next few minutes, we're going back."

"Come on." I tug his arm. "Look. There's a place over there, with tables outside. One drink and we'll go back to the hotel."

We sit down and I order a Coke. Dad has a beer, which he attempts to order by saying, "*Una thairvaytha, por favor,*" but the barman looks confused for quite a long time, so Dad points and says "beer?" and is immediately handed a bottle. Mum has a pale green cocktail with mashed-up limes in it. It's not a drink I've ever seen before, at home. Not even at the pub Jack and I sometimes go to. We usually drink lager. Sometimes Lily and I go out and drink sticky-sweet drinks like Southern Comfort. Occasionally I get to tag along with Lily, Mollie and the twins, and we have cocktails with silly names and I am always the first to leave.

As far as my parents are concerned, of course, I've never drunk anything more outlandish than the occasional glass of wine with dinner.

"When in Rome," Mum says, and she starts to drink her green cocktail through the straw. "Oh my *God*, I need this."

I've seen her drink wine. I've never seen her drunk. This will be interesting to watch.

Some other English people are talking loudly nearby. They have the air of being straight off the plane, too. They are drinking beer but eyeing Mum's cocktail.

"This doesn't feel scary," I say. "You have to admit—this is a lot less scary than Wetherspoon's."

Dad tilts his head in a way that means it might not feel scary, but that this fact doesn't mean we're safe. He tries to look at me as if he knows everything and I am a little girl who needs protecting, but it doesn't work. He knows everything about why we're here, and still he is terrified of the very air that we're breathing.

I am not.

Dad drinks half his bottle of beer in a couple of gulps. I close my eyes and draw in a deep breath. I woke up this morning, had a shower, played with Humphrey, and went to school feeling bored. Now I am sitting outside at a table in Rio de Janeiro, watching as my mum drinks a cocktail very quickly through a straw and orders another one.

I have no idea what has happened.

CHAPTER FOUR

SOMETHING STRANGE HAPPENED. I have had a weird and messed-up dream that ended with me crawling into a bed in Rio in the same room as my parents, who, by the time I got into bed, were comatose after chucking back three drinks each, which they never do.

I need to wake up. It's time for school. The light is coming in through the curtains, and that means I've overslept. Even before I open my eyes, I can tell that it's brighter than usual.

I'm too sleepy, but I have to get up, because I need to go to school.

I yawn, and open my eyes.

I am not in my bedroom.

My parents are in the same room as me.

I'm in Rio.

It happened. This is Brazil. The room is light because the curtains weren't closed properly. My dad is sitting up in bed reading a book, with the air of someone who wants a cup of tea and has had a look around for the kettle and found it missing because of our being Abroad in a Foreign Place.

If he wanted a cup of tea in bed, he shouldn't have made us leave the country.

Mum is still asleep. Her hair is all over the pillow, and her mouth is open. She was too tipsy to take her makeup off, so there is mascara all the way down one of her cheeks. It's probably on the pillowcase too, even though she has always told me that if I must wear makeup (and I don't need to because I am so pretty, etc.), then I must always take it off before bed because of pores and bed linens and things. She doesn't often wear makeup herself, and she is not looking like such a classy lady now. If I had my phone, I would pretend to Dad that I was going to take her photo (though I wouldn't really be that mean: I would mime it to make him laugh). But of course I don't have it because they took it away from me and now it's locked in that safe.

I have to get my phone. Yesterday was one thing, but actually living daily life with my parents and without a phone is something completely different. I don't know what to do with myself, knowing that I can't look at what's happened in the world or just put on my headphones and listen to music or an audiobook.

Everyone else listens to music. I do, but I listen to books more. I don't know why everyone doesn't want to be read a story, all the time. I listen to the exam texts over and over again, and that's how I know them so well. If I could, I would read one book with my eyes while listening to another one with my ears.

Dad sees me looking at Mum. He looks down at her too, sleeping off her cocktails, and smiles. I smile back and haul myself out of bed and into the bathroom.

This is Copacabana.

There is a beach nearby.

No one robbed us when we went out, and no one looked as if they might be thinking about it, either, even though it was dark and we had absolutely no idea what we were doing or where we were going.

These are things I know.

What I don't know is how long my parents and I are going to be here and why.

Today they have to tell me.

I am going to make them tell me.

Even if it's something awful, I have to know, because I am starting to imagine things.

I brush my teeth and comb my hair with my fingers. I am far too pale to be here. I need to get a tan.

An hour later I trail into the dining room after my parents, trying to look independent and cool.

No one cares.

The room is informal, with a huge bank of buffet tables on one side, televisions high up on the walls, and tables with white tablecloths. The staff is wearing black-and-white uniforms, but they don't look stuffy in them. I watch Dad talking to the woman at reception, and then follow him and Mum over to a table.

"We just help ourselves, darling," says Mum.

The buffet is enormous, covering table after table. I stare at it.

"Nice."

"I know!" says Dad. "Right? As much as you like. Go for it."

I pile a plate with scrambled eggs (or "mixed eggs" as the label calls them) and some balls coated in breadcrumbs that turn out to have lovely melted cheese in the middle, and a roll. I put that on the table and go back for a glass of fresh orange juice. A woman comes around with a jug of coffee and pours it for us, though Mum shakes her head and goes to find herself some kind of pathetic homeopathic tea from an otherwise-unvisited table around the side of a pillar. Dad, usually another massive fan of horrible weak tea, joins me with the coffee.

"This is an awesome breakfast," I say, and it is. The cheese-ball things are wonderful: for some reason I don't want to eat meat at the moment. I love animals, so I don't really know why I've always eaten them. I look at Dad's bacon and things, but I don't take any from his plate even though he would let me.

Mum is just eating fruit (she always claims to like only things that grow from the ground), and it looks so nice that I go back when I've finished all my eggs and cheesy things, and get myself a second plate of breakfast from the grown-from-the-ground part of the table. I end up with a pile of mango, watermelon and pineapple slices, all juicy and all gorgeous. I could eat like this every day.

Perhaps we *will* eat like this, every day, now. Perhaps this is the rest of our lives.

"So," I say to them as we finish our drinks. "What's the plan? What time do you need to be at work, Dad? Did your suit get crumpled in the suitcase? Because it must have been in there, since you're going to work."

I stare from one of them to the other. This would be a good time for them to admit they made that part up, but of course they don't.

"Oh, Ella." Mum is using her put-upon voice, which I think is a bit rich, considering. "Ella. Just give us a bit of space to think, please, darling. Dad's work isn't today."

"Of course it's not. How surprising. So what do you need to think about?"

70

Mum looks hurt by my tone. I am getting annoyed, and I can feel Bella beginning to stir. Hiding Bella from Mum has, I realize, been the single greatest achievement of my life. I would be horrified if Mum found out what I'm really like. Bella cannot come out right now.

"We just need to make a plan. I know we need to buy you some more clothes, and we will. Let me talk to the front desk about the best place to go for that."

I sigh. "OK. Can I have the room key? I want to go and read my book. I'll watch some Brazilian TV. Or am I not allowed to be out of your sight in case someone kidnaps me?"

Mum looks at Dad, who laughs.

"Much as you're adorable, Ellie, I don't think you'll be kidnapped between here and our room. Here you go."

He extracts the room key from his wallet and hands it over, and I walk as quickly as I can out of the breakfast room, to get away from them.

Something happened when I meantioned being kidnapped. It was only a fraction of a second, but Mum's face gave it away. Dad gave a look too, though he covered it instantly. I have no idea what the fuck that could mean. To everyone other than me, I am a normal girl, and no one in their right mind would want to kidnap me. Who would want Ella Black? I come with baggage, and although my parents have enough money for this trip, apparently, they're not exactly the global super-rich, so it can't really warrant a ransom situation.

All I can think of is that I might be ill, and Mum and Dad have arranged for some doctors to come and take me away for some special kind of treatment. I don't want to be ill. I want to get out of school (which I appear to have done, for the moment) and have adventures. I want to see new things, have new experiences. I want to make myself

71

better, in my head, and do things in the world. I want to do good things, for other people as well as for myself.

That is a new thought.

There is something in the safe that will help me figure out what's happening. I know there is.

I will get up to the room and try all possible codes until I open it. It has to be my birthday. They always use my birthday. If it isn't my birthday, I'll know there is something they really really *really* don't want me to see, but somehow, I will find it.

And then I see him.

Three people are coming through the door from the lobby to the breakfast room as I'm charging out. They are Latin-looking, chatting in what seems to be both Spanish and English. It's the boy at the back who makes me stop.

It is like being electrocuted. I recognize something in his eyes. He's a stranger, but I know him. This boy is one of the main characters in my life. I know in an instant that the feelings in the books and the poems and the songs are real. I know him: I just haven't met him yet.

It is the strangest feeling.

He has dark brown hair and olive-y skin, and he is tall and broad and muscular. I never knew it before, but this is what my ideal boy looks like. Jack flits through my head, and I smile. Jack would like this boy too.

The boy stops and looks at me. He smiles. Our eyes meet. I could not look away if I wanted to.

He looks older than I am, but not much, and he's wearing cut-off denim shorts and a plain green T-shirt. His smile is the most perfect smile. He has even teeth, and his smile takes over his whole face. I am smiling too.

"Hola," he says. He is staring at me in the same way I am staring at him. Am I imagining that? I don't think I am. I hope I'm not. No one has ever looked at me like this.

"Hola," I say. I don't know what to do, so I grin a bit more. He is looking into my eyes, and although I want to freeze this moment and save it forever, I have to be the first to look away. I need to get into the elevator before my parents come along and ruin everything.

I break the eye contact and try not to fall over as I walk across the small lobby. I press the "up" button and turn back. He is still looking. Our eyes meet again. I say everything I can through my eyes, and he says it back.

Then he gives a little nod and turns away, catching up with his friends. I step inside the elevator.

If anyone else were here, they would see a girl grinning like an idiot at her reflection in the elevator door mirror. In fact, I am being serenaded by cherubs with harps. I am being struck by that angel with the arrow. I am gasping for breath.

I have to talk to that boy. I don't know what I'd say, but I don't care.

The elevator chimes, and I am on the eleventh floor. I open our room and sit down on the bed, and relive the almost-wordless encounter over and over again without stopping.

He is staying at the hotel. I have to speak to him. He is with two friends, a boy and a girl. I, however, am with my mummy and daddy. That might be the thing that spoils everything.

I cannot let that happen.

All I want is that boy. I have no idea whether we will be able to speak to each other directly, but I'm pretty sure one of his friends was speaking English.

We both said *"Hola."* It is not really very much to work with, but I replay it again and again.

He was going to breakfast at eight thirty. Tomorrow I will go to breakfast at eight thirty, too, and I will do whatever it takes to get there without my parents.

First, I must find something new to wear. The dress I am wearing right now, packed by Mum, is all right, but it's the only thing I've got that is. It is purple like my hair, made from T-shirt material, and although it's very plain and cost almost nothing, it's nice. Still, I need to do some serious shopping today in order to have something better to wear to breakfast tomorrow. At home I always wear sleeves even though I know I don't need to. Here it's too hot to do that.

Now, though, I'm in the room alone, and I need to see what's in the safe.

I stand in front of it. It wants a four-digit code, so obviously I'm going to try to give it the exact one it needs. As well as all the big, important-looking envelopes, my phone is in there, and I would really, really like it back. I try my birthday: 1711. It doesn't work. The fact that they didn't set it to my birthday means they were trying hard to keep me out of it. I try my year of birth, and Mum's birthday, and Dad's, but literally nothing works.

Whatever is in here, my parents *really* don't want me to find it. I start to panic.

SMASH IT UP.

I shake my head. I can't actually smash it up. Can I?

IT'S NOT REALLY SECURE. IT'S JUST FOR REASSURANCE. WE CAN EASILY BREAK IT.

We can't. I mustn't. I look around for an implement, just in case, but someone is knocking on the door. Bella fades away as I stare at it, picturing the gorgeous boy on the other side of it, abandoning the safe. He has asked reception for my room number and come to find me.

If I opened the door and found him standing there, I would step right up and kiss him. I would kiss him without knowing his name or anything about him.

I pull my hair over my shoulder, arrange my body to what might or might not be its best advantage, take a deep breath, and open the door.

"Oh," I say, slumping. "It's you."

Dad laughs. "Who were you expecting?"

"No one. We have two keys, don't we?"

"Yes. And both of them are here. We didn't think we'd need two keys for breakfast."

"Ella," says Mum. "Are you all right, darling? You look pale."

I turn on her. I can't help it. "You always say I look pale. I'm pale because we live in a cold, rainy country, and even though we're in Brazil now, we haven't actually been outside in daylight. We're like the vampires of Rio."

"Ella!"

I cave instantly. "Sorry. I'm just desperate to get outside, because we're actually here. You know?"

She caves too. She hugs me, pulling me tight so my face is in her hair.

"Oh, I'm sorry, darling. I know it's a lot to deal with. Let's get ourselves together and get out into the sunshine. I know you need to see the beach, and it ought to be safe enough in daylight if we don't carry valuables. There are shopping malls and things like that, so after you've seen the beach, we can get the hotel to call us a taxi to a mall and get you all fixed up." She flicks her eyes at me and away. "And if you wanted to get your hair dyed back to your lovely blond, we could do that too. I'm sure it would be easy."

I frown. I don't need to answer that part. "Clothes would be good," I say. "Thank you." I am going to keep being nice. No outbursts, even though my parents are annoying and boring and right now they are forming a constant human shield around me that will keep me from opening the safe and talking to that boy.

I know Mum is trying her best, but I am very nearly eighteen. They have trusted me to walk around town on my own since I was eleven, and now they've gone completely, freakishly weird on me. However, I do need new clothes, and I am desperate to get out into the sunshine and see the beach and breathe the air and embrace the fact that I am actually here, so I pull myself together. I'll try the safe again later.

"Thanks," I say. I make myself smile at her. "Sorry. The beach would be wonderful. Thank you."

The relief that swamps her face, just for a moment, makes me feel bad.

It is the middle of the afternoon. We have been to the shops, and now I am sitting on the real, sandy, gorgeous Copacabana beach, a sketchbook on my lap, drawing the beach and the rocks and the mountains in real life. The sun is on my face, and I am doing my best to look entirely absorbed by my drawing while secretly listening to my parents' whispered conversation. I am frowning and concentrating hard (but not really), and after a while they start talking a tiny bit louder. I strain to catch the words, and then I hear Mum saying, "The cattery is asking for a fortune."

Dad says, "Well, they always do."

I keep listening, but it turns out they really are talking about how much it will cost for Humphrey to go to his own hotel. Apparently our housecleaner, Michelle, is coming in on Thursday, and Mum says she's asked her to drop Humphrey off when she leaves.

They didn't plan this trip *at all*.

I feel bad for Humphrey. I bet he'd rather stay out in the wild, catching his own dinner, than go to that smelly place and be shut in a cage, having to listen to the yowling of all the other cats, every one of them asking loudly why the humans have sent them to prison. I would never have chosen to go away without saying good-bye to him. I would have cuddled him and talked to him, and I would have explained why I was leaving and when I would be back. He will be missing me, and he will also be missing Bella. I have had an almost Bella-free day today. I love that. I can't remember the last time that happened, if it ever has.

I have to find out what's happening. And I have to find that boy.

I watch a tiny child splashing in the shallow water. Copacabana is not how I expected it to be, even though I knew exactly what it looked like—even though, in fact, I made a huge painting of almost this exact view in art last year. Then I was painting from a still photo, and now I am sketching from life, and it is wildly lively. Everyone is here. A group of enthusiastic boys is running up and down nearby, wearing tiny swimming trunks, and I cannot stop staring at the chiseled contours of their bodies. They are all black and glistening. Their muscles are defined, and none of them has an ounce of fat. They don't look like humans in the way that my parents and I are human. I have never seen anyone who looks like this, not in real life.

I think back to the boy in the hotel again. Every part of me longs to be close to him.

The toddler's mother comes and takes his hand. Vendors come past all the time, selling peanuts and sunglasses. Up by the pavement, a string of little cafés sells food and drink, coffee and beer. Everything anyone could want is right here.

I cram as much of my surroundings, as much life as I can, into my drawing.

A woman runs past wearing a tiny bathing suit, her body jiggling all over the place, and no one seems to notice. I know that on a British beach, people would be snickering at her, but here they really don't look or care at all.

I fill in some detail of the bumpy little mountains that are out in the water. Mist floats around in the distance, and the green hills are sometimes hidden, sometimes revealed.

"Nice to see you happy," says Dad. I try to make a sulky face, but it doesn't work, because both my parents laugh. Mum is now more relaxed than she has been since we got here, and it's actually nice to see that. I actually do want her to be happy, because if she's less haunted and stressed, that means the sense of emergency might have lessened a bit.

"You always said you'd love it here," she says, looking at my picture and smiling. I want them to think that this is enough, that Rio and the sunshine and the little denim shorts and tops and sandals they've bought me are enough to keep me from trying to figure out what is going on.

I put my book down and smile at them.

"So," I say. "We can fit in some sightseeing now. Let's do something."

They both laugh and look at each other. Mum shrugs.

"I suppose," says Dad, "that this could be a good time to visit the famous Jesus up on the hill. What's its name? You know—the Christ statue."

"Yeah—the *Cristo Redentor*?"

"What?"

"The taxi driver said it last night. It was lit up on the hilltop. He said it was *Cristo Redentor*."

"I missed that," says Mum. "Christ the Redeemer. Well. The morning might be better, really. I'm not sure the hotel will be able to arrange us a trip immediately."

"They organize all kind of trips," says Dad. "I asked about it. They book the Cristo thing, and Sugarloaf Mountain, and any number of walking tours. He said there are even tours to the favelas. The slums. I think we can skip that one, don't you?"

I remember the film *City of God*. We watched that a few months ago, as part of Mollie's education.

"A tour of the slums?" I say. "That sounds like a horrible idea. Stare at the poor people! Point at them and take photos and then go back to the lovely comfy hotel? I actually think that's disgusting."

"And those favelas are absolute no-go areas," says Mum. "We need to keep you safe."

Her words hang in the air.

The man at the hotel, whose name tag says he is Pedro, tells us that this is a good day to go up the mountain because it's so clear, but that we'll have to hurry because it's late in the day.

"You don't need a tour," he says, smiling the conspiratorial smile of one who knows that he's supposed to be pushing them at us. "You just need a taxi. Then you buy tickets for the train. It's very easy. Don't speak to anyone trying to sell you a trip when you get out of the taxi, OK?"

"Will it be OK that we don't speak Spanish?" I say, and he laughs.

"Well, that won't matter at all. Here in Brazil we speak Portuguese. But no, you'll be fine with English."

"I meant Portuguese," I say, my cheeks flaming. I didn't really: I had no idea. But now I do.

The doorman flags down a yellow cab and tells the driver where we're going, and we are off, weaving through the streets again. I sit in the front, like before. I just go and get in and no one stops me.

The driver grins at me.

"*Hola,*" I say experimentally. I have just repeated everything I have ever said to the boy at breakfast.

"*Hola,*" he replies with a nod. We set off into the traffic, and I stare out the window, trying to see everything.

I could look at Rio forever. I think you'd see new things every single time. There are people in Lycra. There are gyms with huge windows looking out to the streets, filled with people flinging themselves into weightlifting. There are old people and children, black people and white people walking around. There are juice bars and coffee shops and restaurants. There are drag queens and old men in suits, fat people and thin people. There are old people sitting in parks playing chess. Everything is here.

At school, I thought I was pretty much educated. I barely scraped through the social side of things, but when it came to the education, I thought I was doing all right. I thought I knew the things you need to know. Now I'm not sure I know any single thing at all. The world is much larger than I realized, and there is much more to life than my small existence back home. These people, and their language. When I listen to Brazilian people speaking, I can't make out a word of it. The sounds are different: there are lots of "shh" and "chh" things going on. If we stay longer, I'm going to have to puzzle it out.

Yesterday, everything in my life was mapped out. Now it's not. No one seems to hate me in Brazil; I am coming alive.

All I need now is to know why I'm here. I have to get online. I must find a way to get my phone so I can find out what I'm doing here.

I try to remember anything I've read about parents running away with their children. One parent does it to keep the child away from the other, but that's not us. Some parents ran away with their child a few years ago, I think, because the child was ill and they didn't want to take him for chemo; they wanted him treated with crystals or something.

I would know if I were desperately ill. There would have been doctors' appointments and hospitals.

With a lurch of my stomach, I remember that there *were* doctors' appointments.

My vision goes a bit fuzzy. This is important. I can't have Bella stirring. I need to focus. I force her away using all my willpower.

I remember. I was small, and I hated them. I remember them only in a fuzzy way, but I know that they happened. I remember being upset, crying and crying, and everyone trying to comfort me and tell me it was all right. I remember a woman talking to me in a nasty pretend-kind way, but I didn't like her eyes and I wouldn't speak to her. I remember my mother crying along with me.

Until now, I had forgotten it all.

I remember my mum saying, "We'll always look after you." I remember that making me feel better. What if I have a genetic condition? It could be getting worse. Perhaps I won't be able to live much longer before I start to deteriorate. That could be a reason to bring me to Rio.

I try not to think about that.

Instead I try to think about the last things I heard on the news as we drove away from school. Something about a nuclear standoff, I think. Maybe we're here to hide out from that. There was also something about the simian flu, which has been vaguely around for a while. Perhaps, without my knowing, I have tested positive for it and my parents have brought me here to keep me from being dissected and used for medical research.

Though Rio is not a place you go to get *away* from terrifying viruses.

It all seems unlikely. Everything seems impossible, but the doctors' appointments feel like the biggest clue. I am probably very ill. I whisper that under my breath.

I am probably very ill.

The driver looks over, but he doesn't say anything.

If I am ill, it might explain why I have Bella. I could have something in my brain, something real, a tumor with a name. I wish I had my phone. I would use it to google possible conditions I might have. I would wade through medical papers. Or I could use it for distraction, if Rio wasn't distraction enough.

I stare out the cab window into a bus, where a woman is holding a tiny dog up to the window. I wave at the dog, and the lady lifts its paw to make it wave back.

I focus on my toes. They feel fine. My legs feel OK. So do my knees. Of course they do: this thing is in my head. I concentrate as hard as I can on each part of my body, inside and out, to try to diagnose anything that might be out of the ordinary, but it all, as far as I can tell, feels all right. If I were ill, or some kind of medical time bomb, they wouldn't be letting me out and about in Rio. Or would they? Perhaps they would. I don't know anything.

The secret illness is, weirdly, the most plausible of the possibilities. I feel sick.

I want my phone. I want my book. Before we left, I was reading a sci-fi trilogy about a place called Area X that changed people when they went into it. I am in my own Area X, and I want to go back to the fictional one, please.

I want to listen to music.

I want to talk to Jack and Lily.

I want to see that boy.

When we get out of the cab, scalpers descend, as Pedro said they would, trying to sell us trips up the mountain. I swat them away, striding on to the ticket office ahead of my parents because I know Mum would be swayed by anyone telling her the trip would be too dangerous unless she bought a special expensive tour. I ask for the tickets myself, and Dad pays, and we go into the waiting area, where a man is painted silver, standing very still with a hat set out for coins.

I sit a little ways away from my parents on the train, staring out the window. I want them to feel like they can talk without me overhearing them. But in fact, I'm concentrating hard on listening to whatever they need to say to each other, because I am consumed by the need to know. If I am going to die soon, this might be my last able-bodied trip out into the world. I imagine my brain melting away until I can't read or speak or think or feed myself. I would kill myself now rather than let that happen.

The train judders into action, and I stare out at the rain forest. *Live every day as if it were your last, because one day it will be.* That was a meme that used to be passed around at school. It felt like an easy thing to say, trite but kind of true. It was superficial and easy.

Now it feels terrifying.

After a while, I see that Mum and Dad are leaning toward each other, muttering in their fight-y way, so I slide over onto the seat behind theirs, and they don't notice.

"Yes, I know," Dad is hissing. "But Ellie's not demonstrative. She never has been. She's not the hugging type. It's not *you*. It's because she's—"

He breaks off quickly, because Mum stiffens. She has sensed me there and looked around.

"What?" I say. "It's because I'm *what*?"

"Nothing," says Mum. "Don't creep up."

I'm not the hugging type. That is true. It's been so long since Mum has even tried. She will never know that my good self has often kept away from her so Bella can't hurt her.

Bella absolutely hates my mother.

I want to cry but I can't because I'm not really the crying type, either. Right now, though, I think it would feel really good to cry.

The ringing starts low.

"We went to the doctors a lot when I was little." It is hard to get the words out, but I say them carefully, one by one. "Why?"

Both of them look straight ahead. Neither of them so much as blinks. I feel the panic coming off their backs; at least I think I do. I think I feel them utterly frozen because they don't know what to say. I think I feel them wondering how on earth to handle this.

I wish they'd turn around and look at me, puzzled, and say something like, "What are you talking about? No you didn't." But they don't, and the time ticks by, and still they don't turn around or say anything at all.

Mum has been protecting me all my life—the closed-circuit television camera outside the house, the quadruple locks on the doors, the burglar and fire alarms. I have no idea what I'm being protected from. Or maybe, like I always thought, she really is scared of the outside world and felt safest knowing that I was inside with her.

Unless they were protecting me from something else.

Regardless, I'm nearly an adult now. If I'm ill, they have to tell me, because that is what people do. Little children get told when they've got leukemia, and yet somehow I am forbidden from knowing what this huge thing is that's wrong with my life.

I want to tell them I'm scared. I long to be the hugging type. I want to ask them to take care of me, now, but I can't. It's easier to be nasty. It is getting easier and easier as my head is filled with a high-pitched ringing. Bella is blocking out the rain forest and the train so that all I can see is my parents. Like me, she knows they have the answer and that there is something about me they are choosing to keep secret because they don't trust me, or because it's too awful.

I want to let my parents protect me, to have them stroke me and tell me that everything is going to be all right, that I'm not terminally ill, that this trip to Brazil is just a weird treat because they love me so much.

THAT'S NOT WHAT IT IS.

I know.

THEY'RE LYING.

I know.

DO SOMETHING ABOUT IT.

I don't even want to be nice now. Blotches dance across my vision.

"I'm nearly eighteen," I whisper. They both have to lean back to hear me.

SAY THE THINGS THAT WILL HURT THEM THE MOST.

"I'm not your baby. I'm an adult now, and I could get up and walk away from here and never speak to either of you ever again." *I am holding the hammer, hitting the bird.* "And I will. You don't have the right to keep this secret from me. If you don't tell me what's going on, you don't get to be my parents anymore. You don't trust me enough to tell me anything—I don't trust you enough to live with you. That's how it is."

A part of me gasps. I have never spoken to them when Bella has surfaced before. Not since I was tiny and I had what everyone always called "tantrums," before I learned that I had to hide this other part of myself.

"Ellie," says Dad. He puts a hand on my arm. I shake it off. I cannot let him close to Bella.

"You . . . should . . . tell . . . me," I say. I bite my lip until it bleeds. I clench my hands into fists and push my nails into my palms. I inhale deeply. I cannot shout and rage on a train that is juddering up a Brazilian mountain, that is otherwise filled with content tourists idly staring out of windows. I can't attack them in public even though Bella is begging me to let her. I walk quickly away to stop myself from exploding, and when I get close to the back of the train, I sit on an empty seat, slide over to the window and press my forehead against the glass.

There must be some medication that would stop this from happening.

Maybe it's Bella that's made me ill. She might be a symptom, or she might, somehow, be a cause.

Go away

go away

go away.

I close my eyes and recite the words. I need her to leave.

The universe the universe the universe.

I picture outer space. I am not even a fraction of a dot. I am tiny and insignificant.

As we judder on, she recedes. She goes just far enough for me to take control of myself. It would have been better to cry. Then they would have come close and they would have hugged me. They are my parents and I know I love them. Of course I love them. Everything I do is about trying not to disappoint them, about being the respectable daughter they deserve and hiding the bad things. And I have just said terrible things. I am crying now, staring out at the wild greenery. I wipe my eyes with the back of my hand and sniff. My eyeliner must be everywhere. I cannot fall to pieces. I try to breathe.

Stay

away,

Bella.

S
t
a
y
a
w
a
y,
B
e
l
l
a.

Someone taps me on the shoulder. I look around without bothering to tidy my face up, and see that a man who is wearing a baseball cap with "Venezuela" on it is holding out a pack of tissues. I shake my head but then reach out a trembling hand and take them anyway. I wipe my eyes and blow my nose. I can't look back at him again, but I am grateful.

I wrestle myself under control. I can tell that my parents are looking at me, and I want to open up to them, but I can't, because I cannot tell them that I am possessed by my own demon, and they still haven't told me what I'm doing here. Dad's right: though he and I have always shared an understanding, I've never been one for hugs and kisses. I built that barrier up myself by trying to protect them, but they've strengthened it now by bringing me here with a huge secret.

I started it and they've made it worse. I hate myself and now I hate them, too.

There is a couple in front of me. They are men with tattoos who are smiling at each other and laughing and pointing things out and laughing at their own private jokes, and I want to ask them if I can walk around with them when we get to the top of this mountain. They probably don't want a strange foreign girl tagging along with them— least of all a strange foreign girl with purple hair and white legs and a tearstained face, who didn't even know until a few hours ago that Portuguese is the language of Brazil.

The Venezuela man taps me on the shoulder again, and I hand back the tissue pack, but he gestures for me to keep it. He says something that I don't understand, and then when he sees I don't understand, he says, "I'm sorry you sad."

I manage a little smile and nod. That feels like the kindest thing anyone has ever said. I bet my parents don't like me talking to a strange man, but I don't care. I see them looking back at me, but they don't come over, and I'm glad.

The forest parts, and then I am looking at the most breathtaking view in the world. The sun is glinting off the sea. There are little mountains out in the water, and I can see the beaches, the sprawl of buildings, the tiny cars. I gaze and gaze and gaze. I breathe. I stare and breathe, and I'm not ready for the train to stop when it does.

Outside, my parents come and stand beside me, and I want to say the right thing. I want to say sorry, but the word sticks in my throat and I can barely breathe around it. I move instead, along with the crowd, and they walk on either side of me.

"Ella," says Dad. I'm glad it's him speaking, rather than her. "Look. I know this is frustrating. There are a few things we just can't tell you right now. It's nothing terrible. Please just trust us for a while. You're not ill."

I don't answer because I don't believe him, and I don't know what to say. I give each parent an awkward little hug—the best I can manage—and walk away.

The huge statue of Jesus towers above us. A crowd of people is gathered at a distance from him, standing with their arms outstretched like his, while each one has a friend lying on their back on the ground in front of them, taking a photograph. I suppose the angle makes it look funny. In a way I want to try it out, just to be normal. But I can't, of course, because I am the only person on this mountain without a phone. A little kid of about three is sitting on the ground playing with one. I am literally the only person who doesn't have the piece of technology that connects you to the world, and your friends, and the things you love, and your life. And I don't even know why I don't have it. Because I don't know anything.

But I can't forget that Bella said horrible things to Mum and Dad. That has happened now. It is there: they have met her even though they don't know it. I want to say sorry to them, to make it up to them, to thank them for bringing me here to the best place in the world. But I can't: I don't know how.

So I decide that I'm never going to be horrible ever again; the rest of the trip is going to be amazing.

There are souvenir shops and stalls selling everything Christ the Redeemer branded, and I want to get a fridge magnet for our kitchen to remind us of this trip. Except, of course, that I don't know how many days are going to pass before we'll be back in our kitchen, or if anything will ever be normal again.

A stressed-looking man wearing a Jesus apron and baseball cap strides past me into the café, and Mum appears, taking my arm and guiding me out of his way. I shake her off and move away when I actually want to sob in her arms.

I want a hat. I want an apron. I want things with this place on them, to anchor me. I look at Jesus. I wish he actually would redeem me. I stare up at him. His arms are open. His skirt has lovely pleats in it.

I take a deep breath. I need to be able to make myself be nice. I do it at school every day. I can compliment Jesus on his drapery, but I can't say anything kind to my own mother.

I will try.

I walk closer to my mum. "Sorry," I say. My voice comes out very quiet indeed. "Mum. I'm sorry I was horrible on the train. Really sorry."

She puts her arm around my shoulders and tries to pull me into a proper hug. This time I let her do it. Because she is my mum.

CHAPTER FIVE

I WALK INTO the breakfast room, carefully dressed in my new outfit with my hair blow-dried and what I hope is just the right amount of makeup to make me look "natural." I scan the room, my heart fluttering, every atom of me longing to see him and also scared that if I do see him, the magic might be over. I imagine looking at him and just seeing someone ordinary. I imagine his eyes looking over me and then, bored, focusing on something else. It felt so magical yesterday that it might not have been real at all.

I look around the room, and I know that none of these people is him.

"Are you sure, darling?" Mum said when she saw me ready to go downstairs. "I mean, that outfit is a little more 'beach' than it is 'hotel breakfast.'"

I took a deep breath and reminded myself to be nice.

"It'll be fine," I said. "It's Rio, and I'm dressing for the day." I wanted to snap at her, but I didn't.

Because it's our second morning, I feel like someone who totally knows the way things are done around here. I go straight to the buffet for a glass of orange juice. I stand by the table of food on my own, wondering whether I could really attract the attention of the most gorgeous boy in the world, over breakfast at a hotel in Rio de Janeiro.

If he turns up.

What if he went home yesterday? What if he isn't here at all? What if I never see that boy again? Yesterday morning's glance might be the only experience of love that I'm going to have, for my entire life.

The idea gives me a pain in my chest. It makes my brain hurt, my heart hurt. It would be unbearable, to stare into a stranger's eyes and feel everything and then never see him again.

I put the juice on the table. Both parents are sitting there waiting for the coffee lady to arrive, and I know that I should have offered to get them some juice too. I don't know why I didn't.

"D'you want some juice?" I mutter. They both look delighted to be asked, but they say no. I go and get them each an orange juice anyway and put them on the table in front of them, just in case they want them.

I go back to pile up a plate of fruit, which I eat with a knife and fork while Mum goes to get the same thing for herself and Dad helps himself to bacon and, oddly for breakfast time, toasted ham-and-cheese sandwiches. I still don't want to eat meat. In fact, right now I am eating a raw vegan diet, consisting only of fruit, which would make my skin glow and my eyes sparkle if I kept it up, so I keep it up for several minutes, until I drink some coffee and then remember the cheese balls and go and pile a plate with them.

I have a cheese ball in my mouth when he looks at me. Not only do I have a cheese ball in my mouth, but I am talking to my parents about whether it is too cloudy for us to take the cable car up Sugarloaf Mountain. I am saying, "We probably don't need to go up a mountain *every single day*." When I say the word *day*, however, I put so much emphasis on it that a big piece of cheese ball flies out of my mouth and onto the table and stays connected to my mouth by a string of melted cheese, and that is when I look up and see that the boy is standing nearby, looking at me.

It is the worst thing that has ever happened.

He is standing waiting for the buffet, beside the very next table to ours, with his two friends, and he is smiling at me, though his smile is now frozen. This is the worst moment of my life.

He was watching as I spat food out on the table. He saw that, and he can still see it because the string of cheese still leads from the table to my mouth, and there is absolutely no way around that.

I want to die right now. I want the hotel to catch fire so we can all run into the street and down to the beach and into the sea and swim forever. I want a long-dormant volcano to rise up from beneath this dining room and push us all away on a tide of lava. I can feel that I have turned so red, my lipstick must be camouflaged against my face. All my hair is probably dark red too.

I move my hand enough to break the cheese string, but I can't pick up the piece of cheese ball because that would mean admitting that I spat it out. Dad raises his eyebrows in an annoying way, and I see him do it only because I am looking anywhere but at the boy. Mum tsks and picks up the piece of food with her napkin, folds it away and puts it at the end of the table in the imaginary fourth person's place. She shakes out the fourth person's napkin and puts it on her lap, all in one smooth move.

I will never be able to speak to the boy. Any romance we might have had is over before it could start, because of me. The whole room should be pointing and laughing.

I keep my eyes on the table and tune out my parents while they continue droning on about the cable car. I eat the rest of the cheese balls silently. I drain my juice. I have no idea whether the boy is looking at me, because I can't allow my gaze anywhere near him.

After a while I go back up to the buffet to get more juice, because the embarrassment has dried my throat right out. There are six different jugs there, but I go straight for the orange because it's delicious. I am pouring it when, behind me, a voice—and I know whose voice it is before I even look around—says, "I love your hair."

He has an American accent. His voice is warm and honeyish and it goes right through me. It makes my knees weak. I close my eyes. Maybe it doesn't matter that he saw me spit out a cheese ball.

I turn just a little bit, and look at him. My face is smiling its biggest smile, the one it has been holding in reserve all my life just for this moment.

"Thanks." I manage to stop pouring the juice before it overflows, so that's good. "It just grew like this."

"Seriously?"

"No."

"Oh—right! Ha. Are you on vacation with your family?"

"Kind of. Are you on . . . vacation . . . too?"

I've never said "vacation" before. I feel that if I said "holiday," I would sound silly to him. I would sound like Mary Poppins telling him that it was a jolly holiday with you, Bert.

"Yeah. I'm with my friends."

"I don't normally go away with my mum and dad," I say quickly. "It's because of my dad's work."

"Oh, that's nice."

95

"Yes." I want to keep talking. I want to get us closer to the places we have visited in my head. "I'm Ella."

"Hey, Ella. It's great to meet you. I'm Christian."

I want to say something cool. I want him to think I'm funny.

"You're a Christian," I say, "or your name's Christian?"

I see, at once, that he doesn't realize I was attempting a joke. I wish I hadn't said it: the words hang in the air.

"Um, my name," he says, with a grin. "I'm not really much of a religious person."

I nod. Neither am I.

"So what are you guys up to today?" he asks.

I stare into his eyes. "They're talking about going up Sugarloaf Mountain," I say, though my words could be anything. "But they're worrying about the clouds."

"Us too. The clouds, I mean. Apparently the sun's going to be shining on us tomorrow, and to me and my friends that means 'beach.' So we're going to get the sightseeing in today before it's too hot. We're doing the Christ statue."

"We did that yesterday," I say. "It was cool."

"Well, maybe we'll run into each other back here later."

"I hope so."

His eyes tell me amazing things, and the sun comes out and the walls and the ceiling melt away, and we are standing on a sandy beach in the golden sunshine with those cherubs cavorting around us, serenading us on little harps. I am smiling so hard that I probably look deranged.

He turns to pick up a glass, and then turns back.

"Oh, hey. Ella. We're going downtown to Lapa this evening, to catch some music and do a bit of bar-hopping. If you'd like to . . . You know. You could—?"

"Yes!" I answer before he's even finished speaking. "I'd love to!"

"Cool. Catch up with you later, then. Maybe in the lobby, around nine?"

"Perfect."

As I sit back down, I know that my parents are looking at me and that they are not enjoying the fact that I spoke to a strange boy. In fact, they will hate it. It's lucky they don't know that I have just arranged to meet him at nine o'clock to go out to "catch some music and do a bit of bar-hopping" in downtown Rio.

I will find a way to do it.

"Everything OK?" says Dad.

"Ella." Mum is frowning. I don't care. I have a date tonight. Our eyes met yesterday. He asked me out today. We're going out tonight. I knew that Rio would be my place.

All of a sudden I am thinking of Jack. I wish I could tell him. I wish Jack had been able to come to Rio with me, to meet people, to come out dancing. Jack's parents think a woman's place is in the home. They don't like him being friends with Lily because she's not white. They think homosexuality is deviant and an abomination. The last thing they'd want is a gay son: I hated visiting his house, being approved by them, particularly when I still had my blond hair, as the ideal mousy little girlfriend.

Now I hope Jack will feel this lightning bolt, too, one day. I hope he goes out with someone who makes him feel that he is on fire in a good way. I hope he meets his Christian.

"Yes," I say. "Yes, everything's fine. They might be going to Christ the Redeemer today."

"Well," says Mum. "They should have gone yesterday when it was clear. Anyway, we'll think about Sugarloaf Mountain. Perhaps ask for advice at reception. Maybe we'll leave the trip for this afternoon, at least, to give it a chance to clear up."

"Whatever you think," I say, and I notice Mum giving me a sharp look.

At nine o'clock, after another day of sightseeing with my parents, my voice both casual and trembling with the importance of getting it right, I say, "I'm going to go down to the lobby for a bit."

Mum frowns, because of course she does. "Are you, darling? Why?"

"I want to pick up some leaflets from reception. I'm sure there are more things we could be doing since we're here, and I'd like to see what they are."

Dad gets up as if to come with me.

"On my own," I say. I smile and try hard to look casual. "For once. I'll be back in less than five minutes, and if I'm not, then you can come down and find me. I promise I won't leave the building."

They look at each other. They sigh. I grab a key and leave the room.

Christian and his two friends are sitting on the sofa in the lobby, waiting for me.

I look at him.

He looks at me.

Time freezes, and I hold my breath, and everything is as glittery and magical as it was this morning.

"Hi, Ella," he says. They all stand up, ready to go.

"Your hair is so cool," says the girl.

"This is Susanna, and this is Felix," Christian says, and he walks up to me and kisses me on the cheek, right next to my mouth. All my skin quivers. It is the strangest thing.

They think I am coming out with them. I could. I could just follow them and get into their taxi and worry about everything later.

I wish I could.

I can't.

"I can't come now," I say. "Sorry. But I'll get away in a couple of hours. Can I come and meet you? Where are you going? And hello. Sorry."

I think he looks a little disappointed. "Sure you can," he says. "You'd need to get a cab. Ask for Lapa. Meet us in a bar called Antonio's. It's on a corner. If you can't find it, ask anyone. I hope you can make it."

"Eleven o'clock," I say, and he nods, and they go.

Later, when I know that both parents are properly asleep, I slide out of bed. I have changed and done my makeup in the bathroom when they were in bed and the light was off, so they wouldn't see me, and now all I have to do is grab my shoes and check my pockets (money in one; the spare key card in the other) and open the door as quietly as I can.

It makes a swooshing noise as it brushes the carpet, but my parents don't stir.

I stand on the threshold of the room for a moment, but all is calm and peaceful, and I step out into the corridor, pulling the door very gently closed behind me.

It clicks and locks itself. I stand still, listening, but nothing happens. I walk down the stairs to the floor below, because I know the elevator makes a loud ping when its doors open. I walk down another floor, just to be sure.

I call the elevator to the ninth floor. When it arrives, I stand inside and look at my reflection. I pull my hair over one shoulder. I pout as if I were posing for a photo. I look critically at my body, but it looks all right. I am wearing little denim shorts and a light blue beaded vest.

I'm worried that whoever is working at reception will see me sneaking out and call up to my parents, but the man barely looks up as I cross the lobby. The bright lights glint off the marble everywhere: the whole place is dazzling. I smile at the night doorman, who nods and steps aside to let me out of the automatic door.

"Taxi?" he says.

"*Si,*" I say. "*Por favor.* Yes, please."

He steps out onto the warm pavement, and I follow him into the hot night. He holds his hand out, and within half a minute a yellow cab has pulled over. The doorman opens its door for me, and then he slams it and the taxi starts up.

"*Hola,*" says the taxi driver.

"*Hola.* Lapa, please. Antonio's?" I say it as clearly as I can, and we are off.

I have escaped.

I am in a taxi in Rio.

I am on my own for what feels like the first time in my entire life. The world is filled with possibilities. My parents don't know where I am; I am not sure that has ever been the case before. They have always known, approximately, what I am doing. I have always been locked in, watched over. And now I am not.

I hope I find Antonio's. I said eleven, and it is now ten fifty, so, depending on how long this journey takes, I should be all right.

I gaze out the window. I am actually here. This is happening. I am out alone, being properly independent for the first time in my life. This is me. This is the real Ella Black.

Everything feels hyperreal, and I want to hold on to this feeling and keep it forever.

As we drive, I see mostly darkness, with occasional spots of night-life. The road is huge—six lanes wide—and there are not many other cars. The taxi goes faster and faster, swerving between lanes for fun, edging through red lights when there's nothing coming in the other direction. Bright lights come the other way, speeding closer, flashing past.

I got away from my parents. Sitting in the back of this cab, I can breathe. Whatever happens next, at least I will have this.

I watch the road as we follow signs to Lapa. Eventually the driver slows and drives under a set of huge white arches. I look out at the scene and gasp.

This is where all the people are. On either side of the road, there are tables, and people are sitting at them and standing around and drinking and talking and laughing and dancing. It is so packed that I am not sure I will ever find Christian and his friends, but that is OK. I almost don't care. I took two hundred reales from Dad's wallet, so if it comes to it, I'll get a taxi straight back to the hotel.

The driver pulls over into the forecourt of a closed garage.

"Lapa," he says, with a laugh.

"Antonio's?" I ask, and he shrugs, so I do too, and the meter shows forty reales, so I hand him a fifty note and he gives me change.

I say "*Gracias*" and he corrects me.

"Obrigada," he says, and I repeat it as I step out onto the pavement. I am enveloped in noise and music and instant acceptance.

No one comes to rob me. No one threatens me. No one particularly takes any notice of me at all. I walk slowly past all the people, trying to see the names of the bars. There is loud Brazilian music coming at me, clashing, from different directions, and it is heady and joyous and makes me feel wildly alive.

Even if my parents have woken up, they will never find me here. Never. I can stay as long as I like and no one will know where I am. I inhale the warm night air, the heat, the music, the life.

I find Antonio's down the road, on the other side, on a corner like Christian said. It is frantically busy, with every table taken, and hundreds of people standing up among them. The whole bar is open to the street on both sides of the corner.

If the boy of my dreams is here, as well as everything else, I will be the happiest girl in the world—the happiest girl there has ever been.

I weave between the tables, looking at each one of the people with their bottles of beer and their glasses of the green cocktail that Mum seems to enjoy.

This is nothing like going out at home.

People smile at me as I push my way through them. They move out of my way if they can. Several men say *hola*, or hello (I clearly look foreign), but not in a threatening way, and they don't seem to expect me to reply. I push my way around the whole bar, and I don't see the gorgeous boy, but that barely matters because I am happy. Even if I just walk around here and don't find them and go and get a cab back to the hotel, this outing will have been a massive success.

Someone says, "Ella!" I look around, but I don't see him. It was his voice. I'm almost sure of it, and anyway it had to be him, because no one else here could possibly know my name.

"Ella," he says again, and this time he taps my shoulder, and when I look, he is right there, standing beside me, and I am so happy that I just turn and hug him. He hugs me back, and then he is holding me. My face is pressed against his T-shirt, and I can feel his heart beating against my cheek.

He strokes my hair and keeps a tight hold of me. I don't let go either. He kisses the top of my head. I think we have skipped quite a few stages of getting to know each other.

I feel just like I did the first moment I saw him, that he's always been there, and that all my life has been leading up to meeting him. I knew him already; I just hadn't been in the right place until now.

"You made it!" he says quietly, just above my ear.

I pull back just far enough to be able to speak. "Yes," I say. "I did. I waited for my parents to fall asleep, and then I crept out and got in a taxi."

"My friends were so sure you wouldn't show. I knew you would, and you did."

I nod.

"But hey. We'd better make sure you get back without your folks finding out. I don't want your dad to freaking kill me."

"He wouldn't. If they're awake when I get back, I'll just say I couldn't sleep and I went for a walk. They'll be mad and tell me I'm stupid." I shrug.

"Hey—you're good at this."

Briefly, I picture them awake now. Even if the doorman tells them he put me in a cab, he slammed the car door before I said "Lapa," and so my trail would go cold right there. They'd probably think I'd gone to the airport.

I look at Christian. His arms are still around me. I want to stay like this, pressed up against his chest, forever. I look at his beautiful face, his cheekbones, his glossy hair, everything about him. I need to keep looking at him for the rest of time.

"Let's get you a drink," he says, and we disentangle ourselves and he leads me to where his friends are. He reaches a hand behind him and I take it and walk close, attached to him, through the crowd. They have a tiny table, a high round one, and one of his friends (Felix, I remember) gets off his stool to let me sit down. Or rather, to let me climb up.

Both Felix and Susanna grin and say "Hey" and things like that. Susanna, who has beautiful long black hair, says, "You made it! Great to meet you properly, Ella!"

I try to say the right things back. No one seems to mind what actual words come out of my mouth. Christian says he'll get me a drink and would I like a caipirinha? I say, "Yes, please," even though I don't know what it means. A waiter appears, and the three of them talk to him in Portuguese, and I sit back and let things happen.

Soon after, a drink arrives: it's the pale green one with the straw in it. I sip it and try very hard not to cough or splutter or to betray in any way the fact that this is my first time drinking one of these drinks. I try not to let on that it is far stronger than I thought it would be and that I wasn't expecting it to be so sour and to taste of limes. I can't believe Mum has been drinking these, one after the other, right in front of me since we arrived.

I seem to get away with it, or perhaps nobody is interested in what I'm doing. I am not the center of the universe: I am a hanger-on, but it's OK, because I am all Ella with no hint of Bella, which is amazing and makes me feel full of joy and possibility. The alcohol goes straight to my head and I feel so dizzy that I don't think I could stand up. I take another sip.

Then Christian is beside me, his hand between my shoulder blades. I sway toward him, and he steps closer so that we are touching all down the side. His hand is on my shoulder. I lean on him, so the side of my face is pressed up against his side.

I don't even know what he and his friends are talking about. I piece their story together a bit: they are Cuban Americans and they live in Miami, and when Felix asks where I live, I say I'm from close to London, because I am, close enough, and when he asks what I'm doing in Rio, I just say, "I have no idea."

They all laugh, and Felix says, "Right?" and raises his glass.

"No," I say, shouting so they will hear me. "I literally don't know. My parents came and picked me up from school and took me straight to the airport and I still don't know why we're here."

Saying these words is the most liberating thing that has ever happened to me. These thoughts have been going around my head without stopping, and now I can say them out loud. I tell them about all my fears and suppositions, and they listen. They are quite surprised when they realize what I mean when I say "school."

"You're still in high school?" Felix is incredulous. "Hey, Christian. She's in high school."

Christian shrugs. "She's not there now." Then he turns to me. "So when do you think they're going to tell you?"

I suck on my straw. That drink vanished quickly.

"Soon, I hope."

Susanna leans across and kisses my cheek.

"God, that must be strange for you," she says. She smells lovely.

A little while later we leave. Christian and I are walking, his arm around my shoulder, my arm around his waist.

"How long do you think you'll be around?" he asks.

"No idea. You?"

"Oh, we're here for weeks."

The streets are packed with people, and we are walking on the edge of the road. I am woozy and happy and I need to go back to the hotel soon.

A man is standing on something, visible above the crowd, and singing into a microphone. The backing track is coming from a speaker somewhere. It is all about the drumbeat. It is infectious. My feet want to dance. The people gathered around are dancing. I watch a woman's feet. She is stamping fast, dancing irresistibly, the top of her body calm as her feet do wonderful, crazy things. I want to do that too. I pull away from Christian and follow her feet, trying to make my feet do the same. I'm not getting it right, but the movement clears my head and I feel wonderful. I sense Christian watching but I can't look at him because I cannot take my eyes away from the woman and her feet. She's a million times better at dancing than I am, and I like it that way.

The music vibrates right through me.

I feel amazing.

I continue stamping, feeling the rhythm, trying to get the steps.

Then the music stops.

Christian takes me in his arms.

I know I'm going to kiss him.

I know he is going to kiss me.

I have never kissed a boy before. Everything about this feeling is new. I have never held on to someone who is holding me and pressed my body up against his and felt myself pulled to him as if we were magnets.

This is the only thing in the world, and we are the only people. I never knew it could be this way. I never had any idea.

I tip my head back. He leans down. Our lips touch, gently at first. It goes through me: an electric shock that harnesses all the power of the universe. Then we kiss more deeply, two people joined at the lips, and time stops and I want to stay here, now, in this place with this boy, forever.

At some point the music starts up again, but I barely hear it. People are dancing around us, but I don't care. We stand in the middle of it all, in the hot Brazilian night, kissing.

This is all I have ever wanted, and I never knew. I am outside in Rio on a hot autumn night, and I am a new person. I am happy Ella, dancing Ella. I am Ella In Love.

Later Christian buys us each another caipirinha from a stall under the arches and asks if we can spend some time together tomorrow. I am desperate to see him tomorrow. I never want to be away from him. I want to stare at his perfect face, the little mole on his cheek, forever.

"Yes," I say. "I can't tell my parents but I'll figure it out."

"You will? You're sure? I don't want to be the bad guy."

"You couldn't be the bad guy." I think about it. My head is clear. "Maybe I'll pretend to be sick. If I could get them to go out, I could meet you at the hotel."

Those words hang in the air.

"Yes," he says. "Yes, that would be awesome. I'll maybe see you at breakfast? You're a fabulous girl, Ella."

I laugh. No one has called me a fabulous girl before. No one has come close. It is a strange phrase, but I love it because it's Christian who said it.

"And you're a fabulous boy."

He smiles. "If you do manage to send your parents out," he says, "then maybe you could just come over to my room. You know?" He takes my hand, and our fingers interlock.

I am so pleased he said it. I remember, vaguely, Jack and I implying to other people that we were having sex. I never actually wanted to—obviously not with Jack, but also not with anyone else. It was just not on my mind. But now that I have Christian, it's the only thing in the world I want to do.

"Yes," I say. "Yes. Yes, please." I will tell him it's my first time. I'll tell him everything. I want Christian to know all of me.

The cocktail from the stall is rough and boozy and I can't drink any more of it because I know it will make me sick. The first sip is enough to make me see that.

"Can you get me a cab, please?" I ask. "I need to get back. This has been the best night of my life. Truly, it has."

We stare at each other.

"Of your life?" he says quietly. "That's quite something. Yes. Let's get you safely back. I'll come with you."

"No. Don't. If they're looking for me, you can't be a part of it. Put me in a taxi, and I'll say I went out on my own. I'll see you in the morning."

He looks at me, smiling a lopsided smile that makes me want to stay right here and kiss him all night long.

"You fabulous girl."

Christian puts me in the back of a yellow cab and tells the driver where the hotel is. He gives me a fifty-real note for the fare even though I have money left since I haven't paid for anything this evening except for the cab that brought me here in the first place.

I try to sober up as I go, but I am glowing and dancing and I don't want to feel ordinary ever again. I will never be the same. I kissed a fabulous boy. I will have this evening forever. It really is the best night of my life. It has changed everything.

Tomorrow I am going to Christian's room, and I can't wait. I want to tell Jack. I know he'd be delighted for me. I want to tell Lily. I know she would squeal with excitement, then tell me to be careful.

Eventually, the taxi pulls up outside the hotel. The same doorman as before comes and opens the car door. I pay the bill and give the driver a hefty tip because I love everyone.

My stomach is churning as I step onto the pavement, but there are no police around. I can see into the reception area, and my parents are not there. No one is behind the desk. The doorman does not look remotely interested in my arrival. I say good night to him and walk across the deserted, half-dark lobby to the elevators, and as I wait for one to arrive, I look at myself in the full-length mirror.

I look like the happiest girl in the universe. I look like a girl who has been dancing in the street and kissing in the street and falling in love.

Falling in love.

I have fallen in love.

I

have

fallen

in

love.

Nothing will ever be the same.

CHAPTER SIX

"I'VE GOT A headache," I say, closing my eyes to shut out the sight of her. I feel terrible. I cannot get up.

"You poor thing," says Mum. She sits on the edge of the bed and puts her hand to my forehead in the way she used to do when I was small and feeling ill, or, later on, when I was trying to get a day off school to avoid Tessa, or because I was afraid of Bella and knew that soon I would need to be in my bedroom, alone.

Mum is leaning forward with her hair tickling my face, and that means she is close enough to smell the fumes. She's had those caipirinhas for the last two evenings: she must know the smell. I leap out of bed and run dramatically for the bathroom, where I sit on the toilet for long enough to make her think there must be some form of illness going on, and then flush it and brush my teeth very thoroughly for a long time.

I crept back into the room last night and clicked the door closed quietly. Mum groaned a bit in her sleep, but I slipped into bed, got under my sheets and changed into my pajamas.

I totally got away with it.

It's thrilling.

While I'm in the bathroom, I decide to take a shower.

My feet are filthy.

My feet are filthy because I danced in the street in flip-flops.

I danced, with Christian at my side.

There must be an alcoholic smell coming off me, or a smell of the streets, or grime on me where there was no grime last night. I need to be fresh and innocent if I'm going to keep it all normal.

I scrub myself clean.

"Better?" Mum says when I emerge, back in my pajamas, with wet hair and clean teeth and an altogether fragrant demeanor.

"Yes, thanks."

"Were you sick?"

"No. I've just got a bit of an upset stomach."

My parents are lying to me about something, and now I'm lying too.

"Could you manage breakfast, do you think?"

I have to go to breakfast. I have to see Christian. I hope it's not too late. He and Felix and Susanna will be getting up late, I'm sure.

"Yes. I'll try."

"Sure?"

"Yes." I say it weakly, but I am firm too. I am desperate for food. I am quite sure it will chase away the hangover. I need to eat all the cheese balls there are, and to drink lots and lots of coffee and plenty of water. I'm glad I came home when I did.

. . .

I feel ill in the elevator down, and I can see Mum worrying that I have come down with a terrifying tropical disease (a mutation of the simian flu, perhaps). I want to reassure her, but I can't.

Dad gives it his best shot.

"You look all right to me," he says, sizing me up in the mirror. For a moment I think he suspects the truth, but the moment passes. The elevator stops at floor eight, and we move back to let more people in, but when the door opens, it turns out to be Christian, Felix and Susanna.

My legs go weak. My skin electrifies.

I stare at him. He stares back. I smile a little bit. He grins. I sense both parents stiffening, disapproving.

"Hi," I say, but I address it to Susanna.

"Hi there," she says, and I really, really hope she remembers that all of it has to be kept secret. I hope she doesn't ask if I got home all right, or tell me about the rest of their evening.

No one says anything, and then we are on the ground floor. My stomach is flipping over because all I want to do is kiss Christian again. I want to be alone with him. I hate my parents for being here and for stopping me.

I hang back in the elevator when it stops, and Christian does too, pretending to look in his pockets for something. Mum and Dad get out, and so do Felix and Susanna, and Christian and I brush silently past each other. Inside me, everything bursts out singing.

Mum and Dad are, of course, waiting right outside the elevator, so Christian and I can't kiss or speak, but our bodies touch and I am alive.

I try to convey to Christian the fact that we need to talk and plan, but we all troop into the breakfast room and give our separate room numbers to the woman at the door. She crosses them off her list, and then my parents and I go to sit at one table, and my gorgeous boy and his friends go to another. But every time I look up, Christian is looking at me, and I gaze back.

"You'd better stay off all that fruit this morning, darling," says Mum, who did not notice that I spent the whole elevator ride down staring at the boy that every molecule of me adores, that I am still staring at him now. "If you've got diarrhea. Stick with the carb-y things."

I'm glad she didn't say that in the elevator.

As it happens, the carb-y things are the exact ones I want. I go straight up to the table and fill a plate with cheese balls, a big spoonful of scrambled eggs, and two white bread rolls. I put that down on the table and go back for a glass of water. When the coffee woman arrives, I get her to pour me a black coffee, which she does, though Mum frowns, since coffee is bad for upset stomachs. I pretend not to notice, eat everything on my plate, drink the coffee and water and feel much better. So I go back and get the same things all over again.

"Your appetite's all right," says Dad.

"Yes," I say.

We sit in silence. I look at the Brazilian news on the television screen that is at the other end of the room. There is footage of a rain forest shot from a helicopter, and thick clouds of smoke. I can hear Christian and Felix and Susanna laughing, and I hope they're not laughing about me, sitting here with my mummy and daddy. _My mummy and daddy._

"What are we doing today?" I say.

They look at each other. "Well—that rather depends on you, darling, doesn't it?" says Mum. Dad isn't speaking much. I think the

114

two of them are silently arguing again. He wants to tell me the thing and she doesn't. They have told me that there *is* a thing. They are not even remotely remembering to pretend that Dad has to go to work anymore. That was the most half-hearted and pathetic lie ever.

"I feel crappy," I say. "I think I'm going to stay in bed. But you two should go out. You should just go down to the beach or something. I'll sleep in the room. You can talk about your secret and I won't hear you."

I say that, just in case it makes Dad so annoyed that he tells me the secret to get it over with, but he doesn't. He just closes his eyes. Mum takes a deep breath.

"If you're sick," she says, "then I am *not* leaving your side."

"And if I'm well, you also don't leave my side. I want to spend the morning in the room, resting. Are you *really* going to sit on the edge of the bed and stare at me? Are you going to stay in a darkened room, on an actual sunny day in Rio, one block back from Copacabana beach, just because you don't dare to leave me in a locked room? Really?"

Neither of them answers. On the television screen a highly made-up blond woman is in conversation with a parrot puppet.

Christian is on his feet. When our eyes meet again, he inclines his head toward the elevators and arches an eyebrow.

I clutch my stomach. "I need the room key," I say. "Got to get to the bathroom."

Dad holds out the key. I take it and walk very quickly out of the room. I press the button to call the elevator, and when it arrives, I step into it. I hold down the "doors open" button, and Christian appears. I press "doors close" as quickly as I can, before anyone else can get in, and hit the button for the top floor.

"You made it back," he says as the doors close.

"They have no idea."

Then we are pressed against each other, kissing, kissing, kissing. I push my whole body up against his. He reaches behind me and feels the contours of my body. I want to go straight to his hotel room, fling off all my clothes and stay there all day and all night and all day and all night and all day and all night. I want nothing but Christian.

Instead, the doors open with a ping, and we are not on the top floor but on the ninth. There is a very pale couple standing there all ready to go out for the day, looking annoyed to find that the two people already in the elevator are entwined, and that the elevator is on its way up rather than down. All the same, they get in, and Christian and I stand close together, giggling a little bit. When we arrive at the top of the building, we get out and walk down to floor eleven, hand in hand.

"I'll get them to go out," I say. "I haven't got my phone, so I can't text or anything at the moment, but I'm working on it."

"No cell phone?" he says. "OK. Maybe you should call my room when you're ready. Even if they're only out for, like, a half hour, you could come over. It would be really good to see you. Room 816."

I grin at him. He's smiling back.

"I'd better go in," I say, outside our room. "I know that my mum's going to appear here in a few minutes to check that I'm OK."

"Understood." He smiles and kisses me on the lips, and then I am in the room, and Christian is gone, and I wander around the bathroom a little and make sure I mess things up a bit. I leave the toilet lid down and flush it, and brush my teeth again and stare at myself in the mirror.

My eyes are shining. My cheeks are flushed.

"My boyfriend is named Christian," I say out loud. "He's Cuban American."

I am longing to tell Jack, but I can't. Christian is my real boyfriend: today I'm going to visit him in room 816. I have no idea what has happened to my life, but right now I like it.

Someone is knocking on the door. It will definitely be Mum, and I assume an "ill" face before I go to open it.

"Oh, darling," she says. "Look. Come downstairs and sit on one of those sofas in the lobby and read those leaflets you like, and I'll explain that we need one of the chambermaids to make up the room right away. So you can have lovely fresh sheets. Then we'll get you tucked up in bed. All right?"

I nod, looking as sad as I possibly can. That breakfast certainly washed away my hangover, and I am feeling wonderful. It is important that I don't look wonderful.

"You look a bit feverish," she says.

I nod. Yes. I feel a bit feverish too.

Once our room has been cleaned, I lie down and pretend to be sick. Mum sits on their bed, reading and looking over at me. I blissfully sleep away the last of the street cocktails, and when I wake up, she's not there. The bathroom door is open, and I can see that she's not in there either. I sit up. There might be time for me to visit Christian before she comes back, or there might not. If she comes back and I'm not here, I can just say that I went for a walk down to the ocean to get some fresh air.

She has left a note beside my bed. It is in her fussy calligraphic handwriting:

117

Darling Ella—Dad and I have gone for a stroll to the
beach for a coffee. Won't be long! It's lovely to see you
peacefully asleep. Hope you're feeling better.

Love, Mum xxx

She didn't put a time on it, and I am completely disoriented, and the bedside alarm clock says that it's twelve thirty in the afternoon.

I pick up the phone and make an internal call to room 816, but it rings and rings. I cannot really expect Christian to be sitting in his room staring at the phone for the entire day, just in case I managed to call him, but all the same I am disappointed. I'll keep trying: he might be in the shower, or he might come back into the room in a few minutes, or he might be standing right outside this door right now, trying to find a reason to knock.

I open the door. No one is there.

I sit in bed for a while, but my parents don't come back. I call Christian's room again, but he still doesn't answer. I think about my night out last night. I try to recall every single detail. I relive our ride in the elevator this morning. I call his room again. I call again.

Then I realize that I am alone in a room with all my parents' stuff, and I know that the answer to everything must be here, if I can only access it. I am alone in the room with the secret, and if Christian's not in his room, I can at least use this opportunity to find a way to open the safe while I wait.

I have already tried my birthday, 1711, but I put the numbers in again, just in case. It's still not that. I try their wedding anniversary: 0606. It's not that either. Her birthday is on October 21, and his is May 4, which enables him to make endless Star Wars jokes. I try both of them again just in case, but it's neither of them, and it's not 2104 either.

Mum has not used a number I would guess. If it's something truly random, I won't get it. I try 1234, just in case, and then 4321. I try 2468 and then 8642.

The machinery clunks and the door swings open. She tried to make it impossible for me to guess, but she's never really going to be a superspy.

I snatch up my phone and put it in my pocket. Now I can get my fucking life back. I can't wait to tell Jack and Lily everything that's happened. I take my passport too, on principle, and put it in my other back pocket.

Then there are the official envelopes: my hands tremble as I leaf through them. My head and vision are clear. That's a relief.

I pause. I don't actually have to do this. I could put everything back. I might not want to know.

I legitimately have no idea what I'm going to find out. Dad told me I'm not sick, but I don't think I believe him. I can't think of another thing that it could be. I wish I could. I would take anything other than that.

I might be better off not knowing.

I bolt the door so that if they come back, they won't be able to get in, and then I empty the contents of the envelope onto the bed. There is something about travel insurance and a receipt from a currency exchange. There is also a letter on official paper, from a lawyer.

I read it. Then I stare at the words. They go fuzzy and blur into one another. I sit on the bed and read it again like a small child, running my fingers under the words as I speak them aloud.

Dear Fiona and Graham,

Since our conversation last week, I have made inquiries regarding your understandable concern about Ella and the legal changes that will take place on her upcoming eighteenth birthday.

As you know, an adopted child has a right to look for her birth parents on the Adoption Contact Register when she turns eighteen. However, I have spoken to the caseworkers involved and everyone has assured me that, because of the exceptional circumstances of Ella's adoption, her birth mother will not be eligible to add herself to the register, and although we are all aware that she would like to meet Ella, she will emphatically not be able to do so.

However, because of the fact that she has clearly found your identities and your address, I would recommend that if you are able to go away for a while, this might be an advisable course of action while Ms. Hinchcliffe is made aware that attempts to make direct contact will have extremely serious consequences. I am confident that she can be compelled to stop contacting you, and the law will step in when necessary.

I hope this puts your minds at rest. Don't hesitate to call if I can do anything else for you.

Yours sincerely,

David Vokes

I run to the bathroom and throw up my entire breakfast. My eyes are burning. My head is ringing, and I gasp for breath. Everything is fading to black, and I struggle to make it stay. This is not the time to lose control. It is too important for that.

I breathe in. I breathe out. There is just this moment and nothing else. No past, no future: just now. My head is ringing. Everything is blurred around the edges.

Hello, Bella, I say.

WE'D BETTER FIGURE THIS OUT.

Do you understand what we just read?

WE'LL FIGURE IT OUT.

The exceptional circumstances of Ella's adoption.

Ella's adoption.

Adoption.

I am adopted. They have never told me.

People who are adopted know that they are adopted. It's not a big shameful secret. It's a good thing. But they never told me.

That woman is not my mother.

That man is not my father.

Other people, people I don't know, are my parents. Not these people. I do not come from them. I do not have any of their genes. They never told me.

We have run away because my birth mother wants to find me.

My

birth

mother.

There were *exceptional circumstances*, and because of them she's not allowed to see me. I don't know what the exceptional circumstances are.

Everything swirls around. I am just standing in the bathroom.

I am utterly lost.

. . .

Time passes, and I am still standing here.

I have to tell them that I know.

I have to try to find out more. I sit on the bed and try my very hardest to pull myself together and to make a plan. There is only one thing I can think of.

I pick up the hotel phone, figure out how to make an international call, and ring our house. Michelle might be there, I think, and this might be my only chance of finding out more. Michelle is nice. She is always kind to me, and she told me she liked my hair when I dyed it.

"Hello?" she says.

I use my mother's voice. Everyone says we sound identical on the phone.

My mother. This is not my mother's voice. It is my adoptive mother's voice. We sound the same on the phone because she raised me.

"Hi, Michelle," I say. "It's Fiona. Calling from abroad."

"Oh, yes," she says. "Hello there. Are you all right?"

"Yes, thanks. Is Humphrey OK?"

"Oh, he looks just fine. He's in the living room, so I've closed him in there until I've finished. Didn't want to put him in his basket before I have to."

"Oh, of course. Good idea." I want her to put Humphrey on the phone even though he would be silent, but I have no idea how to ask that while still pretending to be Fiona Black. I just want to hear him breathing.

"Michelle," I say, instead. "Could you do something for me? A little favor?"

"Of course, love," she says.

"Right. Well, you'll need to go to the study. Is that OK?"

"I'm on my way."

"There's a filing cabinet. Could you open the top drawer?"

"What am I looking for?"

"Ella's birth certificate." My voice shakes.

"Right you are. Putting you on speakerphone. Hold on."

I don't say anything, because I have no idea how the filing cabinet is organized. I just leave it to her to look.

"Here we go," she says after a few minutes. "You *are* organized, aren't you? I've got yours and Graham's, Fiona. Would this be Ella's? It's an envelope that says Ella on the front?"

"Yes. That's right. That's the one. Could you open it?"

Oddly, I am managing to talk in Fiona Black's composed manner while tears course down my cheeks.

"Right. Oh. It's an adoption certificate? I didn't know Ella was adopted."

"No. It's not something we ever talk about."

My voice cracks at that, and I have to hold the phone away from my face for a few seconds until I regain control.

"But it's not a secret," I say. It's not a secret now. "Is there a birth certificate with it? Or just the adoption certificate?"

"Just the adoption certificate that I can see, love."

"Could you read it? I just need to check something."

"If you like, dear."

I'm pushing my luck. I know I am. I don't care.

"It says *Ella Charlotte Black, female, born November 17, 1999, in Birmingham. Adopters Graham and Fiona Black* . . . and it gives your address. Let's see. *Date of adoption order: January 8, 2000.* I had no idea. I won't go advertising it. Are you all right, my love?"

I cannot speak, and so I drop the phone on the floor. I curl up on the bed and hug my knees. I never knew. I never had the faintest idea. They never told me. It's my own life, and they never told me. It was in the filing cabinet, easily found, all along, and I never looked.

I was born in Birmingham.

Not Kent.

I was born in 1999 and adopted in 2000. A millennium passed and they never told me.

Everything I thought I knew about my life is a lie.

There are noises outside the door. I stare at it. They are pressing the door handle down, and it isn't opening because I bolted it. One of them knocks, and my so-called mother's voice says, "Ella?"

My world has fallen to pieces.

My world has always been in pieces. The pretense has fallen away and my real life stands there, looking completely different.

I hate them. I hate them completely. I hate everything about them. I hate them for lying to me. They had to know that one day, I would find this out. That letter said there will be "legal changes" when I turn eighteen. Well, I'll be eighteen soon. And eighteen-year-olds can do whatever they want.

My birth mother is looking for me, according to that letter. She's not allowed to find me, so I am going to find her. I try to breathe. I need my dark side.

GET AWAY FROM THEM.

I know. I can't see them. But they're here.

TELL THEM TO FUCK OFF.

I need to focus. I have to do this right.

I know that I *do* have to get away from them. This is too much. I pick up the phone off the floor and put it back in its place.

I already have my passport and my phone. I take all the cash I can find, and some clothes, and I shove all of it into my bag. I take the credit card that is in the safe, hoping that I will be able to crack the PIN as easily as I did the safe code. I take my toothbrush, toothpaste and deodorant. I put it all in, and only then do I unlock the door and stand and stare at them, at these people who, for almost eighteen years, have pretended to be my birth parents.

"How are you . . . ?"

Mum's voice trails off as she looks at my face. Then she stares into my eyes for a long time, and I stare right back. Tears are pouring down my cheeks, but I don't say a word because I need them to say it. Only Dad—or not-Dad, the man I thought was my father—seems to be functioning. He looks past me at the open safe. He closes his eyes, breathes a few times, and opens them again.

"Right, Ella," he says, and he puts an arm around my shoulder. I flinch and push it off. "OK. Let's go out and get a coffee at the café across the road. Or something stronger. And we'll talk this through. I'm sorry. We never meant for it to be like this. You had to find out someday, and we should have told you."

I don't speak. I don't think I am ever going to be able to speak to either of them again. I watch not-Dad put the paperwork back into its envelope and back into the safe. The letter from Mr. Vokes is in my bag, but I don't tell him that. He doesn't seem to notice that my passport isn't with the others. I watch him close the door and lock it. His hands are shaking.

I take a piece of hotel notepaper and a hotel pen and write my phone number on it, with a +44 at the start. I fold that and put it in my pocket. Neither of them particularly seems to notice.

Mum is a statue. There is no color in her face. She looks like an old lady. She looks, in fact, as if she's had a stroke. I hope she does have a stroke.

I hope she dies.

I pick up my bag and follow them out the door. Each of them tries to touch me; I flinch and pull away. I don't look either of them in the eye. I don't care if they're looking at each other over my head, because I'm not part of their family and I never was.

I was a charity project

an experiment

and it failed.

I can't hear anything but the swooshing of my blood and the ringing noise that is now so loud that it sounds like a fire alarm. The fire is my whole life. I stand waiting for the elevator, having an internal conversation with Bella that is different from any way we have ever spoken before.

KILL THEM.

Shall I?

YES.

I can't. How and what with?

COULD YOU PUSH THEM DOWN THE ELEVATOR SHAFT?

There's an elevator in the elevator shaft.

I wobble because I can't see very well, and my dad reaches out to steady me. I walk away and stand at the other side of the landing, leaning against the wall, until the elevator arrives.

I look calm, but I am on fire. Bella is right here with me. Everything that is in me, that is part of me, my whole self, is going up in flames. I am like someone's house on the news: at the moment the flames are leaping, the drama is going on, the change from what used to be there to the blackened ruins is under way. Soon I will just be charred remnants, a wasteland, nothing. Right now, however, Bella and I are burning.

I have no idea who I am. Bella feels like all I have. These people are not related to me. I have no family. I have a feeling I am going to need to embrace my dark side. Bella is not scared of anything.

I want to stop the elevator at the eighth floor. I try to remember Christian's room number, but everything from before-the-safe has gone fuzzy and blurred. It began with an 8. I think it had a 6 in it. But I can't slide my number under the wrong door. I will give my piece of paper to someone at reception instead.

However, as we walk out of the elevator on the ground floor, Christian is standing right there in the lobby, and his face lights up when he sees me. I look at him. He is all I want. I want to tell him this, to tell him about me, to make a new life away from these people who have lied to me all my life.

I was born in 1999. I went to live with the Blacks in 2000. I lived with my birth mother across millennia.

Maybe she was young. Perhaps she was ill. It probably wasn't her fault she couldn't manage a baby.

I want to be a grown-up now. I want to be with Christian. I walk up to him, hand him the piece of paper with my number on it, and kiss him on the lips. I feel his surprise, and then I feel his smile.

"Call me," I say. "I've got my phone back."

My parents don't say a word as we leave the hotel. I don't think they are really focused on anything.

It is warm and sunny today, and this is the first time I have been out. The clouds are gone. It would be a perfect day for going on a cable car up a mountain.

The man I thought was my father puts a hand on my shoulder and guides me down the road to the traffic lights. I push his hand away without looking at him. The woman who is not my mother walks on the other side of me, but she's not looking toward me, either. We are both looking straight ahead.

I know that I have asked her about her pregnancy, about my birth, about what I was like as a tiny baby, about how they celebrated the arrival of the year 2000. In fact, they didn't have me then. The story of my birth (a dream birth, apparently, in a water pool with no pain relief) was a fantasy. Breastfeeding cannot have happened. All of it made up, just to keep me from suspecting the truth. And of course I didn't suspect anything. You believe your parents when they tell you that you're their baby.

We cross the road. The sun is hot. I know why they brought me to Rio. They brought me here because my real mother is looking for me, because I'm nearly eighteen. Boring Mr. Vokes told them to go away, and assured them she won't find me. I would like to assure *him* that I will find her. I want to look at the woman who gave birth to me. I want to meet my real family, whoever they are, whatever has happened.

"Come on, Ella," says not-Dad, and he ushers me to a table at a café, on the other side of the road from the hotel. I sit on a chair because I don't know what else to do. Not-Mum sits on one side of me, and he sits on the other. They still think they can keep me under their control. I hold my bag between my feet.

"Coffee?" he asks. "Or a beer or something?"

I would like to get so drunk that I obliterate all of it. However, I won't: I cannot let my parents think they can win me back by buying "medicinal brandy," or whatever they are thinking of, and trying to pretend we're all in this mess together.

"Coffee would be fine," I say. "I got drunk last night, by the way. I sneaked out of the room and got a taxi to Lapa and met the Americans from the hotel. That's why I was sick this morning. I kissed Christian in the street."

"You didn't," says Mum. Her voice is tiny.

I shrug. I don't need to pretend anymore, because nothing they do or say can affect me. They can believe what they like. I had the best night of my life, and I am glad I did it, just before everything collapsed.

This is the strangest feeling. For years I've separated myself out into Ella and Bella, but now, Bella has stepped in to help me. She is making me strong: Ella would have fallen apart, but now that I am letting myself be Bella, too, I am going to do something. I just don't know what it is.

Not-Dad goes inside to order at the counter. I see Christian coming out of the hotel with Felix and Susanna. He stands still on the other side of the road and looks at me. I raise a hand. I can see from the way he is standing that he is worried. I make a "phone" sign with my hand, and he nods and walks away, looking back over his shoulder.

The woman who did not give birth to me wants to say something.

She keeps opening her mouth and closing it without speaking, and I don't do or say anything to help her. I see her from the corner of my eye, but I won't look at her.

"We always . . ." she says, but then she trails off. I don't respond at all. I act as if she didn't say a word.

Not-Dad comes back and sits down. He takes a deep breath and begins talking.

"Your mother and I were desperate to have a big family," he says, and every word is a sharp little knife, so much so that I think he must be doing it on purpose to hurt me. "But it didn't happen. There were plenty of pregnancies, but they never made it beyond the first few weeks. Every time, we hoped it would be different, but every time, it wasn't. And after it had happened seven times—"

"Eight," not-Mum says very quietly.

"—eight times, we agreed that it wasn't meant to be, and that perhaps we were meant to find our family somewhere else."

"Second best."

"Not second best. Best. Best and only. So we were assessed for adoption. Went through a lot of hoops."

He stops. This is the bit that I need to hear them say. It cannot be real until they say it.

Neither of them says anything. Time ticks on, and still they don't.

"And then a baby turned up." I say it because somebody has to.

"Yes," says not-Dad. "Then a baby turned up, and it was a baby girl, and she was the most perfect and adorable baby that had ever lived, and we both knew from the moment we set our eyes on her that this was the reason why it had never happened before: because this baby was always going to be out there and she was always going to be needing a home, and we were the people who were going to give it to her. We were going to take her away from the . . . difficult . . . start that she'd had, and we were going to give her the closest thing to a perfect life that we possibly could."

I shiver. He is talking about a baby, and it's me.

"That's worked out well," I manage to say.

"It has!" not-Mum is whispering through tears, staring down at the table, barely audible. "Ella—you have no idea how much we love you. I've loved you from the very moment I saw you. I'm your mum and I always will be. We've always adored you."

"Well, it was kind of you to save me from a difficult start in life."

"Ella," says the man pretending to be my dad. "We did try to tell you you were adopted, starting when you were three. You refused to hear it. We took you to psychologists and tried to figure out what to do. This is complicated and hard to explain, but you found it so difficult and distressing that we ended up deciding it was better not to try. We decided that because the circumstances were so . . . unusual, that you were better off thinking you were our biological daughter, for a while, at least. It's not the standard way of doing it, but it made you so happy and secure, and that was the only thing that seemed to matter. Because as far as we're concerned, you are our birth daughter anyway."

"I thought I was here on a bucket list thing. I can remember those appointments, a bit. I said so the other day. I thought I had some genetic illness and that we were here because I was going to die."

"Oh, darling," says not-Mum. I see her start to move toward me, but I lean away and she doesn't even try.

"You're our little girl," she says. "Our precious, wonderful girl. I'm so sorry. Everything we've ever done has been because we love you."

"You've lied. All my life. Ever since I can remember, you've lied to me. It's not such a big deal being adopted, but it is if no one ever bothers to tell you."

I cannot look at their faces. They don't know it, but the girl I have been pretending to be for so long has gone. I am still here in body, right now, but I've gone. Everything I thought I was, I am not. Everything. I have never felt like this before. I knew I had a dark side and I gave her a name and she is in me now. She *is* me now.

HURT THEM, says Bella.

I don't try to push her away. I don't reach for the mantra about the universe.

How?

IT'S EASY OUT HERE. LOOK. HE'S GOT A BOTTLE, RIGHT THERE.

I am shaking all over. My jaw is clenched. I need to get away from these people. I shouldn't hurt them. That wouldn't help.

YES IT WOULD.

It wouldn't really. Would it?

Not-Mum reaches across and runs her hand down my arm. It is a stupid feathery touch and I hate it, so I give Bella an internal nod and she uses my hand to grab not-Dad's beer bottle and smash it on the edge of the table. Bella and I are lunging at her—at the only mother I have ever known—with a broken bottle. The only father I have ever known grabs my arm.

There is all sorts of shouting going on, but I don't care. I am Bella and Ella has gone, and I want to hurt this woman and I don't care what else happens.

I spin around to shake the hand off my arm, and the waiter is standing behind me. I need him to go away, so I turn and swipe the broken bottle at him. It cuts across his face and a line of red springs up. My vision is clouded and I have to run.

I grab the bag from the pavement and drop the glass, and I am gone.

I am running.

I run and run and run.

My feet pound the pavement. One foot. The other foot. One foot. The other foot. I can't stop. I can't think.

I swing around the corner so they won't see me, and sprint faster than I have ever sprinted before. I run down the middle of the road, and cars can hit me if they like but they don't.

I run to the beach without any thought other than to get away. The cars are coming from the wrong direction on the road beside the beach—they are going in the opposite direction from the arrows. I dodge between yellow cabs and buses and cars, and they honk their horns but I don't care.

The other side of the huge road is closed off, and then there is a lot of shouting and whistles are blowing and I think the police can't have caught up with me this quickly, but when I stop to look in the direction of the commotion, I see that there has been a zombie apocalypse, and that a huge crowd of zombies is making its way toward me.

It is possible. Anything could happen now. The zombies have come.

I run over to the beach side of the road and straight into the crowd. It's not really a zombie apocalypse. It can't be. These are people *dressed* as zombies. It must be a Rio thing, and suddenly

I am in the middle of it. It engulfs me and I let it; they won't find me here.

I walk up to a zombie who is covered in blood and gore, and I want that blood and gore, so I take her by her face and kiss her on each cheek. She is laughing and laughing, so I press my cheeks against hers and she kisses me on the mouth. All the old rules have gone; they were never really there in the first place. I rub my face on hers until the makeup is all over me, and I know that I can be a part of this crowd. I can be a zombie. I can absorb my dark side and become someone new, someone brave.

I smear the goo over my face with my fingers, and then I rub my fingers down my T-shirt, and I put my arms up like other people are doing, and I walk like a zombie.

No one cares. Fellow zombies and spectators smile at me. No one knows I just slashed a man's face with a broken bottle. People are watching with cameras, and I don't care if my parents or the police see me on the Internet or the news by some freaky chance, because by the time they see it, I will be gone. I don't know where, but I will be gone. I don't care what I'm walking toward.

I have enough money to keep me going for a few days, and that is all I need right now.

WE'RE NEVER GOING HOME. Bella is triumphant.

I know we're not, I tell her. *We should get some water, though.*

WHO CARES ABOUT WATER?

I hope I see Lily and Jack one day.

NEVER MIND ABOUT THEM NOW.

There is a drumbeat somewhere at the back of the march. The sun is heavy on my head. I know that I should be drinking water, but

Bella stops me from caring. Now I know who I am for the first time since I was a tiny baby, when they took me away from my real mother and gave me to the Blacks.

A pregnant woman is walking close to me, with a plastic baby's head and arms bursting out of her real baby bump. A little child is in a Snow White outfit and covered in blood, holding a doll with a severed head. Two small twin boys are both dressed as zombies from the old movies, lurching along in ragged clothes with their hands out in front of them, laughing helplessly. I keep walking, up the beach and up the beach.

I keep walking. I snarl at photographers. I take my hair in both hands and twist it around itself, tying it in a knot on its long side to get it off the back of my neck. I try to smear my makeup more, but the gore has dried up. I keep going with the crowd, and after a while, a boy passes me a pot of some kind of green greasepaint. I cover myself with it, rubbing it all over my face to make me as unrecognizable as I can, though I know my hair will give me away instantly if they see me.

I wait for a hand on my shoulder, every moment.

Every now and then the procession pauses, and there is a battle staged between zombies and people dressed as police and soldiers. Zombies grab bystanders and pretend to bite them, and they turn into zombies too, either joining the parade or melting back into the crowd. At one of these performances, a monster zombie grabs me and pretends to bite my shoulder, even though I'm already a part of the zombies, and I scream as loudly as I can. As I do, I find that everything I am feeling—all these feelings I cannot put names to and all the horror and all the fury—comes out in that scream. I scream so long and so loud that people begin to gather around me. At first they are concerned, and then they are laughing. They are admiring me for getting into character, and I realize that this is a place of extremes where I can do anything, anything at all. I can be anybody. I do not have to be Ella Black, because I did not come into the world as Ella Black. I am not Ella or Bella.

And I realize: I don't know my own name.

I keep on screaming.

After I am a zombie for a while longer, I know that I need to go. The waiter will have called the police, and my fake parents will be mobilizing everyone they can to look for me, even though they're clueless in Brazil.

I need to find a place with an Internet connection and start the process of discovering who my real mother is. This Mr. Vokes is weirdly determined to keep her away from me, and I don't know why, but it's not going to happen anyway because I'm going to find her myself. No one has asked me what I want, so I don't care what they want.

If I hadn't just attacked two people, I would go to the airport and get myself home and wait for my real mother there: she knows where we live and is supposedly coming to look for me. I could just sit in our house and hope she arrives. But I can't do that, because I hurt a man with a piece of glass and there was blood all over his face. I knew Bella would do that one day, and she has.

I don't want to go to prison.

I duck out of the parade as it reaches the top of Copacabana, and cross the road, dodging between cars, turning and giving them a zombie snarl if they beep at me. I run down a street and find I am back on the road that has our hotel on it—Avenida Nossa Senhora de

Copacabana. This road is the worst place to be. I need to get off it as quickly as I can. There's a bus, so I get right on. I find some coins in my pocket and pay the driver, push through a metal turnstile, sit down by a window and stare at everything.

After a couple of minutes the bus passes the hotel. I look out as we bump past, then quickly lean down to fiddle with my shoe. There is a police car parked outside, in the space where the taxis stop. I glimpse two police officers inside the hotel reception, and a crying woman, and a man who I think caught my eye for the fraction of a second that I looked before I ducked out of sight.

Then I am past, and they are gone.

I want to get off at the next bus stop and run back to them.

THE POLICE WILL ARREST YOU.

I know, but I want to go back anyway.

YOU ARE A CRIMINAL. DO YOU KNOW WHAT BRAZILIAN PRISONS ARE LIKE?

No. Do you?

SHALL WE FIND OUT? WOULD YOU LIKE THAT?

I hold my breath and try to imagine it. Much as I have always been sheltered and treated like a baby, I'm pretty sure the Brazilian justice system would consider me an adult responsible for her own violent actions.

No, I tell Bella. *No, let's not.*

I hold my bag on my lap and look through it. I packed in such a rush without concentrating, but now that I focus, I discover I have assembled a reasonable bag for running away. I have some clothes and a toothbrush. I have my passport and what I think is quite a lot of money. I have a credit card without a PIN. I have the letter from boring Mr. Vokes, who knows a lot more about me than I do myself. I have a phone without a charger. I have nowhere to go and nobody to talk to. I have no friend in the world. I would give anything to have Lily here. To have Jack.

All I can do is find a place to hide and track down my birth parents, so they can tell me who I actually am. I am going to look into the eyes of the woman who gave birth to me and tell her that it's OK that she gave me up, because there must have been a good reason and at least she was honest about the fact that she couldn't look after me. At least she's never lied to me. At least she wants me back.

When I've done that, I will happily hand myself over to the police.

Will I?

I don't want to go to Brazilian prison.

I gave Christian my phone number. I switch on my phone, making sure the volume is off because I know it will start pinging with messages from everyone and I don't want anyone on this bus to notice me. I ignore all voice-mail messages for now and look at the texts. There are loads of them from my parents, of course, and I don't read any of them. There are messages from Lily, Jack, Mollie and even Tessa. There is nothing from Christian.

I turn the phone off.

If they trace it to this spot, they will know I was here, though they won't know I was on a bus or where it was going.

Tears are running down my face, and when I wipe them away with the back of my hand, they leave green and black trails on my skin. I must look like a mess, but there's a zombie apocalypse and I look undead and nobody cares because that is the point. I stay on the bus, staring out the window, feeling my heart pounding, and seeing nothing, until it stops and everyone gets off. This is clearly the end of the line. I get off too.

I am on the sidewalk, in the hot sun, in some suburb of Rio. The air is very still and nothing is happening. I have no idea where I am. Everyone who got off the bus has gone. There is nothing particularly here. Cranes are poking the air nearby. The buildings are big and warehouse-y, and there are no cafés, no houses and no people.

Everything I thought I was has melted away.

Every bit of me is a lie.

I should be feeling a lot of things, but all I am is numb.

I start to walk.

I walk and walk, and I would really like some water and some sunscreen. I follow all the tourist-looking signs, and after a long time I find myself on a huge road with cars and buses traveling in each direction. It seems to be lined with banks and things, and all of them are empty and deserted. I am the only person walking, and I am very, very tired and very hot and the thirstiest I have ever been in my life.

I feel like a character in a computer game, on a quest, knowing where I'm trying to go (to my real parents) but not having a clue how to pass this level. Sometimes I get confused and tell myself that if I just press the right part of a wall or the sidewalk, a new level will open up and I'll be closer, but when I try it, that doesn't work, because I am an actual human girl and this is really happening.

I pull myself back from that. I can't look around for some magical solution that might work in a dream. I can't indulge in anything. I need to focus and find a way to walk into the next stage of my life.

I keep walking, and I try to do it normally. One foot in front of the other. Soon I am in a part of town with more people around, and then there is a shop and it is open, so I buy a huge bottle of water and drink it in one big gulp. I buy a little bottle of sunscreen, too, and smear it on my pink arms and legs and face. I look for a phone charger, but there isn't one here.

Then I need to go to the bathroom. There are no cafés anywhere nearby, and as far as I can see, no public toilets either. It feels so urgent, suddenly, that I contemplate finding a corner and just doing it right there.

Across the road is a square surrounded by huge buildings, and at the far end of the square I can see a kiosk selling tickets of some sort. There are pictures of boats, so I walk toward it. If I got on a ferry, it would probably have a toilet. I ask for a ticket on the next boat, in English, and the woman frowns and tries to figure out what I mean. I think she is trying to ask which boat I want, where I want to go, and I try to convey that I just want the next boat and I don't care about the destination.

She passes me a plastic ticket shaped like a credit card, and I slide a large bill under the security screen. She sighs and pushes lots of change back, and points to a set of turnstiles, off to my left.

I manage to say "*Obrigada*," and she says "*De nada*," and then I push my ticket into the turnstile, but I'm doing it wrong. A man comes and does it for me, and I push through the barrier and walk straight onto the back of a huge metal boat, where I see a sign for the ladies' room and follow it, because that is all I can think about right now.

I open the metal door, and at first all I see is that there is indeed a bathroom in there and that I will be able to pee. Then I smell it and note that I am very definitely not the first person to use it. I can hardly walk close to the toilet because the smell is making me gag, but I have to, because I need to use this bathroom more than I need anything else in the world. I want it, right now, more than I want my real mother, and that is a lot.

I have to breathe through my mouth because I cannot bear the smell. But I know that breathing through my mouth means that I am gulping particles of sewage, and that makes me gag even more. I hover over the metal toilet, that is, of course, blocked and clogged and full almost to the top with strangers' shit, but I pee because I have to. Of course the flush doesn't work, and then I stumble to the basin and stare at myself in the tiny mirror that is nailed to the wall.

My face is covered in blotches of green and black. My eyes are bloodshot so that the whites of them are actually pink, and I truly do look like a zombie. My hair—my lovely purple hair—is slicked back with sweat and grime, tied at the side of my neck in a knot. I'm wearing a dark red T-shirt and a pair of small denim shorts, and I could be anybody.

I breathe deeply. There is something calming about that because it's true.

I could be anybody.

I

could

be

anybody.

That means I can be whomever I like.

Though the most notable thing I have done so far since I found out that I could be anybody is lunge at someone with a broken bottle and cut a man's face and run away.

There is a jolt and a small crash and the boat begins to move. I hope we're going somewhere far away. If it is a place that has somewhere to sleep, then I will sleep there. If it has an Internet connection, I will try to track down my birth mother. When I can't stay away any longer, I will go back and hand myself in to whoever wants me.

I step out of the bathroom, smiling apologetically at the girl who's waiting (hoping she doesn't think its rancid state is entirely my fault) and find a small deck at the back of the boat. I stand on it and fill my lungs with gorgeous fresh air as I stare at the water. The engine is roaring, and there is land receding behind us. I don't care what happens now; I only care about the fact that I am putting water between me and everything else. No one can come after me, because no one knows where I am. The air is hot on my face. The boat is moving slowly, noisily now, and the stretch of water between me and the land grows as I stare at it.

I am leaving. I am running away.

My legs feel weak. I walk back to the inside of the boat and find a place to sit beside a window. There is a huge bridge up ahead, with arch after arch after arch. We are going to go under it. It looks like a bridge from a story, a bridge that spans the whole ocean.

I close my eyes, and the movement of the boat rocks me, and although I know that I will not actually sleep because I am too jumpy, I find myself yawning. I will just close my eyes for a moment. I will just shut it all out. I will rest for just a few seconds.

Waking on a random boat that is taking me to an unknown destination while made up as a zombie feels like it's part of a strange and horrible dream.

Then I remember.

My parents are not actually my parents.

I attacked my adoptive mother with a broken bottle.

I cut a man across his face.

Those things are real. That is my new truth.

They brought me to Rio because my mother was trying to find me. My mum. My birth mum—the unknown woman who grew me.

She wants me back.

She could be anyone.

I could be anyone too.

Until now I have paid no attention to the people on this boat, and they, in turn, have left me completely alone. It is about half full. There are families with young children. There are young and old men, on their own and in groups. There are women, with babies, with children, alone. People are walking around offering things for sale, but they're not pushy about it, and it's easy to shake my head. A woman sitting nearby is spending ages looking at big pieces of jewelry. The man with her drapes them over his arm, and she fingers each in turn, holding the big fake rubies on cheap metal chains.

If I can sit still like this and watch the world going on without having to interact with anybody, ever again, then I might be all right. I would miss Lily and Jack and Humphrey, but really I could live on a boat and go nowhere forever.

The boat, of course, stops even though I am willing it not to. We are at our destination, wherever that may be. I stand up when everyone else does and file off the boat with all of them. A man grins at me, and I know I look ridiculous, with my face all covered in smeared zombie gunk and my eyes red and a cloud of desperation and running-away all around me.

"*Hola,*" I say to him, just to see if my voice is still working.

He says something back in Portuguese, but there are too many words and I don't understand them, and so I smile and shake my head and walk off the boat behind a family with two children—a girl and a boy who are fighting and bickering until their mother tells them to stop.

They are a family. That woman is their mother, and they are brother and sister, and I bet that none of those facts are lies. Though they might be. Most people don't think to question the basic foundations of their existence. I never did.

A crowd of people is waiting for the boat, but none of them are the police. A young man walks up and hands me a flyer, and I force a smile and keep walking. Another man, an elderly one, does the same. He laughs and points to his own face, and says something and makes a scary face. I think he's saying that his face is scarier than mine without any makeup, and so I laugh too and keep going. I push both flyers into my back pocket and keep walking, because I don't want to look lost or vulnerable. I don't want anyone to talk to me, to ask if I'm all right, to report me to the police as a teenage runaway or as the criminal they saw on the news. I look fierce right now, and I want to stay fierce.

But I know I will never blend into a crowd with purple hair. I need to change that.

I don't know what to do. I don't belong here, or anywhere. The part of me that is Bella is crowing. She is telling me that she always knew it.

She doesn't blur my vision or make my ears ring anymore. She doesn't need to.

. . .

The ground under my feet is sandy and stony. I walk over to a display board and look at a map. This place seems to be an island: according to the map, it is called Ilha de Paqueta.

I walk down the street in front of me, breathing the warm air, walking on the stony road. I pass restaurants and cafés and souvenir shops, and step aside to let a horse and cart go by.

I am not the real Ella Black.

I try to process that fact, now that I have escaped. The child I thought I was actually died in the womb, eight times over, and I'm the imposter, the changeling, the next best thing. I thought I had come into the world as someone, but I actually arrived as somebody else, and I don't know who that person is, who I would have been if I had stayed where I started.

I wished for this. I wanted to be anyone but myself. Only the other day, just after I killed the bird with the hammer, I wished to be a different girl. I got my wish. I am an entirely different girl from the one I always thought I was. And there is someone else out there who wants to find me and be my mum.

I want to find my mum. I want my real mother.

There is a bike rental shop on my right. I stop.

"*Hola*," says a boy sitting behind a desk. He has little round glasses and curly black hair, and if he had a scar on his forehead, he would look like Harry Potter.

I take a deep breath and say, "*Hola*." That is pretty much all my Portuguese, used up already.

"Hi. You speak English?" he says.

"Yes." I smile my relief. "Yes I do."

"Are you interested in renting a bike? Special rates for zombies."

"Yes, please."

"Good call. No cars here, so it's the best way to see the island."

His English is fluent. He speaks like an American, with the very smallest of accents. His voice is a bit like Christian's.

"No cars?"

"That's right. Did you notice? That's what makes it cool."

I am thinking of Christian now, and I have to stop for a moment and pull myself together. Christian will have told my parents about our night out in Lapa. I'm sure of it. It was only last night. I told them already, and they didn't believe me. They'll believe Christian, when he's saying exactly what I said.

"Is there a place to stay?" I manage to say.

"Sure there is. You're backpacking?"

He looks dubiously at my little bag. I look at it too.

"I left my backpack with a friend in Rio." That sounds convincing, and anyway he won't care.

"Sure," he says. "Well, there are a few hotels. Are you looking for a hostel?"

"I'm looking for a place that's cheap. I don't care how basic."

"Right. Look, take the bike and go explore. One of my friends rents out rooms, and I'm sure she'll have a bed for you. I'll give her a call while you're out, OK? There are many places to sleep here. It's a touristy place. It's totally easy."

"Thank you!"

"How long do you want the bike? It's ten for an hour."

I shrug. "Two hours?"

"Sure." We both look at the clock on the wall, and I realize I have no concept of the time at all. It is just after five o'clock. "We close around seven," he says, "so be on time if you can."

"Got it," I say. I hand him twenty reales. He asks my name, so I say Chrissy because I am thinking of Christian, and he writes it down.

"I'm Alex," he says.

Then he shouts to his colleague, and they both look at my legs in an objective way, and then a bike is produced that is approximately the right size.

"We got you one with a basket," he says, "so you can carry your bag."

I stare at him, this wizard boy who is making everything all right. I don't know what to say to his kindness.

I wheel my new bike into the dusty road, and turn and wave to Alex. Then I get on it and start to ride toward the sea at the end of the street. I am wobbly at first, and the road is a bit stony, and the sun is harsh on the top of my head. There are people riding huge tricycles, two people side by side, laughing, but those things look like gimmicks for the tourists. I am glad I'm on a real bike, the kind you could ride in Rio or London or Hong Kong. A bike is a real piece of independent transportation, and I am on my own now. I pedal hard, making my legs burn. I have always loved biking.

I turn right at the end of the road and ride alongside the sea. I take a path leading inland, and then I ride furiously around the island, to different beaches and inland past huge crumbling houses with trees with drooping vines and plants with massive tropical leaves. The breeze makes my hair stream out behind me and blasts warm air into my face.

People watch me pass, and sometimes they say *hola*. I ride and ride and focus on the details—on the insects and the tiny birds and the flowers and the peeling paintwork of the houses. All the time, though, I am thinking about my biological parents.

She was young when she had me.

She was forced to put me up for adoption.

She has missed me every day, and she's looking for me now, because she knows I'm nearly eighteen.

She wants to find me. I know that that part is true.

I want to find her. I want to know where I came from.

The real mother who takes shape in my head as I ride is someone like me (of course—because I am her daughter). She was young, she got pregnant, she had no family support, and she gave me up for adoption because she had no other option. I forgive her. Over and over again, I forgive her.

After some time I stop and push the bike onto a beach and lean it against a tree. I kick off my flip-flops, which, I realize, have rubbed between my toes and given me a blister, and I walk to the shoreline and step into the water. It is brown, which I wasn't expecting, but there are some girls farther down the beach who are splashing and swimming, so I am sure that it's fine. I paddle into the water, and then I reach down and scoop it up and wash my face in dark, possibly polluted, Brazilian seawater from a strange corner of the edge of the Atlantic.

I have no idea if the green and black and the crusted zombie blood have actually come off, but I probably look a bit more human. The water is cool on my feet, and I stand in it for a long time. When I stare out to sea, I see there is some land, but I don't know whether it is another island or this island curving around or the Brazilian mainland. I could probably figure it out if I tried. But I don't feel like it.

I try to feel things, but I'm really just numb.

The sun is as hot as ever, and the rules don't apply anymore. There are no grown-ups to tell me what to do. I don't want to be arrested, so I sit in the shade of a tree and look at the sand that is glued to my feet.

I take out my phone, take a deep breath, and switch it on.

It has full reception. I watch as new texts drop in, as the number of voice mails goes up and up as it counts them. I don't want to look at any of the communications from the Blacks, so I skim past them all. I want to hear from only one person, and he still hasn't texted me.

I need to listen to the voice mails, and I do it, deleting them as soon as I hear "Ella, it's Mum," or "Ella, it's your dad." I am cold with horror when I imagine what those messages might be saying.

Then it is there.

"Hi. Ella. It's Christian. I'm really worried about you, because your parents say you've run away and the place is swarming with police. I know everyone is trying to find you. I hope you're OK. Um. Thanks for giving me your number. I guess you got your cell phone. So. You'll need to do the plus one for the States, and then it's 305-555-5923. I hope you're safe, Ella. I miss you."

I draw the number in the wet sand by the shore, with the +1 in front. I take a photograph of it and save it in my phone. I call it immediately without stopping to think about whether or not it is a good idea.

"Ella?"

It is his voice. It is Christian's voice.

"Hi." My voice barely comes out at all.

"Jesus. Ella, are you OK? Where are you? They're going insane looking for you."

"Would you . . . Could you come and meet me tomorrow?"

"Could I? Yes, sure. Of course."

I close my eyes and make myself breathe deeply. He said *of course*. He didn't have to stop and think about it. He has no idea what I did.

"You have to tell your parents you're OK, though, Ella. You really do. They've been talking with the police. They're insanely worried."

I cannot tell him.

"Listen, I have to go, but I'll tell you everything tomorrow."

"OK. Where are you?"

I hesitate. I can't tell him I'm on this island. He might tell everyone I'm here. And if he finds out that the police aren't looking for me because they're worried about my safety, but because I've hurt someone's face, that will ruin everything. If he doesn't know where I am, he can't say anything.

"I'll text you in the morning at nine. Promise you'll come without telling anyone. Until I've told you what's going on."

I listen to him thinking.

"Sure," he says, in the end. "Sure. OK."

At seven, I am back at the bicycle place. The sun has set, but the light is hanging in the air. The boy, Alex, looks up from an old-fashioned laptop.

"Right on time," he says. "So, Chrissy. I've got you a bed at the Hostel Paqueta. It's not far away. You can rent a bike for a couple of days if you like. I'll draw you a map of how to get there. The lady who runs it, Ana-Paula, is expecting you." He pats his stomach when he says her name, as if her main feature is being fat.

"Thank you." I beam at him. I have a bed, and in the morning Christian is coming and I will tell him everything, even the bad things.

A short while later, I arrive at the hostel. It is actually a big house with crumbling plaster and yellow windowsills. A huge tree in the garden trails vines over my head as I walk down the path. I can hear insects making wild little noises from all directions. The grass is short, and the plants have huge leaves. I watch a beetle walking along one. The air is perfectly still.

When I feel ready, I knock on the door, first softly, then, when nothing happens, a bit louder, and then, eventually, when that still doesn't work, as loudly as I can. The silence is oppressive, and I can smell ripe things beginning to rot. Even though I know that the sea is all around us and that literally just across it is a huge, wonderful city, this could be anywhere. It could be in the middle of any tropical place. It could be any spot in Latin America.

It couldn't, of course. I know nothing about Latin America. But this place reminds me of Gabriel Garcia Marquez, of the stories of weird things happening in strange fertile places. Anything could happen here. Strange things do happen. That much I know.

Nobody answers the door. It doesn't matter. I have nowhere to go, so I sit on the doorstep, which is warm and stone and cracked, and put my bag next to me and lean back. My parents might find me here. The police could track me down easily enough, thanks to my hair. Christian might tell them I'm here the moment I tell him.

My plans have been forming while I've been riding around the island. Tomorrow I will see Christian (I hope he comes I hope he comes I hope he comes). And unless anything else changes, I will stay here and be Chrissy, because there must be an Internet connection, and that means that I can try to figure things out, as far off the beaten path as it feels possible for me to be. As soon as I get online, I will do everything I can to help my real mother find me, and then I will go back.

I will go back to the Blacks so they know I'm all right, and I'll go back to England and see what happens.

A woman comes around the side of the house, and I see what the Harry Potter boy meant when he patted his stomach. She is heavily pregnant, and I think of the zombie woman in the parade earlier today, with the bloody baby doll bursting out of her bump. This woman has very long black hair, and she is wearing a little vest and a long skirt that she has pulled down to go under her belly. She looks exhausted, but she smiles when she sees me and says "Oi" and then some things in Portuguese.

I stare at her baby bump. I try to imagine what it would be like to grow a baby like that, inside your actual body, and then give it to someone else to take care of. I feel sad for my mother: she has probably missed her baby for nearly eighteen years.

I wish I spoke Portuguese. For now, the pregnant woman and I manage to communicate by speaking our own languages while miming, and she says her name is Ana-Paula and I remember that mine is Chrissy so I say that. Then I follow her around the house and in through a side door.

It is dark in there after the bright sunshine of the outside world, and the floor is covered in cool tiles. She opens a squeaky door and shows me into a dark room with trees outside the window, and there are four bunk beds in it and no sign of anyone else. I put my bag on a top bunk, because why would you choose to sleep on the bottom when you can sleep up in the air?

Until a year ago, I slept on a top bunk of my very own, or rather, in a "high sleeper," which meant that, in the absence of a sibling, I had a desk under my bed. I think high sleepers are supposed to be for rooms that don't have much space, but there was plenty of space in my bedroom at home. I just wanted to go up a ladder to get into bed. Then I got older and realized that my high sleeper was a bit childish. But still, I missed it when it was gone.

I have a little wooden ladder to climb to go to bed tonight, and I am so exhausted and so confused that I want to go to sleep right away. The last thing I want is to have to go out and find something to eat, but I cannot ignore the fact that I haven't had anything since the hotel breakfast back in my other life. I am absolutely starving.

Ana-Paula looks at me and asks something, miming eating. It's like she can read my mind.

Some time later I am sitting in the kitchen with her, eating rice and beans. The beans are in a delicious meaty brown sauce, and this is legitimately the best thing I have ever eaten in my life. I smile at Ana-Paula, and she smiles back and says things to me. I want to ask about her baby, but I can't, and anyway if I think too much about her baby, I will fall apart. A woman was this heavily pregnant with me eighteen years ago, and I don't know her. I don't know her face or her voice. I don't know anything beyond the fact that she was forced to give me up. That is not a good only-fact to know about your mum.

She must have looked at me. I must have looked at her. We must have been each other's worlds, for a moment.

I blink back tears. Ana-Paula pats my shoulder. I know she would let me sob on her shoulder, but I can't do it. I need to control myself.

Soon after, I go to bed, but I wake up in the middle of the night and stare at the ceiling, replaying the day's surreal events. I lie awake for the rest of the night, certain that I will never sleep again.

CHAPTER SEVEN

AT NINE IN the morning, I send Christian a text.

Ilha de Paqueta, I write. You can get a boat here from Rio. PLEASE DON'T tell my parents that I'm here. And particularly don't tell the police. Come and talk to me first, at least. I promise that I'll contact them all if you think I should, after you've heard the story.

I stare at the words *my parents*. I don't like writing that, but I have to if I don't want to tell Christian what's wrong just yet.

I will tell him everything when he gets here. It will be a relief to say it out loud, to have someone here who knew me before I knew the truth about myself, even if it was only for a day.

A magical day.

I stare at the phone until he replies. It takes an agonizing seven minutes, but then there is a text from him that says the words I most want to hear.

On my way.

I stand at the ferry terminal and just stare at every person who gets off each boat, waiting for Christian to arrive and hoping the police won't turn up. In between the boats arriving, I get a bottle of water and drink it. Other than that I just stare. I shut off my brain and look at the sun glittering on the sea and try to think of nothing at all. I don't think about who I am. I just exist.

Christian might be bringing my parents with him, or worse. If the Blacks arrive, I will tell them I don't want to see them yet. If they bring the police, I'll admit to what I did and take the consequences, because I'll have to.

I hope they don't.

I run through things in my mind. I must have needed my birth certificate at some point, to get my passport or something, but I've never seen it. My parents—my adoptive parents—must have made sure of that. It never occurred to me to look. But I'm about to be eighteen and to leave school. They would not have been able to keep this a secret much longer, no matter what. It was always a time bomb.

I'm sure that if you grow up being told that you were adopted, it would be perfectly all right. At least you'd know, then, approximately who you were. You would have the right feelings about your adoptive parents, so you would know all along that they weren't the people who gave birth to you, but the people who rescued you and gave you a family and a better life. Adoption is a great thing. There are two girls at my old school who were adopted from China. Adoptive parents are wonderful, in theory. Other ones are, but mine are not, because they deferred to me when I was younger, when I refused to hear them say that I was adopted. They let me have my own way, when actually they did know better than me because I was a tiny child. They were the grown-ups, and they should have forced me to listen.

I feel second best. Actually, I am ninth best. I cannot get over this. The real Ella Black, the one they told me I was, actually died, many times over, in the womb. I am her shoddy replacement, the best (the only) one they could get.

They told me I was her because that was who they wanted. They didn't want someone else's castoff baby: they wanted me to be their actual child come to life. And so they bought me everything I needed and sent me to a posh school and got me a kitten and made me eat the right things and took me to ballet lessons and did all the things they would have done for their real child, if they'd been able to have her.

By the time Christian steps off the boat, I am determined to move out of the Blacks' house and get a job, if I manage to get home. TV-drama phrases like *actual bodily harm* and *aggravated assault* chase each other around my brain, and I have no idea what is in store for me when the authorities catch up. Luckily, Christian is on his own, and even more luckily he walks straight over to me, takes me in his arms and kisses me deeply.

I allow it all to drift away for a few minutes. I relax into his arms. I feel his mouth on mine. I smell his smell. He knows me for who I am—or rather, he doesn't actually know me very well at all. I can be any Ella I want with him. He doesn't care who gave birth to me.

I love him, even though I hardly know him.

I love him.

I nuzzle into him as close as I can, wishing I could push against him so hard that we could merge into the same person. In the end we have to break apart just a little so we can talk.

"So," he says. "Ella. It's so great to see you. I cannot tell you how relieved I am. Want to tell me what's been going on?"

"Yes."

"Should we get lunch?"

"Lunch?"

"It's midday. That's good enough for me. Lunch and a beer. How did you find this place?"

I smile as we start to walk down the sandy street. "I think it found me. Literally, I needed the bathroom, and I saw a boat, and I thought there'd be a toilet on the boat, so I got on it."

"That's it? That's what brought you here?"

"That's it."

"Was there a bathroom on the boat? I didn't look for one."

"Yes, but it was disgusting. It was, like, the most disgusting bathroom you could possibly imagine. I was desperate."

I said "bathroom" like an American, and I like that. This is not the romantic conversation I was imagining, but we're both giggling and that makes it better than anything that has happened in my head. Laughing feels strange and wonderful. I wish I deserved this.

A short while later, Christian sits opposite me at a rickety metal table, and I stare at him. I gaze at his cheekbones and his jaw, at his lovely shiny hair and the way it frames his face so perfectly. I stare at his huge dark eyes, and he looks back at me. We both smile.

Sometimes you don't need to say anything.

I pick up my beer bottle and he takes his, and we clink them and take a sip. I wish I didn't have to tell him what I did.

"So," he says, as we put them down.

I did promise him an explanation. "So," I say. "Thank you for coming here. I'd better tell you some stuff."

He nods, and I take a deep breath and start talking.

I have only two actual facts to relate. However, for some reason I talk for hours and hours. I tell him everything. I have never done that before. I've never told the truth about myself. I tell him all of it because I want him to know the truth about me.

We order fish and potatoes and it arrives and we both eat it, but I barely notice because I am so busy talking. I find myself telling Christian about Bella and am horrified to hear the words coming out of my mouth. He reaches across the table and grips my hand as I talk, because the words make me shaky. I have never spoken about her to any human being at all, not even Lily, not even when Lily came into the room and saw Bella killing a bird.

"She's made me do awful things." I stop, wipe my eyes on the napkin he passes me, and take a deep breath. "I've thought for a while that it was building up to something terrible. And then it happened. Yesterday."

I talk him through yesterday, and I don't leave anything out. I tell him about the letter and about my phone call to Michelle, and about the café and the thing inside me that smashed the bottle and would have slashed my mother's throat with it. I tell him about my dad catching my hand, and the waiter being right there, and the line of blood across his face.

"It's the worst thing I've ever done," I say, and I'm not hungry anymore. I feel like I'm going to be sick.

I expect Christian to get up and walk away from me. He looks at me, and I see uncertainty on his face. Then he nods. "And you can make sure it's the worst thing you'll ever do," he says. "Look—I don't know what's going on back there, but your parents didn't tell me any of that. They just said you'd had a fight and run away. There were police around, but they probably weren't . . ." I see that he doesn't know what to say. He wants to reassure me that I'm not in trouble, but he can't. "I don't know," he says, in the end. "I don't know what would happen if you went back right now. Maybe you should stay here awhile. I can go back and find out for you."

"Will you?"

"Can I tell your parents—your adoptive parents—that you're safe?"

He is so kind. He is gentle and lovely. I had no idea.

"Yes, but—please don't tell them I'm here. Find out if I'm going to prison and then I'll figure out a plan. In fact, I'll write them a note and you can just give them that when you get back, so they'll know you really have seen me."

Christian nods. He looks more worried than ever now. "Look. I have to be in Rio this evening because it's Felix's birthday and he's booked a show and shit like that. I'll talk to your parents. I'll give them a note. I promise I won't tell them you're here, and I'll find out everything you need to know. OK?"

"Yes. Thank you. Anyway. You know everything about me now and I know hardly anything about you. But you seem to be so together. Your life isn't falling apart like this."

He laughs, though he doesn't sound as though he thinks it's funny. "Are you kidding?"

"No."

"Yeah. There's a bunch of stuff you don't know. Let's pay this bill. Let's not talk about Bella or anything that happened yesterday. Let's take your mind off it a bit."

I take a breath. "OK."

"So this island has no cars? Are there bikes?"

"Yes. I've got one. I'll take you to the rental place. The owner's nice. He speaks perfect English, luckily for me."

Christian pays the bill even though I try to make him split it with me. We walk down the road hand in hand, and when we reach the bike rental place, I extend the rental on mine again and introduce Christian to Alex.

Alex says, "Oh, the friend in Rio! I knew it would be a boyfriend."

I feel too shy to look at Christian's face. I want him to be my boyfriend. I wish he could be. I know I could do anything as long as he were standing where he is now, at my side holding my hand. He knows everything, and yet he's still holding my hand.

Christian doesn't correct him. In fact, he squeezes my hand and gives me a secret glance, as if we are in this together, which we are, and my heart fills up and overflows with sparkles and joy and love.

"It's ten an hour," says Alex.

Christian takes out his wallet. "Three hours?"

I nod. "Sure."

He takes out thirty reales, and I watch him do it, and I see, because it's in front of my face, that in his wallet there is a picture of a girl.

She is a beautiful girl.

She has long black hair.

She is smiling.

You have a picture of a girl in your wallet only if she's your girlfriend. So Christian does have a girlfriend.

It's not me.

I've just told him everything. I told him all my secrets, and he never told me that he had a girlfriend. I suppose he never said he *didn't* have one, and I never asked.

I am so dumb.

He pays and puts his wallet away and gets on his bike, and I get on mine too, and we pedal down to the end of the road. Except now I don't know what to say because I can't really carry on like normal now that I've seen that picture.

He doesn't say anything either. There are other bikes and the funny trike things and then a horse and cart, so we don't really have the chance to chat anyway. Then we turn off down a stony path, past those peaceful houses, and the world is silent except for the buzz of insects and the crunching under our wheels. No one is here but us.

"Ella," he says, slowing down so we are riding side by side. "I know you saw the photograph back there."

I look at him and then look back at the road.

"Oh?" I try to pretend to be surprised, but there's actually no point. "So I guess you have a girlfriend back home?"

"No," he says. "No, I don't. I really don't. I was happy when that guy called me your boyfriend."

"Were you?"

"I was. Look. Ella. That was Vittoria. My sister."

Immediately I'm relieved, but then I sense something. It's in the tone of his voice, and the fact that no one carries a photo of their sister in their wallet.

"Shall we go and sit on the beach?" I say, and we keep going until we reach a stretch of sand. Then we push our bikes across it and lean them against a palm tree, and we kick our shoes off and sit down at the edge of the water, looking out. He reaches for my hand.

"So let me tell you why, in spite of what you might think, I am not at all *together*."

We sit there, and he tells me all about his life, beginning from his earliest childhood memory of himself and his twin sister, Vittoria, sharing a cot. He tells me how they did everything together, how everyone called them "the twins" instead of their names. They grew up in a nice part of Miami and went to good schools and had their own groups of friends, but they were so close that they felt like "two halves of the same person," he says. He talks about the big house, the emotionally distant parents, the sense he always had that it was the two of them against the world.

"And then she got sick," he says. "I knew it at the same time she did. She got sick, and we knew it was serious, and it was. It was a very rare cancer. Anaplastic thyroid cancer. If you get it, the chances are huge that you'll be dead soon. You can fight it, but it's not one that you beat. Our friends and family tried to be positive, and I did too, because she was my fucking twin sister, and if positive thinking might help, then I was going to do some positive thinking. But it didn't help. I knew it wasn't going to and Vicky knew it too. So."

"Oh God. I'm so sorry."

"Yeah. Me too. It sucks."

I can't think of the right thing to say, so I just hold on to his hand.

"You would have liked her. She'd have told me you were too young for me. I can hear her saying it. But she would have loved your hair."

"How long ago . . . ?"

"A year. One whole year. It's a lifetime, and no time at all. Felix and Susanna came over here with me for the anniversary. Or rather, to get away from the anniversary. My parents would have preferred to have me home with them, and I feel bad about that. But I couldn't do it. Vicky would want me to be here, with you, sitting on this beach, right now. She would."

He is holding my hand, playing with my fingers.

"It's not today?"

"No. You know what? It was two days ago. The night we met up in Lapa. You said it was the best night of your life, and that meant the world to me. It really did. When you said that, I felt like, actually, life can go on. I can be happy. People can be happy. I felt good."

I stare out at the water. "I've just spent, like, four hours telling you all my problems, and they're just nothing next to yours. I'm sorry. I feel like a dick."

He shakes his head. "Your problems are very much not nothing, Ella. My problem is boring. It's about getting through the rest of my life when there's only half of me here. It's about living Vicky's life for her too. It's something I have to work out just through living. Yours, Ella. Yours is immediate, because you're here and your parents—the people who have always acted as your parents, whatever—are a few miles away over there, and I seem to be the only one who can move between you and them and try to help you work it out."

I try to digest everything he just said. There is a lot to process.

"What did Vicky like to do?" I feel self-conscious saying *Vicky* instead of *Vittoria*, but he doesn't seem to mind. He looks at me.

"She was much smarter than me. She wanted to be a doctor. And she loved to dance. She would have been doing the samba in the street with you."

I nod. I want to have a sense of her, in my head.

"She sounds brilliant."

"She was. Always. But I didn't plan to come here and talk about her. I really didn't. Like I said, I've got to go back to Rio tonight. And I'll do everything we said. Can I come back tomorrow? I'll come in the morning. Could I . . . Could I stay the night with you? Tomorrow? Depending on everything else?"

I turn and look into his eyes. We stare at each other for a long time. Then I answer his question by kissing him.

I see his ferry off, and he stands on the back of it, leaning on the railing and waving to me until he blurs into nothing. The boat, huge and white and made of metal, carries my Christian over the horizon and away from me, but only until tomorrow.

He is coming back. I thought I loved him before, but I had no idea, because I didn't know that it was possible for another person to make you want to open up. I have never been open with anyone. I always hold things back because I'm scared of them, but I told it all to Christian. I told him my horrors and he told me his, and we sat on the beach in the sun and kissed and kissed and kissed.

I'll ask Ana-Paula, now, whether she has a double room, and if she doesn't, we can go somewhere else.

I left school just a few days ago thinking I was Ella Black, but now I know I'm someone different.

Maybe that is a huge opportunity.

I am invigorated, and the only thing I want to do right now, since Christian is gone, is find my real mother. Life is short. Weird things can happen. I don't know who I am, and that feels fundamental. Christian and his twin sister were united against the world, but I have no one to unite with. I literally know no one at all with whom I share genes, and I need to find them. Even if I just look into her eyes and see parts of myself there and walk away—that will be enough. I don't want to be anyone's baby girl anymore. My birth mum doesn't have to take care of me. I just want to meet her.

First I need to find a place to use the Internet, and I want to find a computer because I have a phone but no charger. Even though I've been keeping my phone switched off most of the time, it won't survive a long search for a birth mother. Hopefully I might be able to buy a charger here; I'll try to find a shop in the morning.

Until then, I'll see if Alex can help me.

"Could I borrow your laptop?" I say.

He barely looks up from his magazine. "You can try. It's older than you are. You might as well communicate with the world by carrier pigeon."

"Oh. Well, do you know anywhere that I could use one? I've got my phone but I have to do some stuff on the Internet for a family thing, and it'd be much easier on a computer. I'll, like, pay or whatever."

He puts down his magazine and looks at me over the top of his little glasses.

"Most people just use Wi-Fi on their phone," he says. "On the island, I mean. If they need to. I'll give you the Wi-Fi code for this place if you do want to use it. Or you're welcome to have a go at this old thing. I just about manage to keep the bike rental website updated on it, but it's not easy. I could bring my MacBook along tomorrow if you like."

"Thank you. That would be amazing."

"Sure. Your boyfriend seems like a nice guy."

"He's wonderful." I know that I am glowing. I can't believe Alex brought up the subject of Christian. Now I get to talk about him, and I didn't even make it happen. "He's coming back tomorrow, to stay."

"Hey. That's great. You . . . Well, you seem much happier now."

"I am. We didn't have a fight or anything." I don't know if he's just being polite, but I decide to keep it as close to the truth as I can. The new me is going to try to be up front with people. "I'm just going through some family stuff," I say. "The same stuff I need to use a laptop for now."

"Take it, and good luck." He grins and pushes it along his little desk, toward me, then picks up his magazine again.

I sit at the back of the bike rental place, on a step beside a load of bikes, and open the laptop. It is dark back here, because the front of the shop is open to the street and there are no lights on. It smells of bikes and wooden floors and walls.

It takes a long time to connect, but I don't mind waiting. When it is working and connected to the Wi-Fi, I start googling.

I begin with my old name, Ella Black.

My fingers are trembling.

I need to know who I am.

I

don't

know

who

I

am.

Nothing comes up that would suggest my adoptive parents have told the papers that I'm missing, and I guess the police are probably working on bigger crimes than mine.

I look up how to go about finding your birth parents, and fill in a form to apply to join the Adoption Contact Register. I know, from the adoption certificate that Michelle read to me, that I have the right birthday, and I'm glad about that because it would be very strange to have been celebrating on the wrong day for all these years. I navigate slowly through the Internet and do everything I can to help my birth mother find me in exactly two weeks' time, on my eighteenth birthday.

Then I take boring Mr. Vokes's letter out of my bag and uncrumple it. I read the whole thing again. I'm surprised to see that my birth mother's name is there. In all the shock, I must have forgotten.

It says "Ms. Hinchcliffe." That is her surname. That is my real last name. Ella Hinchcliffe. She must have had a name for me that wasn't Ella. I wonder what my first name was.

I want to find *Ms. Hinchcliffe*. Mum. I want to tell her that I'm all right, that the baby she had to give away because she was too young or too poor or too ill has grown up. I want to tell her that they lied to me all my life, but that now I know and I forgive her. I want to tell her that I have been Ella and Bella, that I always knew something was wrong.

Ms. Hinchcliffe cannot have been to blame for what happened. I picture her as a gorgeous, pretty teenager who couldn't handle a baby. Maybe her family wouldn't let her keep me. If I was pregnant (which is not actually a possibility, but it could be after tomorrow—that thought makes me shiver with excitement), I might not be able to handle that either. I might have to give the baby to someone else so that it could have some proper parenting. I imagine my birth mother looking like me, being young and scared, struggling with the idea of motherhood, knowing she had to give her baby to some grown-ups. I want to tell her that although I've had every material thing in life, I've missed her every single day without knowing what it was that I didn't have.

I take a deep breath and type the words *Hinchcliffe baby 1999 UK*. It seems unlikely, but you never know.

The computer works slowly. I squint through the darkness at the sunlight outside. Alex is talking to some tourists who want to rent bikes. I can't understand a word any of them are saying, but I can vaguely follow what's going on through their gestures and the tones of their voices. One of them is so tall that he's looking for a particularly big bike, but Alex isn't sure if he has one.

I look back at the laptop. It's still thinking. The Google search bar comes up, but the rest of the page is blank. I am only half hoping for a birth announcement or something, and you probably don't really put them in the paper or online if you're about to give your baby up for adoption. The year 1999 was long ago, and the Internet was different then. I am sure there will be nothing, but I have to try because her last name is the only fact I have.

The results start to appear, but they are irrelevant, as I thought they would be. All the Google hits are about a recent court thing that has nothing to do with me. That's annoying. I add the word *adoption* to the search, and they keep coming, the same results, about some boring other thing.

The first image to come up is an ancient photo of a woman being arrested. Her name is Hinchcliffe. I look at the picture just in case, but she looks nothing like me: she has a tiny skinny face and thick black hair and she's not my mum. I scroll down the page to the bottom, but all the results are about her.

That is irritating. I want to find my birth mother, and I'm not interested in this woman who has done something to land herself in court . . . I click on one of the results to see what she has done.

"I'm going to close up in a minute." Alex is standing beside me. "Sorry, Ella. But like I said, you're welcome to come back tomorrow and borrow my MacBook."

"Sure. Thanks. I'll just be a second."

"Ten minutes?"

"Great."

The news story has loaded, and I look at it out of curiosity. This woman is called Amanda Hinchcliffe, and she has just been released from prison. That sounds familiar: I've heard her name before. I read that she has been in prison for being an accessory to murder: she found young women in the street and took them back to her boyfriend's flat, where he tortured and killed them, long ago.

She has been in prison since 2000. There are no photos of her now, but there are several of her when she was arrested.

I look at them all, just in case.

I look at them.

I look at her.

And then I see her stomach.

She was pregnant.

She

was

pregnant.

She was arrested in October 1999, and she was pregnant.

My ears are ringing.

My vision is closing in.

I stare at the screen.

I am looking for the words.

Finally I see them.

Her baby, they say.

Her baby was taken into care.

Into care.

The baby was born.

It was taken into care.

It doesn't say if the baby was a boy or a girl. It just says that it was taken away from her. Away from Amanda Hinchcliffe.

Where have I heard that name?

It comes back to me in a flash. Driving away from school. The news. The radio. "Amanda Hinchcliffe released." My mother jabbing the button, stopping the words.

I feel my heart pounding.

I try to think.

It's not easy to adopt a baby. I have no idea how many babies were born in November 1999 and taken away for adoption, but I know that not many of them could have been taken from mothers with the last name Hinchcliffe, at that exact time.

There is an old photo of her boyfriend, the murderer. His name is William Carr. I had not thought about my birth father at all, and I don't want to. I push the man away. I cannot look at him. Because even from the corner of my eye I can see one thing about him, and it is a thing I do not want to see. I want to hide. I want none of this ever to have happened. I can't handle it.

I'LL TAKE OVER.

We can't do anything. It already happened.

WE CAN ALWAYS DO SOMETHING. I KNEW IT. I KNEW WE CAME FROM BADNESS.

I suppose I knew it too.

NOW WE CAN BE BAD. NOTHING MATTERS NOW.

The world has faded away. I am not in it. I can't tell what I can't see, because I'm sitting in the dark anyway. I struggle for a while and then I succumb.

I KNEW IT ALL ALONG.

IT IS WHAT I AM.

IT IS WHAT I HAVE ALWAYS BEEN.

I KNEW IT.

I

KNEW

IT.

I am Bella. The real me is my Hinchcliffe self. I read the news report, every word of it, and I look at the man who murdered five women, eighteen years ago, and who would have killed more if he hadn't been caught.

The man in that photograph is young. It is a mug shot. He looks at the camera, and he looks sideways.

The man has my cheekbones. He has my mouth. He has my original fair hair, and I think he has my eyes. That man is my father.

WILLIAM CARR IS MY FATHER.
AMANDA HINCHCLIFFE IS MY MOTHER.
I AM THEIR DAUGHTER.
I AM A DEMON.

It's nearly dark, and I am on the beach, sitting on the sand staring out to sea. The sun has gone, but its light is lingering. I don't know what has happened. I am exhausted, and I don't want to think about anything because it is a million times worse than I would ever have imagined possible.

I pick up a little stone and throw it into the water.

I need to walk into the water and keep going. That would be the best thing to do. It would be so easy. I could just walk. That water is brown and nasty, and it would come into my mouth and my nose and stop me from breathing.

She should have had an abortion. I have been going for eighteen years too long already.

I thought I wanted to find my birth mother.

I had her last name, and I found her easily. I didn't have to wait until my birthday because she is famous. My parents are infamous.

I cannot meet my real mother.

I cannot meet my real father.

I could go back to my old life, to face whatever's waiting for me in

Rio. I could pretend I never found out any of this and go back to being Ella Black and be grateful for it. For a moment I picture myself doing that. I could go back to school, apply to university, and take my exams. I could grab hold of the stupid orange life ring and let myself be pulled back onto the boat and pretend I never fell off it.

But I know that is impossible.

The Blacks know who I really am, and I never want to look them in the eye again. I cannot pretend I don't know I was adopted, and I cannot pretend to be the baby they never managed to have. Yesterday I thought I could tell Christian everything, but I cannot tell him this. I am absolutely on my own.

This has been the Blacks' shameful secret for eighteen years, and now it is mine. Even though they tried, up to a point, to tell me I was adopted, I know they never would have told me who my biological parents were. No wonder they backed down gratefully when I refused to hear the truth.

I feel a twinge of sympathy for them. Their lies were better than the truth. They did a good thing: it's impossible to argue with that. They did a good thing, but I can't go home to them.

I need to go back online and see the details of the crimes so I know all the horror of my origins. I was clearly conceived right in the middle of it, and I can't even say that William Carr might not be my dad because you only have to look at him to see that he is.

This, finally, is real. I am Ella Hinchcliffe-Carr, child of murderers, and my dark side, my demonic Bella, is my truth. Bella Carr. That would be my birth name.

I lean back against a tree and close my eyes.

I try to think of anything I've ever heard about Amanda

Hinchcliffe and William Carr. I can remember little flashes of newspaper coverage; a sidebar of *other famous serial killers* when something happens, a link on the Internet, a mention here or there. But that's all. I suppose the Blacks must have shielded me from it. If I try, I can revisit my childhood to find scenes of them switching the TV off, or distracting me with cookies and kittens if they couldn't, when anything came on the news. I suppose, too, that if something is in the news when you're a baby, it's faded from the headlines by the time you are old enough to notice it.

In a flash, I realize: my school knows who I am.

Not all the teachers, but I think Mrs. Austen, the principal, knew. I can see her tearing a piece of paper to shreds as she told me that I had to go with my parents whether I wanted to or not. She must have known why.

It must have been strange for her.

She knew, and maybe some other teachers did too, but I don't think any of the students had any more idea than I did. They'd better not have. The idea of any of my friends knowing that about me makes me shiver and shudder.

I made most of the teachers like me by ruthlessly controlling my bad side, pretending to be quiet and nice, and being a good student, but in my heart I am bad. I have always known that. Now I know that I was made from badness and born into badness. I have bad genes, and no amount of education, nutritious food and ballet lessons was ever going to make me good. I tried to be nice, but more and more I had to fight against my real self to do it.

Fiona and Graham Black are, on the face of it, the nicest people in the world. They are never mean to anyone. Those new parents gave me everything I ever needed or wanted or asked for, and yet I still smashed birds to pieces with a hammer and slashed a stranger across his face with a broken bottle. But that is easily explained by the fact that I am the product of a famous criminal partnership. We are up there, us Hinchcliffe/Carrs, with the famous murderous couples of the world. You do not mess with us.

I cannot live with this. I stand up, stretch, and walk to the edge of the sea. No one is around. I can hear the sound of drumming from a house nearby. I step into the water. I don't have a bike with me; I suppose I must have walked here. I cannot remember a thing between surrendering myself to a gleeful Bella and winding up here on the beach. I know why I came here, though. I know what I have to do.

I walk out, in a straight line, up to my knees. I'm wearing the same shorts I've had on for days, so I can get thigh deep before any clothes get wet. I pause with the water just below my shorts. I can walk on, keep walking, and die, and they will find my body easily because this water doesn't seem to be the kind that moves around.

I want to. I desperately want to. I want to walk out and find a lovely blankness. Everything would go away. All of it. I have the power to extinguish myself.

But
I can't.
I want to, but I can't.
I
want
to,

but

I

can't.

OF COURSE YOU CAN'T.

YOU

ARE

NOT

DOING

THIS.

She is right. My feet won't take the steps. My body is refusing to choose to die.

TURN AROUND.

WALK BACK TO THE WORLD.

I can't keep myself under the water, because if I did, then I wouldn't be able to breathe, and I need to be able to breathe even though I don't want to be alive anymore. I can't get past that.

I can't conquer my need to breathe, and I can't override the voice in my head.

I can't die. I don't seem to be strong enough to take those last few steps.

I push myself back through the water's surface.

I've failed at dying.

. . .

I knew that would happen. The one time I tried to harm myself in my old life, a couple of years ago, I took a craft knife into the toilets at school and tried to work out my problems that way. I had read about self-harm: I thought it might be a good way for me to deal with Bella without hurting anyone else.

I stayed there, alone in the stall.

DO IT. HURT YOURSELF.

Just the idea made me feel so sick that I couldn't stand up, and I had to slump against the partition wall. Still I put the blade against my arm and waited.

DO IT!

But I couldn't. I couldn't override my instincts. That's why I just have two silvery lines on my left arm that no one sees. Only I know they are there. No one has ever noticed them because they are almost imperceptible. That was all I could do.

I turn now and walk slowly out of the water. I can't stay here. I can't tell anyone who I really am. I need to start again. The only way I can do that is if I leave everything behind—every single thing—and find a new life.

I pick up my bag and walk back to the hostel.

When I arrive, I see from Ana-Paula's face that something has happened to make her worry about me. I don't know how much time passed between my seeing Carr's face on the screen and finding myself on the beach. I might have smashed the whole town, striding through it like Godzilla. I have no idea.

"Are you OK?" she says, in careful English.

I nod, even though it's a lie. She speaks in Portuguese and I don't understand a word, so we can't communicate, which is all right by me. However, she is not giving up. She takes a pencil and a piece of paper and sits at the table in her warm kitchen and draws a picture of a girl who looks enough like me, with teardrops all over her face. She adds a laptop and some primitive bikes. As she draws, she talks, adding arrows to show me leaving the bike shop in tears and running away.

She mimes flinging the laptop to the ground.

She draws a boy like Harry Potter, with his mouth open in shock.

I try not to cry, but I know I've failed when she puts an arm around me and hugs me tight. She smells of coconuts. Her huge baby bump is pressed up against me, and I feel the baby squirming around.

That only makes it worse.

CHAPTER EIGHT

I SIT UP all night thinking. I spend an hour reading about my real parents on my phone, watching the battery dip. I hope it dies. Then no one will be able to find me ever again. I tiptoe into Ana-Paula's kitchen and write her a note saying, *Sorry I had to leave. THANK YOU.* I put it on the table with some money.

I write a much more difficult note, too:

> Dear Christian,
>
> I love you. I fell in love with you completely. I love you with all my heart. I know I've known you only a few days, but I feel I know you better than I've ever known anyone, ever, and I love you.
>
> I'm sorry I can't stop saying that.
> I'm sorry I'm not here.
> I'm sorry.
> This has nothing to do with you and everything to do with me.

I'll always love you. Thank you for everything.

I can't stay.

Ella xxxxxx

I fold it in quarters and write **CHRISTIAN** on the outside. I don't even know his last name. I hope it will get to him. He will go to Alex when I'm not there to meet his boat, and Alex will tell him where I'm staying. That should work.

According to the timetable, the first ferry of the morning leaves at five thirty. Quite a few other people are waiting for it, but I avoid their eyes and wrap myself in a cloak of misery. I hope I will get away before Christian gets here. I need him to keep the best Ella in his head, the one he loved. That me—the one who was between Ella Black and Bella Hinchcliffe-Carr—existed for only a few days.

She was the one with possibilities.

The engine starts, and the ferry moves with a jolt. I stare out the window. This boat is much emptier than the one I arrived on, two days ago. I lean my forehead against the glass and watch the island disappear in the dawn.

I know what my birth parents were doing, now, during the year before I was born. I read every article I could find. Amanda, my mother, would go to a carefully selected public place and cry, and wait for a kind woman (always alone) to stop to ask whether Amanda was all right. She would say yes but ask the woman to walk her home, just around the corner. She would lead them directly to the flat in which Billy, my father, was waiting. He would keep them there for days, doing things that I have forced myself to read about and will never bleach from my brain, and then he and Amanda would go out together at night to throw the bodies in the canal, because, of course, I am not from a privileged little town in Kent, but from a city far away from there that has canals running through it.

They got away with it for a long time because Amanda made sure to be in a place without closed-circuit television cameras and without witnesses, a short walk from their home. The women would be reported missing, but nobody would link them to Amanda and Billy because they had no connections to them, and they always covered their tracks extremely carefully.

Until, one day, they didn't. One of their victims had a huge family who made a loud and immediate noise about her going missing, and there was a sighting of her walking with a young woman just before she disappeared.

The witness's description eventually led the police to Amanda, and she cracked and told them to look in the canal. There, they found not just the body they were looking for, but the other ones too. Everything unraveled, and in the middle of the unraveling I was born.

Amanda was eighteen and heavily pregnant when she was arrested. The newspaper reports barely mentioned the fact that the baby (name and sex never given) was removed as soon as it was born and taken into foster care. That is where my public story ends.

I was *in care*. I was adopted by people who couldn't have their own baby and were reduced to rescuing one from murderers, and I was named Ella Black and brought up thinking that was who I was, for almost eighteen years.

I was "given a new identity," it says, in one of the glancing mentions of my existence. Ella Black: a new identity. I have a new identity like Jason Bourne. I was brought up oblivious to the fact that there was a fundamental truth about myself that I never knew, like Harry Potter or Luke Skywalker.

I have enlarged the photos of Amanda Hinchcliffe pregnant at her trial until they are as big as I can get them on my phone, and I stare and stare at them and I know that was where I began. I imagine a creature growing under the fabric of her baggy sweater, inside the waistband of her stretched leggings. I grew inside her, and before I was big enough to breathe, she was caught tricking kind passersby into coming home with her to be tortured and murdered.

I stare at her face. She was only a tiny bit older then than I am now. She has a nose like mine. It is a completely ordinary nose. It doesn't turn up at the end. It has no lumps or bumps in it. But it's the same as my ordinary nose.

I study her eyes. I would like a mirror to check, but I think there is something about our chins that is the same. Her hair, in these pictures, is thick and dark, and no amount of looking at it can change that. Mine is straight and fine and currently purple, but otherwise blondish.

I want to look like her because I don't want to look like him.

My phone warns me that it's almost out of battery. It has my old life on it. It has my friends from school, and my enemies from school, and all my photos and texts and emails. It has the truth about my birth in its search history. I was going to throw it into the sea, but I can't do it, because the entire truth of Ella Black is on it and I don't want to lose all of that.

The boat arrives in Rio, and everything is quiet. There is no sign of Christian, because of course he wouldn't be coming back to the island at six thirty in the morning.

I step into the pale sunlight and smile as my ears start to ring and my vision blurs. I welcome it.

I'VE GOT THIS, Bella says.
Thanks, I tell her.

I walk across the square in the cool sunshine and feel my strength surging as I go. The old me drowned in the sea last night. This me has feet that barely touch the ground. This me has nothing to be afraid of, because nothing can touch her.

NOTHING
CAN
TOUCH
ME.
BRING
IT
ON.
I'VE GOT THIS.

I am Bella through and through, and I am strong. I feel the violence beneath the surface, and I know that I could do anything to anyone now. I'm not sorry about the man's face anymore. I'm not sorry about anything. I miss Christian with a terrible nagging ache, but I know I cannot see him again because he is too good for me. I am walking away from the love of my life because I have to, because he loves Ella and I am Bella.

I flag down a yellow taxi, and the driver starts driving before I say where I want to go. I say the only word I can think of that will lead me to a place where Christian and the Blacks will not think to look for me.

They won't look for me because it's too dangerous.

Everything is dangerous.

Bring it on.

I say, "Favela."

The driver wants me to clarify. There are lots of favelas.

"The biggest one," I say.

He speaks enough English for us to have a basic conversation. He says a word that sounds like *Hosseenya*.

"Yes," I say. "There." Whatever that means, it will do.

This is what I know about favelas: they are shantytowns dotted around the city, and they are terrifyingly dangerous. I know that Fiona and Graham Black would never venture into one of them. I know that it would never occur to them to try. Ella Black would have run horrified from such a place. Bella Hinchliffe-Carr, on the other hand, will walk right in.

I need all the money I can get, and I need a place to go. It feels ridiculous to get the taxi to stop at an ATM so that I can get out lots and lots of cash to take into a dangerous area of a Latin American city, but I know I need to do it. Even if they trace me to the ATM, they would have to be very quick to catch me before I got back into the waiting cab, and then they still wouldn't be able to follow me to my brutal destination.

The driver stops outside a bank that is red all over. Although it is still early in the morning, I am able to open its lobby door and get blasted with freezing-cold air-conditioning. I put the card into a machine. It asks what language I would like it to speak, and I press the button next to "English." I put in 1711, my birthday—knowing that it will work because my not-parents use that number for almost everything even though they didn't meet me on that day at all—and it works. I half expect the shutters to come down and trap me in this room, but nothing happens. When it asks which account I would like the money to come out of, I tap the button next to "checking" because it's the first on the list of options, and then it is grinding into action and giving me fifteen hundred reales, which feels like a lot of money.

Of course it gives me money. That is its job.

I get right back into the taxi, and we are on our way again. This is thrilling. I need to stash most of this cash somewhere secret. I can't put it in my shoe, because I'm wearing flip-flops. I can't put it all in my bag in case the bag is stolen. I end up separating it out, and when I think the driver isn't looking, I put most of it into my bra, some of it into my shorts pockets, and a bit more into my bag. Whatever happens to me next, I should still have some cash.

The streets are getting busier as we go, and I stare out the window. Christian will go back to the island to meet me, like we agreed, and Alex will tell him all about my meltdown, and then he will find my note.

I stare at a lagoon that has busy roads and traffic jams all around it even though this is early in the morning. I know that I can only live from one moment to the next right now, and that suits me fine. I cannot stop and consider the bigger picture or even begin to imagine what I will be doing tomorrow. This should be overwhelming, but it isn't. I am made from badness and I come from criminals and I can survive anything.

I am never going back to my old life. I will try to live in the favela. The adrenaline throbs through my whole body. This is madness. It's probably an elaborate way of killing myself, and that's why I don't care.

The cab follows lines of traffic into a massive tunnel. All the noise is amplified and the sun is gone, and everything is tinged with red from the line of taillights in front of us.

Then we are out, into bright sunshine, and the taxi swerves across a lane of traffic and stops.

"*Hoseenya,*" says the driver, grinning, and I take a deep breath and step out of the cab. I pay him through his window, and he smiles and waves and says, "Good luck to you." He drives away, and I am alone.

I am alone in a slum in Rio and I should be terrified

but

I'm

not.

A week ago I was at school.

A day ago I was falling in love.

An hour ago I was on a boat.

Although I am heartbroken in a million different ways, the energy of running away is carrying me through. Ella is hiding inside me sobbing. Bella is going to get on with things, and there's one thing she needs to do before all others.

There are shops and stalls beginning to open up, and people and motorbikes are everywhere, and I don't speak the language. I hold my bag tightly, half expecting someone to snatch it.

I know people are noticing my hair. It makes me stand out.

In front of me is a stall selling cooked chickens: they are lined up under a glass counter. There is a barber working nearby. I walk over to his shop and sit on the bench outside. I smile a hello to the other people waiting, and they don't actually seem that interested, so I just sit there and wait my turn. While I wait, I literally think of nothing. I just stare at the people going by and I feel a surge of power, but I don't let anyone see it.

I open up the browser on my phone and put in my old name again. Ella Black. It takes a while, but then a photo of me comes up, and then, instantly, the battery goes and nothing I do will reanimate it even just for a second.

The barber calls to me, and I tell him I don't speak Portuguese, but I pick up a strand of my hair and make a face, and he laughs. I mime shaving it all off because it doesn't seem like the kind of place that will dye it black for me. The barber checks a few times that it's what I really want, and then he takes some clippers and runs them over my head. Locks of purple fall onto the ground, and he does it again and again until it is finished.

I look in the little mirror and run my hand over the top of my head.

Just like that, I have no hair.

I have no name. I have no family. I have no boyfriend. Now I have no hair.

Actually I have a little bit of hair. I have a few millimeters of the stuff, and it's light colored and fuzzy. It feels nice to stroke it. I must look as if I'm having chemo.

The man sweeps the purple strands into a pile of everyone else's dark hair, and I pay him a tiny bit of money and walk over to the café that is right there. On the way I pass the garbage. I stop and look into it. My recent photo came up on my phone just now, and that didn't happen when I googled myself yesterday. Someone must be looking for me.

I put my phone on the ground and stomp on it before dropping it in the trash. There goes Ella Black. She is now untraceable.

I am starting over.

I wish I had a guidebook or any kind of information at all. Right now, I am thirsty and bald. I am in a slum, but I can put one foot in front of the other and make my way toward a place to sit, and although it feels hallucinatory that I am even here, I am going to manage.

The café up ahead is called Super Sucos, and it is a juice bar. I order a juice by pointing at a picture of a pink one on the menu, and the woman motions to me to sit down. I sit, and am ignored even though I am strange and foreign and have just had my purple hair shaved off.

After a while a plastic cup with a lid and a straw arrives in front of me.

"*Obrigada,*" I say.

"*De nada,*" says the woman.

The Blacks felt sorry for me, because I am the offspring of murderers, and so they wanted me to have a nice life. That was kind of them. I needed parents and they needed a baby. I still managed to grow up demonic.

Maybe they wanted me to like them so I wouldn't kill them. Now I hate them. Perhaps I will kill them. Perhaps they are expecting it.

The juice tastes like strawberries and watermelon. I drink it as slowly as I can, and order another one, a green one this time. I sit and sip at it and keep my eyes on the table in front of me, waiting for time to pass in the hopes that half an hour from now I might know where to go and what to do.

The buildings here are made of concrete rather than corrugated iron and cardboard. It's not the way I thought a shantytown would be. This actually feels like the kind of place that might have somewhere for travelers to stay.

It is less terrifying than it should be.

I pay for my juice and say to the woman, "Do you speak English?"

She speaks enough English to know that I am asking whether she speaks English, and makes a "not really" face.

"Hotel?" I say.

She calls someone over. They talk, and look at me, and talk about me, and I don't like it because I might have been on the news and they might be going to call the police. They might have seen me getting out of the taxi with my purple hair. I decide that I don't need their help after all.

"Actually, don't worry about it," I say quickly, and shake my head and make a "forget it" motion with my hands. I will walk up the hill on my own and see what happens. I try to leave the café, but the man she called over stands in my way. I am breathing too fast. My legs tremble.

"You," he says. I look for a way past him. "You want hotel?"

I swallow. "Yes?" It comes out sounding too weak, so I say it again, bravely:

"Yes."

I am Bella and I am surviving. I am a monster and I can do anything. I have gotten this far and so far it's all right. "Yes," I say again. "I want a hotel. *Por favor.*"

"You come."

I follow him. The man leads me over to one of the men with the motorbikes and talks to him while I attempt to follow their gestures and catch an occasional word. He gestures to me to get onto the back of the bike and I do it, immediately. Then the guy revs up his engine and we are off. The bike vibrates underneath me, the engine roaring as it climbs the steep hill.

My life is in his hands.

Fuck it. Fuck it all.

We swerve in between people, because everyone is walking in the street. They are everywhere: the place is busier than I would have thought possible. There is a bicycle with a tiny child perched on the handlebars as a woman bikes uphill (it's probably her mother, but I know better than to assume anything). Other motorbikes buzz around the place. People sit at plastic tables on the pavement, drinking coffee and Coke and beer. A man carries a huge bag with something with white plastic edges sticking out of it. A group of young men walks, laughing, down the street. Every type of thing is for sale. There is more meat, and there are electrical appliances. There's a man doing some welding with sparks flying through the air, another barber. On every corner, there is a street vendor of some sort.

The entire scene is thrilling.

As we get off the main street, it stops being commercial and becomes more residential. I stare at the houses, packed together, painted in bright colors. Children are messing around with a ball, and they stop to watch me pass. A young man sits on a doorstep having a shouted conversation with someone I can't see. Two girls dressed identically in white T-shirts and blue shorts are doing handstands against a wall.

I pass it all, glad to be removed from it, to be on this motorbike, even though I am entirely in the hands of a stranger in a Brazilian slum and have no idea where he is taking me.

The roads become smaller, and then we are in an alleyway so narrow that I could put an arm out on either side and touch the walls as we pass. When the bike stops, I am ready. If he mugs me, I will hand over the cash from my front right pocket and run away. I should be able to find my way back to the place with the buses and the taxis and the juice bar, just by running down the hill.

However, he gets off his bike, bangs on a door and calls something. A woman comes out. She is tiny like a little bird and looks young, and when she sees me, she smiles and nods. The driver says something to her, and she says, "Hello. I speak English but not good."

"I don't speak Portuguese at all," I say, amazed at how brave I feel. "Sorry. But I'm going to learn."

"My name is Julia."

I pause, unsure of who I am. I can't be Ella. I can't be Chrissy, even though I'd like to remind myself of Christian, and I used that name on the island.

"Lily," I say. As soon as the name is out of my mouth, I wish I'd said something different, but it's too late. I should not say things that have any association with my old life. I am not Ella Black. I should not have used the name of Ella Black's best friend, and now it's too late, because I can't say that what I meant is that actually my name is Jessica, for example. That would be crazy, and my bald head and everything else about me is already crazy enough.

I pay the motorbike driver the small amount of money that he asks for by holding up fingers, and add a tip to show that I'm grateful for the lack of kidnap and robbery. He nods, turns his bike around and drives off. Then I am just here, deep in the slum, following the woman named Julia into her house.

It really is a guesthouse. She leads me into a white-tiled hallway and then opens a door and shows me a bedroom. It is nicer than I expected it to be, as the whole favela has been so far. It is small, with a floor and walls tiled in white, and the single bed has a green nylon cover. There is a window high up in the wall that doesn't let in much light. This feels like a place to hide. I put my bag down on the bed and ask how much it costs.

"How much time?" she asks.

I take a deep breath. "Could I stay for a month?" I ask.

"One month? Yes, of course. You work? Teaching English?"

"Yes." It is much easier to agree with this than it would be to attempt to explain myself any other way, and I'm grateful that I don't have to make something up.

We agree on a rate for a month's rent that I don't bother to convert because I know I have enough money in my bra to pay for it. I insist on paying it up front, because that gives me less cash for anyone to steal. I have money on me now, so I'm not going to use the credit card again for a long time. That is it. I am hiding from my old life and starting a new one, and I have a place to live until December.

The bathroom is next door. Julia shows me that there is one other guest room, currently empty, and tells me that she and her husband,

Anderson, live in another bedroom. The kitchen, with a table in it, is completely available to me, and there is a little sitting room with two comfy chairs. All the floors are tiled in white, and all the furnishings are faded but spotless.

"I go out to work," she says. "I work here, in Rocinha. Anderson works many hours in a hotel in Ipanema."

It didn't occur to me that people who work at hotels live in places like this, but of course they do. Everything I know about slums and shantytowns comes from geography lessons at school, and *City of God*, so it makes sense that the overriding idea I had is wrong. In the school version, a slum, a shantytown, a favela, was chaotic and desperate, with houses stuck together any old way and made from cardboard and corrugated iron. No one would have jobs: they would be beggars, or go rooting through trash cans and trash heaps, or they would sell drugs. They would be different from me. That was the idea I had.

I had to be brave to come here, but in fact it's just a place, like other places, and the people here have, so far, helped me out in every way I've asked them to. They have cut off all my hair and sold me juice and taken me to the exact right place on a motorbike and given me a bedroom.

I remember, again, how a million years and a few days ago, my pretend mother said that "they" did tours of the favela, and the three of us winced at how horrible that would be. In fact, this neighborhood is alive. It is interesting because it is different from anything I've known before, but really, it is just a place with people living in it like any other.

My fake parents would never have imagined that. Because they're comfortably well off, they are scared of people who have nothing. They would not look for me in here, and if they tried, they would struggle to find me. I need to keep my bald head down and stay away, at the same time, from everyone who knows me, and also from anybody who might like the cash I'm carrying. For now, at this moment, I am all right. In fact, I am bursting with adrenaline, and I feel like I could fight anyone and anything.

However, even though I have all the energy in the world, I don't have a plan beyond hiding out. Since I threw my phone away, I will have to find some analog entertainment: I wonder if there is a book in English anywhere nearby. I would like to do some drawing if I could find a sketchbook and some pencils. One day I would like to do a painting again.

I wonder whether a bald girl sketching would be a curiosity or just ignored.

But I need to do something more than that. I need to find a way to live, and I will find it. I'm not really going to sit around reading and drawing for a month, even if I have the materials. I still need to eat, so I will be spending money, and so eventually the money I have will be gone. Then I will have nothing to do and nowhere to live. I'll allow myself to settle in here for a few days, and then I'll figure out how to make some money. I know there will be something I can do. This is my new life, and I'm going to live it.

Julia gives me a glass of water, and I close my door and sit on my bed. Even though I'm really wired, the moment I lie down I fall asleep, and when I wake up, it's the middle of the afternoon.

It's the middle of the afternoon, and I can't find Bella's energy. I desperately need it. I need her to be a part of me, but all my bravado has vanished. I am lying on a bed in the middle of an unfamiliar part of a huge city, and I am entirely on my own.

I have crashed, and I have absolutely no idea what to do. I can't go out. It's too scary. I look at the wall for a while, and nothing happens. I make myself stand up and stretch out all my limbs. I want to stay here, shut away, and I do, for a while. Then, when I know I can't just stay shut away in a little room forever, I go to find Julia. She is watching TV in the sitting room, and she pats the sofa to invite me to sit with her. I want to check that there's nothing about me on the news, but actually she's watching *Seinfeld*, dubbed, and I manage to concentrate on it and not think about anything else at all for several minutes. I pick up a newspaper and stare at it, and flip through the pages, trying to use the French I learned at school, and logic, to figure out the words. It is a lot easier when it's written down than it is when it's spoken, that's for sure.

When I turn a page and find a familiar face staring at me, my head starts to spin and I think I am going to be sick. There are blotches all over my vision. I can't remember how to breathe.

It is me. I am in the paper.

I am on page fifteen, buried but very much there, on display to anyone who picks up this newspaper and flips through the pages. I want to translate the words, but I cannot ask Julia to help. I pick out my old name, Ella Black, and my adoptive parents' names, Graham and Fiona Black. There is no Amanda Hinchcliffe in there, and there are no grainy photographs, no notorious murderers. There is no café man with a mutilated face, though for all I know, he might be featured in the article.

The headline says *O medo aumenta sobre o destino do adolescente desaparecida. Adolescente desaparecida.* Disappeared adolescent? Desperate adolescent? Despicable adolescent? Whatever it says, this is about me and my *destino.* I've seen these stories in the papers at home. They usually end with the discovery of a body. This one won't. Not yet.

It is a photograph that my fake dad—Graham—took on the beach a couple of days ago just after I made my sketch of Copacabana. My hair is light gray in the black-and-white photo, and it is long and loose. I touch the stubble on my head and wonder whether Julia thinks I have been terribly ill. In the picture I am squinting a bit because the sun is in my eyes. I'm wearing my halter top, the one I've got in my bag, so I need to get rid of that. The flat line of the ocean horizon is behind me in the photograph. I look happy. I am actually smiling. I attempt it now, but it feels like a strange thing to do with my mouth. The Ella in that photograph is the same as the Ella I am in my earliest memory, in which I am held up to stroke a horse on its nose. I am two, and I am Ella Black. Last week I was still Ella Black. Yesterday morning, too.

Now I know better.

Julia looks over at me, and I force a smile and turn the page of the paper. It is a newspaper called *O Globo,* and I don't know if it's local or national. Not that it makes any difference. My hands tremble as I turn the page, and it shakes in an invisible wind.

I have to find a way to stay here. I don't even speak the language. The first thing I need to do is learn it.

"Will you teach me Portuguese?" I ask Julia.

"Yes," she says. "You help me with English?"

"Deal."

. . .

I go to bed early, but I can't sleep.

I think of my old life, the one represented by the photo in the paper. I miss Humphrey. It's ridiculous, but I am thinking about my cat.

I miss Lily. I miss my best friend, the one who kept me on track. The one who helped me try to be good, without even knowing it.

I miss Jack, my gay boyfriend, the boy who told me his secrets and helped me out.

I miss having a place to go every day.

I miss my life.

As a baby I must have missed my mother. Before I was born, she was my whole world. I wonder whether they let her cuddle me before they took me away. I think I have been craving her smell all my life. I am a part of her, and I always have been.

I wipe away the tears. I cannot cry for that woman.

I think about my adoptive mother instead. I wish I could say, "She's my mum no matter what and I love her," because that would make everything easy, but I just can't. Not now. She has probably spent the past eighteen years feeling sad about the babies she couldn't have. That must have been complicated, when she did actually have a baby but it came from murderers.

I am secondhand. I come from killers. My fake mother has done her best all this time, but she must have known, really, that I had a bad thing inside me. She must have known all along.

Perhaps that's why she tried too hard to be perfect. She made sure I ate healthfully, always lots of vegetables. She painted my bedroom exactly the way I wanted it and bought me a high sleeper when I asked for a bunk bed. She got me into the best school, encouraged me to work hard, and drove me everywhere I wanted to go. She was driving me to school last week, when everyone else walked or biked or even drove their own cars. She cooked dinner for me and my dad every night and picked at a salad herself. She loved my having a boyfriend, loved having Lily over.

The other mothers were different: mine worked harder at it than all of them. Even Jack's mum would dash around between work and home, and she would make a point of saying how lovely it was to see me, and that we should help ourselves to juice and always leave the bedroom door open. We would laugh about that when she was gone.

All the other mothers seemed like human beings who happened to be temporarily responsible for some children. Mine was the mother who was terrified of everything, who quadruple-locked the door behind me every time I came in, who would never have to drop everything to help me out because she was never ever doing anything that she needed to drop.

I wonder, now, whether she was on Valium like the women in the sixties used to be. I bet she fantasized about her imaginary biological family. The real Ella died in the womb, again and again, and they had to put up with me.

I was the demon, all along.

Real Ella would have had a brother, because they definitely would have had a nuclear family. He would have been called something unimaginative like Tom. Tom Black would have been a blond kid who climbed trees and was cheeky, and whom everyone loved even though he was "spirited." In time he would have calmed down and ended up working in the financial sector like his dad.

But they couldn't have any of that.

Fiona must be devastated that I tried to stab her. They raised me almost to adulthood, so they did their job. It's finished. Soon I will write to them and tell them that I'm fine and that I've got a job and they don't need to worry. Now she can become whoever Fiona Black really is. She can do her own thing and blossom. Her burden is lifted. I can't trust myself to go near her any time soon, because I don't think I can trust myself not to fly at her again.

So all I have to do is become fine and get a job.

I have no idea how you get a job.

I live in the favela.

I need a job.

I will need money. I have never not had money, apart from the fact that I was born into poverty.

I had nothing.

I was taken

into

care.

I stay awake all night. I don't seem to need to sleep in the way I used to anymore.

I hear Anderson coming home. Julia talks to him, and I know she must be telling him about me. As soon as I hear the low rumble of his voice, something changes. I can feel it.

Then I remember: he works at a tourist hotel.

I only realize slowly that I'm not really hidden, being in this house. He works at a tourist hotel, and I am in the paper because the police are looking for me. It must say in the paper that I have purple hair. Now I have no hair. A person with distinctive hair, hiding, would cut it off. My baldness is not really much of a disguise.

I can't even get a wig from somewhere, because Julia will have told him about me by now, and she must have said that I have no hair because that is now the most notable thing about me.

And I have the same face as the girl in the paper, because the girl in the paper is me.

And he works in tourist Rio at a hotel, and that is where people are looking for me.

After a while they go to bed. It is quiet. Sometimes there are voices outside, but there is no gunfire and nothing that sounds like trouble. For a shantytown, it seems very peaceful.

I wish I hadn't told Julia my name was Lily. My best friend Lily might have been in the British papers herself, worrying about me. Julia will have told her husband that I am Lily. He will tell them at the hotel that there is an English girl here called Lily. Since people are looking for an English girl, word could get back to the Blacks that there is a bald English girl here, and when they hear the name Lily, they will know.

I can't stay here.

I realize it with horror. If I want to stay hidden, then I cannot stay in this lovely little room buried in the favela with the friendly landlady who lets me watch *Seinfeld* with her and is going to teach me Portuguese.

I stumbled upon a nice place, and I paid for it for a month, but I have to leave. If I stay here, the police will come and find me. I will have to face everyone, and everything.

I desperately want to stay, but I have to go.

I am terrified. I remember thinking about applying to university or art college: I thought those were the kinds of decisions I was going to have to make. Instead my decisions are to drown myself or run to the favela. To stay here and risk being arrested for hurting someone or run away into the unknown.

I stare at the wall and try to make myself strong enough to go out and find a way to live. I try to get Bella to come back and take control of me. I concentrate every atom I have on finding my strength.

I cannot stay.

I cannot stay.

I cannot stay.

CHAPTER NINE

FOR THE SECOND morning in a row, I get up early and creep away. I walk out into the favela with no plans and less money than I would like. It is dawn and the light is pale. The door clicks shut behind me. I cannot go back to Julia's house.

The early-morning sun is tickling my face, and I am standing on the hard earth of the alley. Then I am walking away, my few possessions and remaining money in a bag over my shoulder.

The only creature I see is a chicken. She fixes me with a glare and struts away. When I get back to the tarmacked road, however, I see that there are plenty of people around. Across the road a woman in a black-and-white uniform with a name tag on is climbing onto the back of a motorbike, and then the bike speeds away down the hill, taking her to work at, judging by her clothes, a tourist hotel.

A man in a green jumpsuit walks past me so closely that I step back in surprise, but he turns and grins and waves a hand in greeting or apology. He, too, is going to work somewhere in the city, out of the favela. All the way down the hill, people are walking down to where the buses stop or getting onto the backs of motorbikes.

Then I see a police car. It is farther down the hill, driving slowly in my direction. I turn away, then duck down the first alley I see. I walk to the end of the alley, turn sharply right, and then follow it farther, turn left, wondering whether I am in someone's garden but always finding a small gap to squeeze through to the next place. No car, at least, can follow me here. All I can do is keep walking and hope I don't stroll into something terrible and get shot.

I take a step, and then another. I can only live from one step to the next.

I pass a teenage boy who looks younger than me, fixing a bike, and he stares as I go past without saying anything.

When I come to a wider road, I follow it uphill, because I know that downhill leads to buses and cars and people who might have seen me in the paper. I keep walking, knowing that I am hungry, knowing that I am going to have to make a plan, and then I come to a stretch of grass that, as I get closer, I see is a little field with goalposts at either end. It has a view of the entire city and the sea and the mountains.

I walk across the grass and stand and stare. The water is glinting and gleaming in the sunshine. The mountains are the same ones I painted at school, but they are a million times more beautiful in real life, and now I am standing on one of them. There is a cool breeze blowing on my face, and although it is early, it is warm. In spite of everything—in spite of the fact that I have exiled myself into a Brazilian shantytown and that I have no particular future in sight—I must be in the most beautiful place on the planet. I am homeless in paradise.

I cannot hear anything except the buzz of distant engines some-where behind me. The air is fresh and smells of the sea. A cluster of chickens pecks at the ground in the distance.

I am thankful it is early in the morning. I have a day to find myself a new place to stay.

And then the exhaustion catches up. I can't last until nighttime without sleep, so I end up on a beach, dozing while trying to look like a typical tourist. If I curled up on someone's doorstep and dozed, the police would find me. If I sleep on the beach, however, behind a pair of cheap sunglasses I bought from a street vendor, and with a cotton scarf wrapped around my head, I look enough like everyone else to get away with it. At least, I hope I do.

For now I'm at the end of a beach that I found by walking out of the favela and in the opposite direction from the city. This beach has enough people on it to make me feel that I can blend in a little, but it's different from the glossy beaches in the city. There aren't as many people selling things. The sand is fine and golden, and there is a lovely breeze in the air. It feels like an easy place to be. It reminds me of being on vacation, and that is strange now.

I don't have a bikini with me, but it would probably be all right to go into the water in my underwear without anyone particularly noticing. My underwear needs a wash, anyway.

My mind races, even as I lie flat on the beach, but I can't figure out where to go or what to do. I go around in circles. I could find another guesthouse and hide out for a week or so, and then go back to the Blacks and face whatever is coming to me, because I can't really hide from it forever. I could find out where people learn English, like Julia said, and try to become a teacher even though I should be at school myself. I could take the credit card back into the city and get more money out. I think I'll try that, and ask at the Super Sucos for another hotel. I should probably sleep before I do anything else, because everything is feeling weird now that I am so exhausted. I'll end up making a crazy, hallucinatory plan that makes no sense if I don't sleep.

I lie so still that I must look like yet another person soaking up the sunshine without a care in the world. Nobody can tell that I'm born from murderers and brought up by liars. They can't tell that I met the love of my life and had to walk away so he would never know what I really am. They can't tell that I cut a man across the face when I was trying to hurt my adoptive mother.

That fact is worse now that I know the truth about myself. I hurt someone, like my birth parents did. I could have killed him. Perhaps I did. I have bad blood. I was showered with every material thing, and I still grew up violent. I kill little creatures. I have tried to hurt myself on occasion, to keep myself from hurting anyone else.

I told Christian about Bella and he didn't hate me. I thought I could tell him everything until I found out the worst thing of all. I cannot tell him this. I just can't.

The thoughts make me too agitated to sleep. I gather my stuff into my arms and carry it to the water's edge. I leave it there, on the last bit of dry sand, take off my T-shirt and my shorts, put all my cash into my bag, and run into the water in my underwear. The water is murkier than it is in the big showpiece beaches, but I don't care. It's cleaner than it was on the island. I walk into the water and sink down so it covers my shoulders. I swim out, even though I'm swimming into murk. I hold my head underwater and rinse the place where my hair used to be. I spring back up and make sure my clothes are where I left them, with my bag underneath them. They are. No one is looking at me. People are probably fighting their own battles.

I swim along, parallel to the beach, and it makes me remember how tired I am, so I walk out of the water and back to pick up my things. The sand is hot under my feet.

I go back to the spot I left, farther up the sand. There are more people around now, but I don't pay them any attention because if I did, I would become paranoid about them looking at my bald head and recognizing my face from the paper. I pull my T-shirt on over my wet body as quickly as I can, and squeeze into my shorts, and I lie back and close my eyes.

When I wake up, I am lying on the powdery sand of a beach whose name I don't know, in the glare of a perfect sun, sweating and overdressed in shorts and a T-shirt. I have no hair. I am in Brazil. I am alone. It all comes back to me in a rush.

The loneliness hits me in the face for the first time because I am not running. I am just here, in a random place, on my own. The excitement of running away has gone. I don't know if I'm Ella or Bella or someone completely new. I'm limp and exhausted, and I try to list the things that are important.

1. I need a place to sleep tonight. So I need to go and ask for another guesthouse.
2. I don't want to go back to the Blacks or to Julia, and I don't want the police to find me, so I must find somewhere else to stay around here, even if it's just for a bit.
3. I'm going to be eighteen soon, so I need to make my own decisions.

I could go somewhere else in Brazil, or I could go home. If I could get through the airport without being arrested and thrown into a scary Brazilian prison, I could go home and find a job and an apartment. But I don't have any qualifications, and I know that Britain will absolutely not hand me such things. And even though there are things I miss about home, I don't really want to go back there.

I could go to the Amazon, up in the north of Brazil. I would be impossible to find up there. Someone would want to learn English, or I could just max out the Blacks' credit card and go off and see what happens. I will need to learn Portuguese and keep my head down.

I reach for my bag to check, again, how much money I have left.

I feel around the inside of the bag where I put my cash and credit card. I will be able to get a bus to the north: that feels like the best plan.

I reach in deeper to find the credit card. It is in here. I put it here. I checked and it was all there when I came out of the sea. My bag has been right next to me the entire time.

I sit up and look around. There are a few groups of people nearby. No one is looking. No one is holding up my money and card and laughing. I turn my attention back to the bag. I take everything out and pile my things on the sand, turning the bag inside out and shaking it, but the only thing in there is clothes. There is no money in there. And no credit card either.

There is definitely no money.

I have lost all my money.

All my money.

I

have

nothing.

Someone stole my money and my credit card while I was asleep.

I try to imagine a human being creeping right up to me while my eyes were closed, and picking up my bag, and taking every last real out of it, as well as a card that I had already stolen.

I run to the edge of the water and scream as loudly as I can out to sea. I scream and scream and scream. I cry. I shout. I swear. My voice is carried away on the breeze. No one cares or notices.

I cannot go on without money. This is as far as I can go. All I can do now is get to a police station, hand myself in and see what happens.

But I cannot. I cannot go to prison. I can't look Fiona Black in the eye, knowing that I tried very hard to attack her with a broken bottle. I can't look at the man I wish was my real dad, knowing that he grabbed my arm to stop me from slashing at his wife. I can't. That is a bare fact.

My head starts ringing. The beach and the trees and the water blur.

It takes me ages, walking along hot sidewalks with the ocean beside me, before I reach Leblon, another tourist beach. I get there, sweaty and smelly, hungry and thirsty, and I know that this is it. I will either flag down a police car and give myself up, or I will . . . do something else. I have no idea, at the moment, which it is going to be, but for now I have found some strength. I walk along the edge of a different favela, which goes up the hillside, and then I head down into the smart, shiny tourist part of Rio de Janeiro.

I don't look like Ella Black. I look like Bella Carr. I don't bother to worry about being recognized, because either I will be or I won't and there is nothing I can do to change that. I have no choice.

The beach is busy, and the water is crystal clear, so the first thing

I do is go for another swim. I wash my head in salt water and kick around listlessly with tired legs. This time I don't worry about anyone stealing my stuff because I haven't got anything worth stealing. For a moment this feels like freedom.

Then I stand on the sand and look around. A man catches my eye. He smiles and mimes stroking my head, but I frown and he looks away.

I begin to walk along the beach, looking at the people. Looking at their abandoned possessions.

DO IT.

I pick up the bag casually, in passing. I don't pause. The people beside it are asleep just as I was when my stuff was stolen. I am shaking all over as I keep walking, and when I reach the wide pavement, I run and I know that no one will catch me because I am Bella.

I run through crowds of people, back in the direction I came from. I wish there was a zombie parade now. I know that by running while looking like what Fiona Black would have called "a fright" and holding what is probably an expensive bag (I hardly looked), I am drawing so much attention to myself that I might as well have "thief" written on my forehead, in Portuguese. But no one stops me.

I take a deep breath and slow down. I pull the bag over my shoulder and try not to look suspicious. The last thing I want at this point is the Rio police picking me up.

I cross the main road, running between cars that honk at me and slam on brakes, and head up a side street and down another. This is tourist Rio: I would be better off in the alleys of the favela.

I stop and head over to a building and let my legs give way so I'm sitting on its marble doorstep, because I realize something that changes everything. I have lost my passport too.

It was in my bag, and now it is not in my bag.

Not only can I not get around, or get any food, but I cannot leave this country. I am trapped.

DOESN'T MATTER.

YOU WEREN'T GOING TO USE IT TODAY.

WORRY ABOUT IT LATER.

That is all I can do, really. I stand up and force my legs to walk down the road. In a tiny park, I sit on a bench and try to look casual as I open this new bag. It is a stripe-y canvas one, bright pink and bright blue, with a gold clasp. It is distinctive, and I need to lose it. I take all the things out of it and drop them straight into my old bag, stuff the new bag into a nearby trash can and walk off.

I keep walking in the direction of the favela, and when I find another bench, I sit on it and open my old bag to take a closer look at what I have stolen.

There is a wallet, but it contains only a small amount of cash. I have one credit card in the name of Jens Bierhoff, but I don't have a clue how to begin to think about getting money from that because its PIN almost certainly won't be my birthday. I have an iPhone, and a book that I think is in German. There are a few other cards in the wallet, but they will be of no use to me. If I was nice, I would just take the cash and leave everything else on the steps of a police station, but I have committed two crimes now, so I am not nice at all. I keep the wallet, put all the cards in the trash except the credit card just in case, and count the money as quickly and surreptitiously as I can.

A group of boys with skateboards on the other side of the street are staring at me. They know what I'm doing. I start to walk away. They follow, so I walk faster. One of them shouts something at me. I keep my head down, and a couple of the others call something else, and someone makes a hissing sound.

I don't think they like my skinhead look. It is impossible for me to tell what they are saying: they could be yelling at me for being a thief, or they could be inviting me to join their gang. When they start shouting at me, all together, I speed up, running back to the main road, and get on the first bus I see. I grab some coins from kind Herr Jens Bierhoff to pay my fare.

The bus takes me away. I don't care where it's going. I stay on it to the end of the line, not looking out the window, with no idea where I'm going, and then I get off in a random suburb, beside a wide road, and sit on a bench to wait for another bus to take me somewhere else.

I stare at the German's iPhone.

No one will find me here.

I STOLE FROM A STRANGER.
I STOLE.
I
AM
A
CRIMINAL.
I
AM
AMAZING.

I'm not amazing.

．　．　．

It all crashes quickly. At home Bella was separate from me, compartmentalized. Now I need her strength, but I cannot bear the badness. I crumple as I stare at the German's phone. My strength and excitement drain away.

My catalog of bad things is growing.

I want to say it was all Bella, and not me, who threatened Fiona Black and hurt the café man and stole the bag on the beach, but I can't, because Bella *is* me.

Before I know what my fingers are doing, they have tapped in Fiona Black's mobile number, with a +44 country code at the start.

I only want to hear her voice. I tried to kill her, and she knows that, and I want to hear, from her voice, whether she can forgive me.

I struggle to breathe as it starts to ring. It rings with an international tone, and then the woman I always thought was my mother actually answers.

"Hello?" she says, sounding fast and desperate. I don't say a word at first. I tried to hurt her, and I really meant it, and she knows I did, and that fact will be there forever.

I form the shapes of the words I cannot say with my mouth.

Hello.

Mum.

Seconds pass. This is the voice I heard from babyhood, the one I believed when it told me who I was. It is not, however, the first voice I ever heard. She used to say she had given birth to me, but she never did. She is not my mother.

But she is my mother. She took me in and cared for me. I hate her and I love her.

I'm hungry. I want to go home. I don't know where that is.

"Hello?" she says again. "Ella? Is that . . . Ella?"

I cannot bear to listen, and yet I cannot hang up. I take a deep gasping breath, and she hears it. A weird animal sound comes from the back of my throat.

"Ella," she says. "Ella, darling. If it's you, then don't . . ."

I press the button. I cannot hear what she was going to say. I throw the phone into a trash can and find a bus that's going to Rocinha, which seems to be the way you spell the name of the favela I slept in last night. It will be easy to get lost there because it was huge, and I need to get lost urgently. I get on it, and I stay on until it goes through the tunnel, and then I get off by the juice shop and this time I walk up the hill myself.

I haven't had anything to eat or drink in a long time, and that doesn't help anything, and I have nowhere to sleep. Still, for some reason it feels better to be here than it does to be anywhere else. I buy a bottle of water and a bar of chocolate, and I eat and drink as I walk. I see a sign for a guesthouse and knock on the door, but the man who answers it says they are fully booked.

I don't know what to do.

CHAPTER TEN

I AM DOZING and then alert.

I am asleep and then awake. I am awake because something bad is happening. I am awake and my heart is pounding because there is something around my ankle and it's someone's hand. Someone's hand is around my ankle and it's gripping me and pulling me hard toward it.

I was asleep in a corner of an alley but now a man I can't see has grabbed me by the ankle. My back scrapes along the ground as he pulls me toward him. Bella is yelling "FIGHT!" at me, and I scream and scream and scream, but he puts his hand over my mouth. I struggle and try to bite him, but it doesn't work because I can't get my teeth around his hand. I kick and kick and flail around with my arms. I wish I had that broken bottle in my hand right now.

I can't scream, but someone else is yelling. Another voice says, "Get off her, you bastard! Get off her now!"

Then the man is gone. I hear his feet running off down the alley. He was chased away because a woman shouted at him in English, but that cannot have happened because there could not possibly have been another Englishwoman out and in this alley at night. I haven't seen anyone else foreign here, let alone another woman, let alone an

English one, and particularly not in a place like this, in the middle of the night. I must, somehow, have shouted at him myself even though his hand was over my mouth.

I don't really know what happened, but the man has gone and there is no one else around. It is still night, but I know I can't go back to sleep, and I can't sleep on the streets anymore either, and that means I am finished.

I sit in the same place, the sheet of plastic I was using as bed-clothes wrapped around my shoulders like a blanket, and wait, jumping at every sound, for it to be morning. I am so so so fucking bored, and scared. I have broken myself and I'm hungry and I need water but all I have is my little bag with sunscreen and a headscarf and a few clothes in it. I threw away everything I stole, bceause it felt too incriminating.

I get through to daylight by sitting in one place and making lists in my head and telling them to Lily. I send them to her in my head and hope that she finds them popping into her brain and knows where they came from. That is all I can do because I can't tell her who I am or the things I have done.

Here are the top three worst things about sleeping in the street, Lily:

1. Danger. It's dangerous: specifically with regard to rape and murder. So that makes it difficult to sleep.
2. Sleep. It's truly impossible to sleep because it's not comfortable. Imagine how hard it is getting to sleep when you're camping, like when we did our Duke of Edinburgh award. Then at least you have a bit of a soft mat. Now I would give anything for a soft mat.

3. Food. You're so hungry all the time. And thirsty. And
    a bottle of water a day may be what you've decided
    you can afford, but it's not actually enough. Food
    and water become impossible luxuries when you're
    homeless: you can't decide you're a bit hungry and go
    and get a piece of toast or a cookie. All the girls in my
    class used to withhold food from themselves to make
    sure they were thin. That feels like a joke now. When
    you're hungry, it's the only thing you can think about.

Then I make another list.
The top three people I miss so much it hurts:

1. Christian. I wish you could meet him, Lily. I fell in love
    at first sight, and I love everything about him.
2. You. Lily. My best friend. I asked you to be my best
    friend forever, and I wish you were here now because
    you would know what we should do. You would help
    me out of this. If I had to go to prison, you would
    come to visit me.
3. Jack. I never told even you the truth about my
    relationship with Jack. I miss him. I miss our secrets.
    I hope he's happy. I wish him all the light and joy in
    the world.

I watch the sky becoming lighter, and as soon as it's daylight, I get
up and fold my square of plastic and walk down to the beach so I can try
to sleep there. The beach is out of action during the night: I know because

I stood in the shadows and looked at it, and there were groups of men, and I don't know what was going on but I knew it was no place for me.

In the light of day I can see that I am filthy. I must smell terrible. I have no idea how Bella and I fended off that man, but we did: I guess you do strange things when your life is at stake.

When I make it to the beach, I walk down to the end that has the cleaner water and leave my bag on the sand, and take off my shorts and top and walk into the sea. I lie on my back and let the dirt wash away. My skin is terrible: it's gone all dry down my legs. I won't sleep outside again. I found the best spot I could, in the shadows away from the road, and still it was no good.

Today I need to steal another bag and hope that this one will have enough money in it for me to sleep in a bed for a few nights and to eat something that will fill me up. I wish I could go back in time. If I had my passport, I could try to leave the country, but as it is I'm stuck.

I get out of the water and pull my clothes onto my wet body and lie on the beach. A man comes over to me. I make a point of not looking but I sense him there, tall and muscular. I feel his gaze.

"*Hola,*" he says. I look up, and he runs his hand over his head and smiles. I thought not having hair would stop me from being interesting to men, but it doesn't seem to work that way. They seem, like this man, to want to touch it. I thought that my skinny body, with its skin that has gone all flaky because of the salt water and dirt and sun, would put men off too, but it doesn't.

I shake my head. I want to shout and scream at him to go away, but I don't want him to know that I'm foreign because that would feel more vulnerable and he might have seen me in the news, so I keep my mouth closed. He shrugs and goes away.

I feel the hand around my ankle again and again. The fingers that gripped me are still there. Someone saw my body and wanted to take it.

I put on my sunscreen and lie back down because I can't do anything until I have slept.

When I wake up, I have no idea how much time has passed. I sit up and stare out at the paradise sea, the gorgeousness of Brazil, and I know that I have to decide, now, whether to give myself up.

There is something next to me that wasn't there before. It is a paper bag, with words written on it. I hold it up to look at the writing.

It says, *Something to help you, Jo. From a friend.*

It is written in English, but I don't think it is written by someone who speaks English fluently, because the letters are too carefully formed. This, though, is from someone who knows I am English.

They think I'm someone else. They think I am Jo, but I'm not. This is meant for her, whoever she is, and they've given it to me. I open the package and find cheese balls, like the ones at the hotel a million years ago, and a little bottle of water and some money. It is enough money to buy a coffee and more food. I drink the water quickly in one gulp and pause, breathing deeply, hoping that it's not going to make me sick.

When my stomach has settled, I take a bite from a cheese ball. It has ham in it and that is one thing I was not expecting, and I have to run into the sea, my legs wobbling, so that I can be sick without anyone seeing. My stomach heaves and empties itself into the water with a surprising amount of vomit, considering how little I have eaten, and it starts to disperse as a shoal of little fish appears and eats it.

I force myself under control and walk back across the beach. All the water I drank is gone, and I am dehydrated again. I know, now, that this food has ham in it, and I eat the balls, one by one, slowly. They fill me up, and I have some strength, and I feel better.

A stranger left food beside me. That is actually scary. Someone has seen me and helped me, and although they have quite possibly saved my life, I wish I knew who they were, and why, and who they think I am and who Jo is. I imagine there being a second homeless girl, a Jo. I would not be alone.

I will go and buy more water because I am so thirsty I can hardly think. I will drag myself back to Rocinha and get water and coffee. I get up and start walking, imaginary Jo at my side, keeping me going.

I get there in the end, hot and with my head pounding and my legs screaming. I stop at the first café I see and force a smile while I ask for a bottle of water and a white coffee, hoping that milk will give me extra sustenance. I drink the water as slowly as I can. I order two cheese balls, which feels like a luxury when I have already had eight ham ones. I don't think about the spoiled girl who piled up food on her hotel breakfast plate without being hungry. I do, though, remember Ana-Paula on Paqueta island, handing me a plate of rice-and-bean stew. Perhaps one day I could try to go back there. I could live with her and help her with the baby. Even Bella would be nice to that baby, because Ana-Paula was so kind to us.

Baby. That thought cracks me open, and I push it away.

I go to the counter to pay when I feel I can loiter no longer. There is a woman at another table, a large middle-aged woman, and she is looking at me with far too much interest on her face. I keep my head down and turn my back. I know I look weird. I look homeless, and pale and bald. Of course everyone stares. There is another woman at her table with long tangled hair, and she stares too, for a while.

"Do you speak English?" I say to the woman at the counter.

"Speak English?" She nods, and shouts behind her. I am expecting her to produce another adult, but instead a tiny little girl emerges. The girl has shiny chocolate button eyes, and she looks away from me, shy.

I realize that the woman is pointing to the girl's T-shirt, which is white and clean and uncreased. It says on it "FAVELA ENGLISH SCHOOL," in red capitals, in a circular logo.

"Favela English School," I say aloud. I try to get the girl to look at me.

"Do *you* speak English?" I ask her, though I know she can't because she's only about three, or maybe five. I don't really know much about children.

Favela English School.

"Twinkle, twinkle, little star," she sings, and I laugh and join in, and she looks me in the eye and laughs too.

"What is your name?" I say. I crouch down so that I'm talking right into her face. This is the closest I have been to anyone for days, apart from the man who grabbed my ankle. I hope I'm not close enough for her to smell me, because I can't remember the last time I brushed my teeth, and I know my breath must be disgusting.

"My name is Ana," she says clearly, and everything about her is perfect and gorgeous. I want to cry. I was a perfect little girl once too. I thought I was. I didn't know I was damaged and secondhand, even then.

I point to myself.

"My name is . . ." I pause. Not Ella. Not Lily. I need a name that could be Latin American so I don't stand out. I have no idea what to call myself, and when I realize that the silence has gone on too long, even for a tiny child, I say the first thing that comes into my head. "Paula." I pronounce it "Powla," the way Ana-Paula did on the island. The girl nods. She is called Ana and I am called Paula.

"Hello, Paula," she says. "I am pleased to meet you."

"And I am pleased to meet you too."

She reaches out and strokes my head, and I let her do it. I am having a conversation, in English, with a toddler. I have food and coffee inside me, and everything feels a tiny bit better.

People who say that money isn't everything have never tried to live without it. Money is literally everything. I used to give money to homeless people sometimes. I would fish out fifty pence and feel awkward and bad. Fiona Black donated food and money to food banks and said that was better than giving someone money when they might be tempted to spend it on alcohol or drugs.

Of course they might want alcohol or drugs. I would love to have something that blotted out reality, even just for a few minutes. If I ever manage to go back to my old world, I will give money to every homeless person I see. I will give them food. I will give them hot drinks filled with sugar, and I will give them alcohol too.

"Where is your English class?" I ask the girl, and her perfect forehead wrinkles, because she doesn't understand.

"English school?" I shrug. I look around, pantomiming a search for something. I point up the hill. I point at the house opposite, raising my eyebrows. I have to make this work.

She giggles and points up the hill. In the squeaky voice of someone who hasn't known how to talk for very long, she explains at great length, in Portuguese, how to get to her English class, showing right and left turns with her hands, talking me through it all in words I don't understand.

I look to her mother, and soon I have a map, drawn with a stubby pencil on a thin napkin.

I want to hug little Ana, but I don't know if that's allowed, so I pat her head instead, as she did to me. I pay for my coffee and cheese balls, and I get a tiny amount of change, which I put carefully into my pocket. I thank them and wave and thank them again and wave again, ignore the large woman who is still watching, and do my best to follow the map to the place that teaches English to tiny children. My language feels like the only skill I have.

"Hello?"

My voice sounds strange. I have not used it much lately, and I'm not used to the way it sounds when I call out. I sound like Fiona Black trying to see if there's a shop assistant in the back room. In fact, I am no one and entitled to nothing.

I am standing at the end of an alley, on ground that is made of compacted earth, and I have no idea whether this is the right place. There is a strong smell of cooking that seems to be coming from a doorway farther back. I cannot walk any farther because the building in front of me is the last one in the alley. There is just a door, which is closed, and I knock on it and call out again.

Nothing happens.

I think I followed the map. It took me ages to get here: I have tried different turnings, interpreted the woman's scribbled pictures and clues about what would be on the corner by the turn I should take, jumped out of the paths of motorbikes, and tried, at all times, to look as if I had some idea of what I was doing. Also, I am not very good at walking today.

I can't get here, find it all closed, and give up.

"*Hola*?" I shout, wondering why I didn't do that in the first place. I am in a corner of Rio. Here, we say *Hola*. Or we say "Oi."

I am in the shade, and it is just cool enough. My clothes are stiff with salt, and I know they have white tide marks on them.

"Hello?" Someone is looking down from an upstairs window. I step back. It is a girl of about my age, as far as I can tell. Her black hair is hanging down, and she looks friendly. She is Asian, and she looks like the girls from my class, with creamy skin and a healthy glow. I know I don't look like that anymore.

"Hi there," I say. I take a deep breath. I have to do this properly. I have to be Ella Black, with Bella's confidence. "Hi—I was just wondering. Do you give English lessons here?"

"Sure. Hang on. I'll come down."

As I wait, I try to line up the words I need. This girl cannot be in charge because she is too young. I need to get her to take me to the person who makes decisions, and then I need to beg them to give me a job as an English teacher. I cannot give my real name or a passport or spend any money at all. I'll also need a place to sleep.

It does not seem likely, and yet I have to make it happen.

I hear a key turn, a bolt being pulled back, and then the girl is standing in front of me. There is a long pause. I see myself through her eyes, and then I try hard not to.

I know that if I manage to make anything happen today, it will be thanks to the person who left food and water and money for Jo.

"Hi," I say. "I'm Jo. I'm wondering if you need an English teacher here at all."

"Oh, hi," she says. "Normally people come out as part of the program. Ben said someone just dropped out, but I don't think . . ."

She doesn't look at me with disgust, and I love her for that. She is talking to me like an equal even though I am a massive horrible mess.

"I'd be happy to do anything," I say, knowing that I sound desperate.

"Great. OK. Well." I see her hesitate. I watch her internal struggle as she tries to decide whether she is allowed to invite me into the building.

I'm not sure where her accent is from, but it's not the Southeast of England. I think she might be Irish, but accents are not my strong point.

"I'm Jasmine," she says. "You'll need to speak to Ben or Maria. I'll see if I can get one of them on the phone. We've no children in until later this morning. Would you . . . ?" She looks at me. "Can I get you a coffee or something?"

The sympathy in her eyes is going to make me fall apart. I have to keep it together. "I would absolutely love a coffee and a glass of water if you've got one." I speak fast, desperately trying to be the person I need to be. "Sorry. I'm sorry if I'm being weird."

"Hey, no problem. Sure. Have a seat and I'll get your drink. Your drinks."

The room is a schoolroom, with murals of Rio all over the walls. The skies are pink, the sea is yellow, and everything is painted in chunks of brightness. I look at the painted Christ the Redeemer statue, wearing a happy smile daubed onto his pale blue face, clearly by a child.

"Thank you," I tell Christ the Redeemer. When I visited him, I had no idea what was about to happen. He probably knew. I could use some redemption right now.

There are laminated posters of colors and numbers, with the words in English. There are finger paintings pegged to a clothesline going across the ceiling. The seats are child-sized plastic chairs with a little desk clipped across the front of each, and I squeeze my body into one. Although my knees are up by my shoulders and I am not remotely comfortable, I decide I will rest my head on my arms just for a moment.

"Hello? Excuse me?"

I hear the words, but I can't move. I don't quite know where I am. After a moment it all comes back. I am Ella Black. We came to Rio. My parents lied about everything. My money was stolen. I stole someone else's money. I'm in the favela. Bella is part of me. I'm homeless. I came to the place that teaches English. I have to make a good impression.

"I'm so sorry." It is a man's voice, and he does not sound sorry at all; even in my befuddled state I can tell that he is deeply pissed off. I am squeezed into a tiny chair. My back, my arms, my neck all scream in protest as I stretch, and I don't dare to try to stand because I would definitely fall over.

The man is smiling, but there is steel behind the smile. He is a black man, dressed casually in blue shorts and a Favela English School T-shirt, and his hair is long and his face is open, but his manner is formal, and I think he is angry. I need to make him like me. I need to charm him even though I am not charming at all and he does not look like someone who wants to be charmed. I have to do what I used to do: I need to pretend to be normal, and hope that that will be enough.

He passes me a glass of water, and I drink it in one go.

"Hi. I'm so sorry." I echo his phrase at him and shake my head to try to make some of my own words come. I beg Bella to lend me her bravery while withholding her nastiness, even though I'm not sure where I end and she begins anymore. I reach across to Bella's side of my brain and take some courage. "I'm so sorry," I say again. "I didn't mean to fall asleep." He might have seen me in the paper. I know I used a different name, but I can't remember what it was right now. "I was really tired."

"I can see that. So, you're looking for work? I'm Ben. I'm sorry, but we don't have anything, and we don't work like that. Jasmine should have said that at the start."

I'm pretty sure he is Brazilian. His English is American accented and fluent.

Jasmine should not have let me in. He doesn't need to say that outright, because everything about him is saying it wordlessly. He wants to shove me out and close the door behind me.

I can't let that happen.

"I could help out. I can teach English, but I can do anything else too. I'll do anything. I met one of your little children today. Ana."

Ben has dreadlocks, and dark eyes that are noting everything about me. I can see every detail being transformed into data and filed away. He is like the teacher we had in year ten, Mr. Richards. He saw me holding a compass point against my arm once, to try to appease Bella, and I saw it in his eyes every time he looked at me. I hated that. I wanted to tell him that I would never have done anything with it.

"Forgive me," says Ben, "but you are clearly down on your luck, and you've plainly been extremely ill. You look, in fact, like someone who should be in the hospital. Our volunteers pay to be here. They pay up front before they arrive—that's how we keep running—and everything is arranged before they leave home. It's highly unusual for anyone to locate us like this. We run a program that's staffed by gap-year volunteers, mainly from Europe, the US, Canada and Australia, not by casual workers who drop in, and also not by ESL teachers. And if I may say so, you do not look like someone who's recovered enough to hold down a job."

I take a deep breath and try to sound believable. I summon Bella, and she comes. My dark side steps in and actually helps.

"I'm not ill," she says. He thinks I've had cancer. I look so awful that this man is assuming I'm terminally ill. "What happened, right, is this: I was traveling, and it went wrong. I was robbed, so I've got almost nothing right now, as you can tell, but I will soon have access to money from home. It's a long story how I've ended up here, but I haven't done anything remotely illegal. I've been sleeping outside while I wait for the money, and I need to stop that. I promise you I'm not ill, and I don't want any charity or anything like that. I haven't got any money to pay you today, but I can get some, and that is a promise. I've taught English before, and I know a lot about art and books."

"Have you? Where have you taught?"

Bella plucks a word at random. "Venezuela."

It was written on a man's cap on the train up the mountain. The picture of Christ the Redeemer in this room has taken me back there. Luckily Ben doesn't follow up on Bella's bold claim, since I wouldn't even be able to tell him the name of Venezuela's capital city.

He is sizing me up.

"The thing is, Jo," he says, "I really can't take you on as a volunteer. It's our volunteers that fund what we do, for one thing. I know everyone has an opinion about gap-year children coming into poor places to do good work, but we've made it function properly here. We're not an orphanage—you met Ana, so you know that they're kids with families. We teach English to the local children because it improves their life chances. We have a relatively high turnover of teachers, but my partner, Maria, and I make sure there's enough consistency for the kids. It's a carefully run business, and I cannot act as a charity for Westerners who need somewhere to escape. Sorry. It sounds harsh, but you do have options. You can go to your embassy, and they'll get you home."

I can't go to my embassy because I cut a man across the face.

"Can I do anything at all?" I say. "Sweep the floors. Cook. Clean the toilets?"

"You can go home and let us concentrate our efforts on the kids. With respect, Jo, we don't owe you anything. And you know you can get home, if you go to the British consulate. They will take care of you. That's what they're there for."

"Someone just dropped out, though." Why not tell him what I know? I have nothing to lose. "Jasmine said so."

"Did she?" He does not look amused. "Well, people often get scared and pull out. It doesn't mean anything."

"Give me a chance. A temporary one. Please. Give me a day."

Something in him changes, as if his refusals have been a test.

"You're persistent." He sighs and rolls his eyes. "Jesus. Look, for God's sake take a shower. Then we'll see, but it would be a couple of days' boring work at most and then you'd be done. You would of course be welcome to apply for the program while you're sitting right here, if you can pay the money, but you should know that it's a lot, and every penny of it goes to our day-to-day operating costs."

I nod to show him I understand.

"But if you can shower and clean up a bit, I might be able to let you fill in a very short gap. If you can teach like you say you can, you'll need to work with Jasmine this morning so I can have a look at you."

I smile at him with every atom of my being. It's a tiny lifeline, but it feels enormous. I am dizzy. He's going to let me do something. I have to do this amazingly.

Pretend to be amazing and then you will be amazing.

He calls Jasmine, and I follow her through a door and up a dark staircase to a corridor with a concrete floor. She doesn't speak because she doesn't know what to say, but she emanates sympathy and niceness. When she pushes a door on our left, it swings open to reveal a tiny, concrete-floored bathroom with a shower and a basin and a toilet.

"Here you go. This is our stately bathroom. Just a sec." She leaves, reappearing almost instantly with a threadbare towel. "Would you, y'know, like some clothes? We've a few that Kate left behind. She just left a few days ago. Off to Argentina. I'd say they'd fit you. They might be a bit baggy."

I look at Jasmine's wide eyes and lovely face. I wish I could ask her for food, but I don't want to push my luck.

"Thanks. What are you doing this morning?"

"Cleaning. Doing the admin. There's a class in at eleven, but that's it. They're the older children, the eleven-year-olds."

When I have the clothes as well as the towel, I lock the door and turn on the shower. Running warm water is an impossible luxury, and I stare in wonder at the fact that people harnessed an element, made it run through pipes and invented showerheads. I think I am delirious. I rinse the salt off my body and scrub my fuzzy scalp with shampoo.

I cannot mess this up. I want to lie on the floor and cry as the water pounds me, but I need to help Jasmine teach some eleven-year-olds English instead. It will take far more strength than I have to get through this, but I have to do it somehow.

I scrub my body with soap. I dimly remember that there used to be different moisturizers for face and for body, and makeup and perfume and all kinds of expensive things, but I know for certain that I have never had a better shower than this one, and I hope I never will. I hope I never will because a shower that is better than this could only come after something worse than my past few days, and I cannot let myself picture a thing in my future like that.

The clothes Jasmine gave me are a pair of shorts that are PE style, almost to the knee, and a T-shirt with "FAVELA ENGLISH SCHOOL" written on it—a big version of the one that tiny Ana wore, a smaller version of Ben's. She has even given me underwear. I don't hesitate to put on another woman's underwear, and they fit well enough. Everything is clean. It smells of basic detergent, and that is the best perfume in the world.

I brush my teeth with toothpaste on a finger and allow myself only the quickest glance in the tarnished mirror. I really do look ill. My skin is darker, and blotchy. I look weird and ugly without hair. I see myself only in the eyes.

I try to remember French lessons at school. How do you teach a language to a class of children when they're too old for nursery rhymes? I have no idea. I will do whatever Jasmine does and try to be confident.

I push everything else aside. This is the only thing that matters. My whole life is resting on getting this right: if I can do this and get a couple of days' work, then I could get the money somehow and end up living here like Jasmine and the invisible other volunteers. That would give me a chance.

"What stage are they at?" I am sipping the second coffee that Jasmine has made me, because I fell asleep before the first one arrived. It is instant, the kind of thing they would scoff at in my class's student lounge, and it is the best drink ever. Everything about this place is the best thing ever. Even being able to say "What stage are they at?" like a grown-up teacher makes me feel warm inside. I feel that I am hanging off a cliff, clinging on with my fingernails. Jasmine has no idea that she's reaching down, hauling me up.

"Oh, it's a tricky age," she says. "It's much easier with the little ones. This is actually art class, so just do an art class in English. Can you do art? It doesn't matter if you can't. I certainly can't."

"I'm . . ." I stop myself. In my old life, the rest of that sentence would have gone, *I'm doing it for A level.* Instead I say, "I love art. I might not be great at it. But I like it."

"Oh, I couldn't do it well at school either. I'm useless. I just let the kids do it. Some of them are good. So. You'll be fine, actually. I was terrified the first time I did this." She looks around, clearly checking that no one in authority is nearby. "I messed it up completely, but it was different because I was already in the program. And don't worry, Ben likes to check out everyone when they get here. He's very particular. But I'll be with you, Jo."

I grin at her. "Oh my God, Jasmine. I love you. So what do we do?"

She has blushed pink. "Oh, we just start off by talking and then let them get paper and pencils. Today they're sketching whatever they like. They're cool. If you get stuck, just ask them about *futebol*."

Twenty minutes later I am running on adrenaline. I'm leaning over a skinny boy's bony shoulder, admiring his picture, which shows a soccer player in action, his leg pulled back to kick the ball, an open goal in front of him, a rudimentary goalkeeper diving in what is clearly going to be the wrong direction.

"Gooooooooaaaaall!" I say. He replies in Portuguese, so I tap his shoulder and say, "In English."

He gestures to the blank space around the edges of his sheet of paper. "The peoples."

I take his pencil and look at the sheet. It would be wrong to do his picture for him, but I can do what Miss Cook, who taught me art in a different lifetime, would have done. I am sure that would be all right. I do my best to fill in some spectators for him. I draw the structure of some seating, roughly put in the top row of a sea of faces, and hand the pencil back to the boy to continue.

I like this. I can actually help someone. I can help him with his picture, and I can help him with his English. Everything I have is focused on him right now. Not being focused on myself makes the whole world feel lighter.

I look around again. I can't even see Ben.

The boy grins broadly. He has a white birthmark down the side of his face, and it changes shape when he smiles.

"Thank you, Teacher Jo," he says. His smile vanishes as he turns his attention back to his work, frowning, using my sketch as the basis and filling in every face, every expression. His spectators are happy, shocked, sad, bored. They become real people: rudimentary ones, but real.

I leave him to it and wander around the room. Dark heads are bent over work, and I look at a cluster of houses all crammed in beside one another, an empty beach, a family holding hands. I stop beside each child in turn and show them how to use perspective to make a house look more realistic, how to sketch out a face, what to do to fill the rest of a blank page. I do something different for each child. I concentrate completely on each of them in turn.

"Talk in English," says Jasmine. She is walking around helping people too.

A girl raises her hand, and I go over and look at her picture, which shows a girl sitting on a doorstep with her chin in her hands, looking grumpy.

"She's not happy," I say. "Is she you?"

The girl nods. "Yes," she says, and she giggles, looking at my head. I help her out with the rest of the picture, showing her, with rough lines, where she can put other houses, the rest of the street, any other people. I put in the perspective lines, lightly. She nods and starts drawing in a shop next door.

If I were properly in charge here, I would teach them how to actually draw. Today they are doing what they like, and no one is ever going to critique these pictures properly because, I imagine, the point is that they are sitting in a room working hard, speaking in English, and concentrating on a task. Personally, I think they might as well learn to draw while they're at it.

I would get them to draw an object that was in front of them, get them to draw each other. I would show them a Frida Kahlo self-portrait and encourage them to do something like it. I would show them how to shade and, if I could, give them the right sorts of pencils. I would teach perspective and vanishing points. We would do silhouettes and clay pots and Jackson Pollocks. I would get brightly colored paints and show them abstract art. I would take them up the hill to paint the view. I would do everything I could to inspire them, to get them to express themselves, to let them lose themselves in art. Art makes life exciting.

For now, however, I walk around the room helping them out one by one. I show a girl how she can draw a face that won't look so childish, because she is in tears of frustration, and she nods and gets to work.

I would quite like Mrs. Browning to see me now.

They are only here for an hour, and when Jasmine claps her hands to bring the class to an end, I want to cancel the rules, to make them stay all day, to keep going with it. Although Ben had said he would be watching, I didn't see or hear him at all. Now, however, he steps out of a corner at the back of the room. As Jasmine engages everyone in conversation about their pictures, he steps forward. The children chant, "Good-bye, Teacher Jasmine. Good-bye, Teacher Jo," and the moment they start to leave the room, chatting in Portuguese and showing each other their pictures, he is at my side.

"That was interesting," he says, and I cannot interpret his tone. "You're an artist?"

"Not a professional one." I feel stupid immediately. He didn't suggest I was a professional artist. Of course I am not. But I am filled with excitement now. I loved that class. I am longing to do it again.

"Even so, a capable one. How would you teach art class, if it were up to you?"

"I know they're here for English, but I would teach them art too.

I'd rearrange the desks into a semicircle and get the group working on the same things, and show them techniques. If you could get other types of pencils, I'd get them using softer ones. If there was paint, we'd be able to do all kinds of things. If there was clay, we could do sculpture and pots."

I keep talking, surprised at the words that are coming out, surprised at Bella for making me strong in this moment without making me mean. I am also aware that while I'm speaking, he is unlikely to interrupt me to tell me to go away. In the end, however, I have to stop because it is not an infinite topic.

"Thanks, Jo," he says. "Look, I'll need to think about this and talk it over with Maria. You can stay and help clean the place up if you like, but that's it; we have to safeguard the kids, and I can't let you stay until I've talked it over."

"OK. And seriously, I'll do anything. I'll clean your floors. I'll cook. I'll do . . . anything. Just anything. Absolutely anything at all."

The hand on my ankle, pulling my body.

I need a door.

I need a roof.

"I need to think about it, like I said." Ben is unmoved. "Come back tomorrow. Midday?"

I do my best not to panic as I help the volunteers clean up.

CHAPTER ELEVEN

I WAKE UP to someone shaking my shoulder. My hand is in a fist, ready to fight and scream and hurt and run.

Jasmine steps back. I stare into her face and remember.

"Sorry," I say. "Sorry, Jasmine. I didn't mean to . . ."

"Oh, you're OK," she says quickly. "I thought it was you. Jo. Look, you can't be sleeping out here. You've been here all night? Come inside, for goodness' sake. You should have said. I'd have let you in."

I stretch out my legs and stand with difficulty. Jasmine helps me up, and I grasp her hand tightly. I like the feeling of her hand in mine.

The sky is light, and drizzle is falling. It is early. I can hear engines on the main street. People are heading off to work. I stretch as many muscles as I can, reaching up for the sky. My back is not happy. Neither are my arms. I wonder whether Jasmine would let me lie on her bed for a while.

"Ben told me to come back at midday," I say. "He wouldn't want you bringing me inside now."

"Well, he's not here, so he won't know, will he? Come on."

I wonder whether Jasmine knows that I chose that spot to sleep in because I knew she could be summoned with a scream. I wonder if she knows that she is my only friend in the Southern Hemisphere.

It's six fifteen. Jasmine makes me coffee and gives me a glass of water, and I am spectacularly grateful. We sit in a little kitchen that I didn't see before, and she hands me two bananas and a piece of bread and jam. I do my best to eat them slowly.

"You're up early," I say.

She smiles. "I always am. What can I say? I just like the early morning. But Jo—you've been sleeping on the streets?"

"Oh, Jasmine. It's so awful. I can't begin to tell you." I stop. I can't break down.

"What is it that . . . ?" Her voice tails off. Jasmine is a nice girl, and I can see that she doesn't quite want to ask me for my story in case I don't want to tell it. I am grateful for that. All the same, I don't want her trying to look me up online, so I had better say something.

"I was traveling," I say, trying to tell it in a way that will be compatible with the version I told Ben. "And it went wrong. I did some teaching in Venezuela before this. I know I look like I'm ill, but I'm not. I shaved my head because I dyed my hair and it looked awful. Then my stuff got stolen, and my relationship fell apart." That is true too. My relationship with my adoptive parents has definitely fallen apart. My relationship with Christian burned brightly, and then I ran away. "I can't go home, because things aren't good for me there. It would be worse. So I've been here for a while, and all I need is to get back on my feet by doing . . . the kind of thing you're doing."

I cannot tell her the truth. I will carry that secret with me forever.

"You're so strong."

239

I don't feel strong right now; however, now that I'm telling another human that I've been sleeping on the streets, I can see that it makes me sound tough.

"I'm not," I say. "Or if I am, it's because I've had to be."

"Jo, you were an amazing teacher yesterday. I was like totally in awe of you. You're so good at talking to the kids. I feel a bit shy when it's not the little tiny ones. You really were far better than any of the rest of us are. Ben kind of despairs about how we're a bit crappy, but he says he just has to train us on the job because he knows he's taking us straight out of school and we're paying him instead of him paying us and that's just how it works. Professional teachers won't pay to work, and the people we teach can't pay for lessons, and since we're all native English speakers, we just learn to make it work. You should have seen him watching you. He thought you were incredible. That's why he's changing his mind."

I smile at her. "That is the nicest thing anyone's ever said to me." I replay what she just said, in my mind. *You're so good at talking to the kids. He thought you were incredible.* I've never done anything like this before, and I did it and it worked.

After I finish my coffee, I use the shower again, and by the time the other volunteers get up for breakfast, I am in Jasmine's bed, hiding there until midday. Her room is basic, with a metal-framed bed, a shelf for clothes, and a little table with a pile of books on it.

I gaze at them. Books are a luxury, another world for when you need to lose yourself. If I had a supply of books, living on the streets would not be quite so bad. I would be able to shut reality out much more effectively.

I pick up one of Jasmine's books. It is a children's book, *A Little*

Princess, and it has clearly been read many times. I remember it from when I was little. I pick it up and start to read.

At midday, I am still woozy with the combination of sleep and tiredness, but I am standing in front of Ben, wearing my own clothes that I've washed in nonsalt water and dried on the windowsill in the newly strong sun. The doors and windows are open, and the school-room smells of hot earth after rain.

"You came back," he says.

"Yeah. I did."

"Have a seat, Jo."

I follow him, and we both sit on top of little tables in a smaller classroom. His face gives nothing away. I have no plan B.

"I've been talking to Maria," he says. "She wanted to come and meet you, but she's teaching all day over in Vidigal, so she can't. Look, Jo. This is unorthodox, and you must understand why we're hesitant."

I close my eyes. He's going to tell me to go away. I know he is.

"However, you did a good job yesterday, and we'd like you to try teaching some art with us, just temporarily, one day at a time. You can also help with the other classes." He takes a few pieces of paper out of his bag and pushes them toward me. "I'll need you to fill all this in, passport number and references and so on, and then we need to talk about money."

I want to hug him. I want to kiss him. I manage not to.

"Of course," I say, trying to be mature, trying not to allow my feelings into my voice. I feel emotions escaping as tears fill my eyes, and I blink them away though I know he sees.

"We can't pay you—as you know, you need to pay us. However, we can feed you with the rest of the volunteers. You clearly need shelter, and although we don't have a bedroom, I've just spoken to Jasmine and she's happy to share with you, so we'll get you a mattress on her floor. I'm sensing that would be acceptable to you?"

"That would be amazing. I mean it. The most . . ."

I have to stop talking, because I am choked up. I screw my eyes shut for a moment and try to take deep breaths. I must not fall apart now that I have a lifeline. I must not. I could ruin it all. I take the pieces of paper. I will fill them in with lies and hope for the best.

A roof over my head. A place to sleep. Food. I am swaying, and there is a ringing sound in my ears, but it's not Bella. I think I have used Bella's bravery over the past few days, because I'm not sure Ella Black would have been able to do any of this. The ringing in my ears is just exhaustion and relief.

"Take a moment." I feel Ben's hand on my shoulder and keep my eyes closed as he holds me steady. I do not speak for a long time. I cannot.

"I'll do anything," I say when I pull myself together. "I'll do everything. I'm a terrible cook, but I'll learn. I'll clean. I'm just so grateful. I'll be the best teacher you've ever had."

He nods and stands up. "I hope so."

I fill the paperwork in carefully, calling myself Josephine Marsh and inventing a passport number, and help with every class for the rest of the day. I make drinks for everyone. I want to cook, but they won't let me because some volunteers called Scott and Clara are cooking today, and I can see I am annoying them by asking for something to do.

In the end I go for a walk because I don't want them to get sick of me before I've officially arrived. I expect, too, that they need space to talk about me, because there are ten other volunteers living there, and nine of them only just met me. I walk to the main street, the Estrada de Gávea, and spend an hour pounding around the pathways. It feels different now that I have a purpose, a home, a job.

I end up in the juice bar at the bottom of the hill, the first place I ever visited in Rocinha. I want to go back to the me who stepped out of that taxi, with her cash concealed all around her body, and tell her to do it differently. I want to send her straight to the English school, to hand her cash directly to Ben and to apply to join the program properly.

I have enough money for a juice, so I order the first one I had here before, the pink one with strawberries and watermelon. I sit at a table and prepare to make it last.

While I drink, I watch people coming and going. There is a man selling goat carcasses, hung up around a doorway. Another is the same street barber who shaved off my hair: he sees me looking and raises a hand in greeting. I can see someone welding, someone selling brightly colored clothes. Buses pull in, and people get on and off them. Power lines cluster overhead. Taxis pull up. Motorbikes buzz around. A family at the next table is having an argument, but they don't seem to be that angry. I like sitting and observing. I like sipping my juice through its straw and knowing that it is full of vitamins, that it will sustain me.

I like knowing that I have a place to sleep tonight, that I have work to do, that I will be part of a community. The relief is so overwhelming that I have to make a conscious effort, all the time, not to collapse.

I watch a taxi pulling up. A man gets out. He is wearing a suit even though he must be hot, and he is half bald, with black hair combed over. He pays the driver through his window and strides off up the hill, clearly with a place to be.

A police car goes slowly by. I look down at the table. They might still be looking for me, and I still don't want to be seen. I don't think I look like my old self at all: I have lost weight, and I feel utterly different with my bare head. All the same, I am the person they've been looking for.

The next taxi to pull in disgorges a pale woman with long hair. She is wearing a lime-green dress and sandals. I watch her pay her driver and set off up the hill, swinging a small backpack. I've seen her before. A little way up she meets another woman, the large one who is definitely local, whom I saw the last time I was at the juice bar, and they walk together, deep in conversation.

The next taxi brings three men in their twenties, who pile out laughing and who come in here and sit at a nearby table, pushing one another and talking loudly. I shrink away: the last thing I want now is attention from anyone at all.

I finish the juice quickly and walk back toward the English school. *Home.*

It feels odd to call it that, but it is my home more than anywhere else at the moment.

Home is a strange concept. I wonder if I actually need one.

CHAPTER TWELVE

I WAKE UP early (I cannot imagine sleeping in ever again) and make my bed quietly so I don't disturb Jasmine, who is fast asleep with her hair fanned all over the pillow. My bed is a mattress on the floor, and it's the best thing ever. I've been here five days now, and although Jasmine does get up early and do stretches and journals with a coffee at her side, I tend to get up earlier still.

I was reading *To Kill a Mockingbird* before I went to sleep. Ben is right that the book collection here is random, but there are some legitimate classics in there, and I'm going to make my way through them one by one.

I take the book with me when I leave the room, and creep downstairs, where I unlock the door and sit on the doorstep looking out at the alley. I slept out here five nights ago, and now I sleep just a few yards away, but it's a different universe.

This is the only part of my day that's not busy. The sun shines down on the alleyway, and although it doesn't reach my face, I stretch out my bare feet into its warmth. Today I am going to be teaching some classes of kids, cooking, showing some of the other volunteers some things about art, sorting through a box of picture books that have arrived from a former volunteer. I like my quiet dawn coffees, but I like the packed days more. I am doing my best to be such a part of life here that no one will ever be able to manage without me. I've told Ben and Maria, who has long gray hair and a kind face, that I don't want any time off.

"I want to work all day every day until I can pay you what I owe," I told her. I will get the money from home, at some point, when I dare. I will have to.

"You have to have at least one day off a week, sweetie," Maria said, but I work through it anyway.

When I got here, everything was bleak. Now I find that my life is Technicolor, and I appreciate every single moment. When there is food, I eat slowly and savor it. That is a habit that I want to hold on to. I am intensely thankful for the luxury of food and a place to sleep, and walls and a roof and a door.

I see, now, why people go to church and why they pray. You don't have to believe in any god to feel the need to stop from time to time and thank the universe for the fact that you are all right. Life is fragile, and to be safe and fed and busy is an incredible piece of luck. I stare down the quiet alley, where a feral cat is pacing about looking for scraps, and take a deep breath. I thank the world for sending me here. I feel safe.

No doubt the universe is unfolding as it should.

But I am not starry eyed about life in this place, no matter how different it is from the way I expected a "shantytown" to be. I know these children, and their families; I know life here is complicated.

I haven't seen any of it myself because I stay firmly where I am. I am done with pounding the streets, even just to get somewhere. When I do go out, I wear my Favela English School T-shirt, and people are friendly because I represent the organization and the local people, who, I now see, are friendly and inclusive, and happy to have a free English school for their children, and for themselves, in the area.

I have stopped eating meat completely, because it turns out it's easy to say "I'm vegetarian," and no one questions it or considers it momentous or even interesting at all. I remember looking at the poor factory-farmed chicken on the plane out here. I don't need to use the corpses of animals to fuel my body. I don't want to damage any creature: I have done quite enough damage already. It is actually easy not to eat meat. We take turns cooking, and the menu often features the meaty bean stew that twice saved me when I needed it. Last night it was my turn, and I tried to cook it without meat for the vegetarians (there are several of us) and it came out just about edible, which was a triumph.

It turns out I don't even know how to chop an onion properly: I started, last night, by plunging my knife into the globe and trying not to let it slide out of control.

"That's an interesting technique," said Jasmine, who was cooking with me, laughing as I tried to steady the slippery onion on the end of my knife. "How have you reached this age without knowing how to cut an onion?"

I shrugged. "Nineteen years somehow passed me by, onion-wise." (I am pretending to be nineteen, and no one questions that either.) I looked at what Jasmine was doing, then cut it in half and sliced it in what I immediately saw was a far more sensible manner. I wished then, and I wish now, that the poor couple who adopted me had taught me this stuff. He used to make a Sunday roast from time to time. She would cook constantly, peeling vegetables, making her healthy soups, concocting bland dinners with lentils and ethically sourced meat, baking cookies that didn't have enough sugar in them. She never taught me a thing.

I try never to think about my Hinchcliffe-Carr heritage. I don't see the news or newspapers here. I am starting to learn to speak and write Portuguese: I got a couple of nine-year-olds to start me off the first full day I was here, after their lesson, when they were hanging around finishing their pictures. They found it hilarious that I was so bad.

I focus totally on the children. Any child in the favela can come to classes here as long as they are registered, and many of them are. They come into the schoolroom from four years old until eleven, but it doesn't stop there: we go out into secondary schools to teach English, and we run adult classes several times a week in different places around the town. I haven't done an adult class yet, and I am a bit scared by the idea of it.

I also know, when I let myself think about it, that if my birth parents hadn't been caught when they were, my life would have been hell. I would never have been Ella Black. I would have been someone else, and they probably wouldn't have taken care of me, and I would have died like one of the neglected children you see in online news stories. They might have thrown me into the canal, too.

I was saved by the people I attacked, and I find myself wanting to save other children, as much as I can, from the troubles their circumstances bring to them. I want every child to have the same opportunities to get places in life, no matter where they're born.

I separated myself out into Ella and Bella, in my old life, because

I knew I was fractured, that I had two selves. Now that I know the truth, I think I have come together, into Jo, who has bits of Ella along with Bella's strength, and a wholly different place in the world.

And I am starting to see how monstrously unjust the world actually is.

As I settle in, I start to understand a little more about Rocinha. It is not actually a favela, but a "favela neighborhood," a city in its own right, originally settled by people who came from the north of Brazil in search of work. It used to be effectively run by drug-dealing gangs, but according to Ben and Maria that was actually less scary than it sounds as long as you weren't involved. Some years ago the police came in and "pacified" the place, which meant they got rid of the gangs and imposed law. People seem to be more ambivalent about this than you might expect.

There's still so much I don't know about this world. I'll probably never even scratch the surface. It's a hill with a huge number of people living on it, and it is energetic and desperate and wonderful and alive. I feel that Rocinha might now be my home, and I am going to stay here as long as I can.

Maybe forever if they let me. And if the police don't catch up with me.

At the end of the first class of the day, Jasmine tells me she and the other volunteers have plans. "Some of us are going out tonight," she says to me. "Nothing massive. We're just going to a bar up the hill for a couple of beers. Do you want to come?"

I love Jasmine, but I don't even think before saying, "No, thanks."

Then, "Hang on a second." The class that just ended was art, and the children are still milling around. I add to the little girl whose portrait I'm drawing, "Stay still. That's right."

"Oh, that's a shame, Jo," Jasmine says. "It would be really nice if you came."

Jasmine is genuinely lovely. She has done me immeasurable good without even knowing it. If she hadn't invited me in when I first turned up, I don't know where I would be. But I need to stay away from social situations because I'm sure I'll say the wrong thing. I have to try hard to remember all my lies: I am Jo, I have been in Venezuela, I broke up with a boyfriend. I also stay away because I literally have no money whatsoever. I used the last of the cash I had to buy a toothbrush and shower gel and things like that. At least I don't need shampoo these days.

"I'm finishing this tonight," I say, nodding to the pile of sketches I've been doing of the children. I don't care that everyone thinks I'm weird or that most of the volunteers are nervous around me, probably because of my shaved head. I just want to stay in and keep my head down.

I finish the picture I'm doing now. It's a sketch of a girl named Gabriella. I shade in her braids and hand her the sheet of paper.

She gasps.

"I can have?" she says.

"Of course you can."

"Thank you, thank you, Teacher Jo," she says, and rolls it up like a scroll to take it home.

That evening all the other volunteers go out drinking. I stay behind and clean the kitchen. It may be weird, but this makes me happy.

CHAPTER THIRTEEN

I WAKE UP smiling because I know it's my birthday. Today I am eighteen, and that is a secret from everyone here. I will celebrate with myself, in my head. I always loved my birthday at home, and today I will love it here in Rio.

Bella sings happy birthday to us in my head, and I like that. I hum along, hoping that it won't wake Jasmine. I'm glad that in spite of everything I know now, this really is my birthday. Eighteen years ago I was born, no matter how fucked up it all was. I burst into the world, and I'm still here.

I have been at the school for ten days, and today is the day on which Amanda Hinchcliffe can look me up on the adoption register. It feels like a million years ago, not just two weeks, that I applied to add my details, when the mother in my head was a gorgeous wayward teen with a strict family and was going to be a big sister to me.

Now I feel like a different person. Time has become very strange.

She will look for me, but the contact details I left with the register were an e-mail address that I will never check and a phone that I stomped on and threw into the trash.

I am safe here.

15 —
DAYS

I am eighteen. I lie in bed and stare at the ceiling. This is me being an adult. It does not feel momentous. I had planned a little celebration for today, at a pub in Kent to mark the fact that I am officially old enough to drink. It was going to be me and Lily and Jack, and probably a few of the others if they could be bothered to turn up. In fact, my best birthday present is the arrival of the tiny child who unwittingly turned my life around when I was at my very lowest.

"Ana!" I say later, when I see her in the doorway. She laughs at the sight of me, and runs into my arms. She giggles as I twirl her around.

"Teacher Paula," she says carefully, beaming at me.

"Oh. Here I'm 'Teacher Jo,'" I say in a quiet voice. "Teacher *Jo*."

"Teacher Jo."

"That's right."

"Teacher Jo-Paula."

"If you like."

Ana sits at the front of the class and gazes at me as we sing the songs and point to colors. I smile at her the whole time. If I could change the world for one person, it would be her.

Later, Jasmine hands me a brown envelope with *JO* written on the front.

"I found it on the doorstep," she says. "Looks like it's for you."

There is something small in it: when I open it, I find two bracelets with pink flowers on them. They are clearly meant for children.

"That's nice," I say. I put the bracelets on my wrist. I have not mentioned my birthday to anyone at all. This must just be one of the children, giving me a present in exchange for my portraits or something. The timing must be coincidental.

"Someone likes you," Jasmine says. "That's because you're so lovely with the kids. Bet it's from one of the little ones."

I check the envelope, but there's nothing else in there.

"Yes," I say. "I guess."

It must be that. It can't be a birthday present, because no one knows it's my birthday. No one knows where I am.

But I can't ignore the fact that someone left food on the beach for "Jo," and now someone has left a birthday present on the doorstep for her too. When I got the food, I wasn't named Jo and now I am.

Something weird is happening. I don't know what to think.

CHAPTER FOURTEEN

WHEN I AM eighteen years and one day old, something bad happens. I am wearing the bracelets, hoping that one of the children will notice and tell me who gave them to me. I am feeling so strange about it that I don't feel like myself. It is horrible. I haven't felt this strange for a long time.

It happens in the first class after lunch. An eleven-year-old called Bruno is cheeky to me to make his friends laugh, and I can't bear it. I did the same thing myself, not very long ago, when I desperately wanted to get Lily out of trouble and somehow told Mrs. Browning her hair looked nice. But I didn't do it to make anyone laugh. No one ever laughed at my jokes. I did it to get myself into trouble, and Lily out of it.

No one gets to act like that in my class.

I am attempting to do some singing, and I know I sound ridiculous blasting out "Humpty Dumpty," and I also know they're too old for such a babyish song, but this is Heidi's lesson plan, not mine, and I don't appreciate Bruno's giggles behind his hands, his whispers, his stirring up of revolution.

"What is this song?" he asks, pretending to be polite.

14
DAYS

"It's about Humpty Dumpty," I say. "I know it's a bit silly. But anyway, let's try it again. *All the King's horses . . .*"

"But who is the Humpty Dumpty?" he asks.

"He's an egg."

There is a moment of silence.

"An egg," echoes Bruno. "A fucking egg?" They all burst out laughing. *Fucking* is one English word everyone knows. Bruno has the audience in the palm of his hand, and they are laughing at me.

I cannot let that happen.

"Do not use that word, Bruno. It's very rude." I sound so fucking lame, when I am actually very fucking angry.

Bruno turns to his classmates and does something with his face that makes them roar with laughter. I am Mrs. Browning. I try to breathe deeply, but I can't let it go.

"Bruno," I say. "That's *enough*."

"But I didn't do anything," he says, in Portuguese.

"You know what you did," I answer, also in Portuguese. I switch to English because my Portuguese isn't up to a lengthy conversation yet. "You swore at a teacher, for one thing. If you don't want to take part in the class and talk politely, then you can leave."

He stares at me, as insolent as Bella. I stare back. He reminds me of myself in the grip of my demon, and I don't like it. Neither of us looks away. I know he wasn't really swearing at me. But still. My head is starting to ring, in the way it used to ring. I push her away frantically. I thought this had stopped happening. I thought we were on the same side now. I mutter the words I use to banish her.

"*No doubt the universe is unfolding as it should,*" I say jaggedly under my breath. I don't know if the children can hear me or not, and I don't care.

"The universe the universe the universe."

Everything swamps me, and I want to do something bad because it's all too much. I was a child in a classroom, and I was rude to a teacher and that same day I was taken away by the Blacks in a panic, and then everything I thought I knew crumbled into dust and I can't bear it.

Bella wants to mess this up. She can see that we've salvaged a life here, and she wants to blow it up because that's what happens.

IT WON'T LAST, she whispers.

It will.

IT WILL NOT. THEY'LL FIND OUT THAT YOU LIED ON THE PAPERWORK. THEY'LL THROW YOU OUT ANYWAY.

No doubt the universe is unfolding as it should.

I have to be the best person I possibly can, because I want to stay here. It's my home. I can't be taken over and do something crazy. This cannot happen.

My vision goes blotchy. Everything disappears around the edges, and I can only see Bruno. I need to attack him. I want to scare him.

I cannot let that happen.

LET ME AT HIM.

No.

HE'S BEING RUDE.

No.

HE CAN'T DO THAT. HE NEEDS A LESSON.

He's a little boy. He's fine.

I'M GOING TO TELL HIM.

"You need to leave." I hiss it in English and then in Portuguese. I have to make this boy go away from me before I attack him. If I hurt a child, everything will be over. I will be homeless, jobless, hopeless, and it will be what I deserve. I am sweating, struggling with Bella, with myself. I point to the door.

"Go on, Bruno. Come back when you can behave and talk nicely. Go home. Go right now." I can barely get the words out.

I watch him hesitating. He has to leave. My hands are twitching, desperate to grab him. I want to push him up against the wall and yell into his face. I want to pinch his skin. I want to hurt him.

I have to get him away.

Strive to be happy.

The rest of the class sits shocked and silent. Bruno, thank God, gets up and walks out of the room, his shoulders drooping, clearly about to cry.

The universe the universe the universe. I have not needed those words for a long time.

"Talk to each other in English," I say, and I run into the kitchen, where Jasmine is making a cup of tea. "Jasmine, can you finish the class?" I say. "I feel terrible."

I don't wait for a reply. I run upstairs and lock myself in the bathroom.

Go away, I say to Bella. I say it loudly.

CAN'T.

Please. Be nice. Help me. This was working. We were good.

YOU KNOW IT'S ONLY A MATTER OF TIME.

That's why we're doing one day at a time.

YOU'LL BE FOUND OUT. YOU'LL STILL HAVE NOTHING. YOU MIGHT AS WELL GO OUT WITH A BANG.

No, I tell her. No no no.

My head clears slowly, and my ears go quiet, and I swallow back the tears and anger at myself and try to take deep breaths.

She's right. I will be found out, any day now. I'll still have nothing. That is all true. She is right.

I wipe my eyes and wash my face. I want to be better than this. I lost control because I saw my bad self in that boy, but that's my fault, not Bruno's. Bella was trying to sabotage everything, and she is a part of me, and I can't let it happen.

Later in the afternoon I find Bruno's registration forms and ask around until I get to his house. It's down a narrow unnamed alley, and impossible to find from the address alone, but people help me and I find it in the end. He is sitting on a doorstep drawing a picture. I stand in front of him in the tight alley, and when he looks up, he immediately looks away again.

"Sorry, Teacher Jo," he mutters. He looks back at the door of his house, clearly worried that I am about to tell whoever is in there that he said "fuck."

I sit next to him. He bristles.

"No," I say. "*Me desculpe.* I am truly sorry. I was mean to you. I was feeling stressed. But it was wrong."

He doesn't understand *stressed*, and I don't know how to say it in Portuguese, so I take his pencil and draw a little picture of myself with claws and fangs and a monstrous expression. I draw Bruno cowering. I draw myself back to normal with a speech bubble saying "Sorry."

He smiles. I give him a little hug.

"Sorry for fucking swearing," he says, chancing his luck, and I laugh and he does too.

"You really shouldn't say that," I tell him, and he nods and says sorry properly.

"Bye, Bruno." I hold my hand out, and he shakes it seriously.

"Bye, Teacher Jo."

When I get back, two new volunteers are climbing off the backs of motorbike taxis. I am instantly scared they might know about the runaway violent teenager with the purple hair, but it turns out they are from the States and have come straight from the airport. They are wearing little dresses and high-heeled shoes. Each of them has long beautiful hair. They stand in the alley.

"Hi," I say. I watch as the blond one's nose wrinkles at my shaved head.

"Hi." She sounds uncertain.

"I'm Jo," I say. "You've just arrived? Are you coming to work here?"

"Hi, Jo," says the other one, who is black with bouncing curls. "I'm Sasha. This is Amy. Um. Yeah, we've just arrived?"

"Cool. Er, welcome."

"That motorbike taxi," Sasha says. "Amy's still a little freaked."

"I mean, what the hell?" says Amy.

"It's OK," I say. "Honestly it is. Come on in. Do you want a coffee or something?"

"Could we get a glass of water?"

"Sure."

Maria turns around as we come into the classroom, on our way to the kitchen.

"Hi, ladies," she says. "Oh—you've met Jo. Thanks, Jo. You're Amy and Sasha? I'll show you to your rooms."

I hand each of them a glass of water and watch as they carry their bags up the stairs. Maria winks at me as we pass, and for the first time since I've been here, I really, truly feel that I belong.

CHAPTER FIFTEEN

IT IS A Monday morning when the phone rings, and I have been living here for twenty days. The phone is a huge wireless thing that looks like an antique. It's kept on its charger all the time, in a corner of the kitchen, and whoever is closest to it answers when it rings. We are supposed to answer in Portuguese, but most of the volunteers don't speak it, and so I grab it more often than not if I'm anywhere nearby. It turns out that in less than three weeks you can pick up some rudimentary conversational Portuguese if you work hard at it.

A class of five-year-olds is coming in for an English lesson, which means we will be reading a picture book and looking at the illustrations and talking about the words. I love the book classes: today we are reading a book about a boy from Cornwall who is captured by pirates and sold into slavery. I love that book, and the kids love to act it out after I've read it.

The children run in, jumping around, chattering loudly, asking about pirates.

Maria, who happens to be here today, claps her hands. "Stop!" she shouts. "Everyone out. Walk, don't run." She says it again in Portuguese, and the children leave the room and file in more sensibly.

5
DAYS

The phone rings. Since Maria is getting everyone to sit in their places and stop being silly, I run into the kitchen and answer it.

"*Alô?*" I say as I walk.

"Oh, hi," says a man's voice.

My legs give way, and I sit on the floor.

My breath isn't coming anymore. I gasp for air.

I

say

nothing.

"Hi?" he says again. "*Português? Español?* Do you speak English?"

I try to breathe. I cannot just hang up. Seconds tick by.

I think of the way Jasmine talks.

"Yes, I speak English," I say in my best, ridiculous approximation of an Irish accent.

"Great. I'm looking for a friend of mine. Just wondering if she might be working with you?"

"Mm?"

"Her name's Ella," he says. "Ella Black. You might have seen her in the press? She's missing. She has been known to call herself Chrissy. It's a long shot, but have you by any chance had anyone that could be her working for you? I could e-mail a photo, because she's probably using another name. Last time I saw her, she had purple hair. I just want to know that she's safe, and I need her to know that she isn't in any trouble and she doesn't have to hide."

I don't know what to say.

"There's no one like that here," I say in Jasmine's voice, when the silence has stretched out too long.

"If you see her, tell her we miss her and we love her," he says, "and she has nothing to worry about when it comes to what she did."

I hang up even though he is still talking. I lie down and curl up into a ball. My body heaves and shakes. I love him. I love Christian with all my heart. He is looking for me. He found me. He said he loves me.

I love him.

He found me.

I hung up the phone.

I have no number for him.

I can hear Maria starting the lesson.

I

am

heartbroken

all

over

again.

I pull myself together, of course, because I have to. I join in the lesson, and as I ignore my red eyes and puffy face, everyone else does too. I get through the day, sit and chat with the other volunteers during my downtime, and go out in the evening to teach the adult class at the municipal hall down the hill. I've done this twice now, and it turns out it's not scary at all. In fact I love it. The energy of it is infectious.

He said, "Tell her we miss her and we love her."

He

loves

me.

As I walk, I pass a group of children playing, and they all stop and say, "Hello, Teacher Jo!" I smile and wave back. A dad I recognize because he drops his four children off for classes regularly shouts, "I speak English!" from across the street, and I give him a thumbs-up. I feel at home. I actually feel like a tiny part of the community. There's nowhere else I want to live.

The sun is low in the sky; it has been a baking-hot day, and the evening sunlight is glorious on my face. As I walk down the hill, I catch a glimpse of the sea.

It shimmers in the sunlight. It sparkles. It is beautiful. In the twenty days I have been at the English school I have never been back to the beach even though everyone else goes whenever they can. I don't want to go there, or to Leblon where I stole a bag, or to Copacabana where I sunbathed with the people who were my kind-of parents. I have not been anywhere, have kept myself within the smallest possible radius of my new home. No part of me wants to go back to the tourist part of the city, or dancing on the streets of Lapa, though that evening will, I am quite sure, remain forever the best night of my life.

I am torn apart with regret. I would give anything to be able to go back and not panic and not hang up the phone. I love Christian. He looked for me until he found me, and I will always know that, even if he doesn't. He is probably looking still. He said I'm not in trouble. That means that the café man is all right. I let myself think about what that means, and the relief it brings me is intense. I feel that the sun has come out inside me. If the man hasn't died from an infected cut, I'm not a killer. If I'm not in trouble with the police, I can get a passport. I can contact the Blacks; I know I'm going to have to do that, one day. I hardly dare imagine the possibilities.

I hope Christian thinks the phone was answered by an odd Irish girl. I hope he is all right.

He told me about Vittoria, and I ran away in the night.

It was terrible behavior. I want to call him back and say how sorry I am.

I could have told him I was all right. I could have begged him not to tell anyone that I'm here, even if the police were asking. I could have told him that I found out the truth about myself and that I had to get away, and I would not have had to tell him what that truth actually was. I didn't do that, and now I never will.

When I get to Ana's coffee shop, I call in to shout hello to her parents, both of whom come out to kiss me on the cheek, and then I keep on going. I have to put Christian out of my mind. I try to think, instead, about what I'm going to cover in this English lesson. We will talk about traveling—booking tickets, catching buses, all of that— in English. The adult class still makes me nervous. We teach them by walking into the classroom and refusing to speak Portuguese for the entire hour. The classes are free and open to anyone who wants to come along: people often look exhausted and stressed, and I know they are fighting their own battles. I am starting to understand that nobody's life is straightforward. I am far from being the only one with demons.

I remember my adoptive mother going out to Italian and Spanish evening classes, anxiously making sure Dad and I would be all right during her short absence, leaving us with lentil bakes and bowls of fruit, with homework to do or instructions to relax. This class, the one I teach, is the opposite of hers. She went because going to an evening class and learning a language was the kind of thing you did to keep yourself from going insane if you'd given up your career (and I don't even know what her career would have been) so you could have a family. When we did actually go to Spain, she would say a few phrases self-consciously, with a terrible accent, and then revert to English. I smile at the memory. Dad and I would cheer her on, encouraging her to overcome her nerves and order for us in Spanish. She was so pleased with herself when she did it.

The memory of it lands somewhere inside, and I miss her.

She tried so hard, struggled with losing eight babies, adopted me in dramatic circumstances, and then gave up trying to tell me. I am flooded with empathy for Fiona Black. She did everything she could for me, and now she doesn't even know that I'm alive.

I am eaten up from the inside by the fact that I tried to hurt her, that she will know that for the rest of her life, that it was the last image she has of me.

If Christian is right and I'm not in trouble, I could contact them. I do love them. It's easier to keep the wall up, to feel Bella's fury at them for lying to me, than it is to remember that, no matter what, they are the only parents I have ever known. And they lied to me for good reasons, even if it was misguided.

By the time I arrive at the hall, I am ready to teach the best class ever. These classes are for people who work hard every moment of every day and who still push themselves. If you can speak English, you can work in tourism. That is why they are here, and that is why

I am teaching them to say, "Would you like a car to the airport?" and "Shall I book you a tour to Christ the Redeemer?" I am amazed by the dedication of the adult learners, who range in age from younger than me to older than God.

When I get back to the school, exhausted and ready for bed, I see the volunteers clustered around someone.

"Look," says somebody. "Here she is!" They part, and I do not believe what I am seeing, so I blink and try looking again.

"Hi there, Jo," says Christian.

My heart stops.

He looks the same.

He is Christian.

He is here.

My Christian.

I love him.

I walk up to him and stare into his eyes. He stares back. Everyone else melts away. I say sorry with my eyes. He tells me it's all OK with his.

"Christian," I say.

He smiles a very sad smile.

"Would you come for a drink?" he says.

The girls (and the two boys: there are fewer boys here than there used to be at my ballet class) are smiling and looking interested. Everyone is waiting for me to say yes. They are all intrigued. As soon as we go, they will start talking about us.

He'd better not have said the name Ella Black when he first arrived. He better not have said that. I am not ready for any of these people to know anything about my old life.

.   .   .

But I can hardly believe he's here, so I say "Yes," and walk straight back out, knowing that he will follow.

"How did you do it?" I say when we are at the end of the alley, on the big road. I am trying to be angry that he tracked me down, but I am delirious with delight. My skin is tingling all over. My muscles are tense. My heart is pounding extra fast. All I want to do is to look at him. I never thought I would see him again.

Bella is happy to see him too. She is agitated, excited. I feel her stirring inside me.

He looks at me.

"Sorry, Ella," he says. "But really. What the hell? And where the hell is your hair?"

He is angry with me. I am busily trying to be cross with him, but he's the one who's shocked at my behavior and, from the look on his face and the sound of his words, my appearance, and he is right to be. He liked the girl with the soft body and the purple hair. Now I'm spiky and bald. He liked Ella, and now I'm Jo.

"Sorry," I say. I take his hand. He holds it tightly. "I'm sorry. I really …"

I don't seem to be able to say any more than that.

"Well. I'll answer your question first, if you like. I did this—I found you here—by trying everything I could think of to figure out where you might be. We'd talked about the favela. You'd talked about teaching English. When you weren't there on the island, I was devastated. Genuinely. And phenomenally worried."

We are walking up the hill together. I'll take him to a bar I've seen up there.

"Sorry." It doesn't really feel like enough.

"But I got the note you left, and look, Ella, I'll just come out and say this, and don't be mad. Don't run away. I know who your birth parents are. The bike shop guy said he'd lent you his laptop, so I borrowed it to have a look, and there it all was in the history. You smashed the screen, by the way: I had to hook it up to my phone to read anything. I gave him money to cover it."

I cannot say a word. I am hot and shaky.

"It must have been horrible. Finding that out. I can see why you felt the need to bolt. I wish you'd felt that you could tell me, though."

"Sorry." That seems to be the only thing I can say.

"I went back to the mainland and told your parents everything. I had to. They were devastated in all sorts of ways. They were looking for you, and I'd found and lost you. I tried to leave them to it, because I knew it was up to you what you did and when you came back, but you had to know that you weren't in trouble with the police." He looks me in the eye.

"Are you sure?"

"I promise. The café guy was mad and he did call the police, but they have bigger things to deal with than that. Your parents paid him some compensation and explained a bit of the situation, and he agreed to drop it. So you had to know that."

I have been living on edge for every second of every day. I was so focused on my new life and on everything I was doing day to day, but underneath I was waiting for the police. I lean back and feel weightless with relief.

"I've been making calls every day. I called about sixteen places I thought you might have gone to, and on number seventeen I found a strange, semi-Irish girl. Was that meant to be Irish?" He puts on a terrible accent. *"There's no one like that here,"* he says. "And there you were. My Ella."

I smile.

"Or my Jo."

"Did you ask for Ella, at the school? Just now?"

"No. Not when you'd made it so clear you were hiding. I just said I was looking for my friend and then I saw your photo on the wall, and even without the hair I knew it was you right away. It was your eyes. I said that was you, and they were all like *Oh, Jo!* They love you there, but they're a bit scared of you."

"They should be. I come from bad people."

He shakes his head. "You are the strongest, bravest, most wonderful person I've ever met, Ella. You are yourself. Nothing anyone else has done reflects on you. You are breathtaking. Maddening too."

It is nearly dark, and the lights are on all over the favela.

"I . . . Look," he continues. "I can't imagine what it feels like, to grow up thinking you know where you come from, and then to discover that you don't, and then after all that, to find out that your parents are in jail for terrible crimes. I really can't imagine that. I'm so sorry. But I'm beyond happy that you're safe. You really are very strong, Ella."

I squeeze his hand. I cannot speak.

"You know, at first, your parents—would you still call them that?—they tried to suggest your running away was my fault, but they stopped that when they realized how much I knew."

"They said it was your fault?"

"They were really, really angry that I'd taken you out in secret, and then far more so that I'd been to visit you on Paqueta. I slipped that note you wrote them in Paqueta under their door, the first night, but I had to tell them when I went back and you were gone. They thought I'd given you ideas. They said you never would have run off like that before. They made it very clear I was responsible. Then you called them from a German phone and your mum was sure you were coming back. That was you, wasn't it?"

I take some deep breaths.

I wait for the onslaught.

Bella?

WHAT?

Aren't you angry?

OF COURSE.

But?

BUT WE'RE IN A BAR WITH CHRISTIAN. FIONA BLACK HAS ALREADY SUFFERED.

I smile. She's right. I am angry that my parents blamed Christian, but I don't want to storm around and lash out. I've done everything I possibly can to hurt them already. They thought they were giving a lovely baby a home; they thought they'd raised a nice girl who had friends and a boyfriend, and who was doing well at school. Now they have a bald daughter who lives in the slums and doesn't speak to them. I can't really think of how it could actually have worked out any worse for them than this.

I walk a little way up the hill away from Christian, just because I have to move. I take some deep breaths. Then I go back and take his hand.

"Yes, it was me on the German phone."

He sighs and looks at me.

"Come on," I say. "Let's get a beer. I haven't had a proper drink since we went to Lapa."

He looks quite nervous. "I can't believe I'm seeing you," he says. "Are you really OK? What's it actually like? Living here?"

"It's good."

"Not scary?"

"No. Not anymore, no."

"Good." He pauses. "They don't blame me anymore, you know," he says quickly. "Your parents. As soon as I told them I knew about the adoption, and then about the birth parents, they just crumpled. No one else in their life knows about it, it seems, apart from their lawyer. They were devastated that you'd found out. They just want to know you're alive, Ella."

"Are they at the same hotel?"

"Yes. In the same room, in case you come back. You could call them there. You wouldn't even have to speak. Um. I wrote the number down just in case you wanted to."

We go down a side street and sit inside a little bar lit by a dim light on the wall. Several other people are drinking beer in there. I recognize a teenage boy who drops his younger brother, Gabriel, off at classes sometimes, and give him a wave. There are flies buzzing around in the doorway.

I look at Christian for a moment, letting everything hit me.

I thought I had lost him, half an hour ago. Now I have him and I need to say it all to his face, because I might never see him again after this, and this is important.

"I meant it," I say. "In my note, when I said I love you. I do love you. I loved you the first time I saw you, and then I loved you more and more. That day on the island. The two of us. It was the most wonderful thing. The best day."

He looks at me sideways and smiles.

"Really."

"We're heading back to the States tomorrow, Felix and Susanna and me. I could not go without seeing you. I just couldn't. I had to find you, and so I did." He hesitates. "Ella—look. You'll probably say no but I have to ask. You could come with me. Back to Miami. Just for a visit, until you decide what you're doing."

I look into his eyes. "I haven't got a passport. It was stolen from my bag. That was . . . Well, I'll tell you about that another time."

He looks at me. "Please do. When you feel ready to be Ella again. Tell me. I'll come back for you. If you like." He is stroking the palm of my hand with his thumb.

I am staring at him. This is the most enormous thing, and my heart fills up and everything goes soft and fuzzy and I will never forget it as long as I live. Christian wants me to come to Florida.

He will come back for me.

He

will

come

back

for

me.

"Yes," I say. "Yes. I will."

"Do you have an e-mail address?"

"No. Not one I look at. I often answer the phone at the school, or you can just show up." I imagine logging in to my Gmail account. It would be full of things from my old life, things I don't want to see. I look into his eyes. "I'll set up a new e-mail. It will be just for you."

"Here. Here's mine. Please write to me. Text me. Call me. Send a letter with a carrier pigeon. Anything you like. Please keep in touch, Ella-favela. You fabulous girl."

He hands a scrap of paper to me. It has the hotel's number on it as well as his details, and I take it and have another sip of my beer.

"I will. My fabulous boy."

"I need to give you one more thing." He pushes an envelope across the table at me. "It's not much. I wish I could give you all the money you need. But it's just something to keep you going. I know those places don't pay salaries."

I stare at it. I have no money, but I have food and the things I need.

"I can't take your money," I say. I got here by myself. I've done all this on my own, and I have food and a home. I can't be rescued now by a handsome prince.

"Don't be ridiculous," he says. "You can call it a loan if you like. When you can, you can send me some money back. Or bring it to me. If it'll make you take it now. I wish I could give you more. This isn't life-changing money. It's just a little bit of cash. That's all."

I take it and smile my biggest smile at him, hoping he can see my soul sparkling through my eyes.

Christian pays for the beers, and I lead him up the hill, past the chickens, right up to the place where the children play soccer at the very top. The city is spread out before us, a string of sparkling lights.

The moon lights up the ocean. The mountains are dark. The city is at our feet, twinkling, alive.

Christian laughs at the sight of it, and then we turn to each other. He takes hold of me, and I take hold of him, and we kiss each other for a long time.

I want the moment to last forever. I am Jo, in the favela, kissing the boy I love beyond all words, on a moonlit night on top of a Brazilian hill.

CHAPTER SIXTEEN

I OPEN THE envelope in the early hours of the morning, lying on my mattress on Jasmine's floor. The light is off, and I hold it up to the moonlight that's coming in around the edges of the blind.

Christian has given me money. I have enough cash to go out for a drink on Friday for Jasmine's birthday. I can buy her a little present. I will have a little cushion now. I'll pay him back one day. I love him.

There's not only money in here, though. When I've stared at the money for a while, I take the other thing out of the envelope. It is a photograph of the two of us together. I never knew that such a thing existed, because in all the time I spent with him I was too busy gazing at him to think about taking a picture. But this is a photograph of Christian and me, in Lapa, dancing in the street. It was the best night of my life, and it was real. In the picture I have purple hair and I am looking at him and laughing, and he is looking at me and laughing too, and we look so happy. I stare and stare and stare at us both.

He has written on the back of it, *Susanna took this. The best night of my life* ♥.

Jasmine turns over in her sleep. I put the photograph under my pillow, with the money, and lie awake for a long time.

4
DAYS

.　.　.

In the morning, I get up early, and while I'm waiting for the kettle to boil, I stare at the English school's phone. I can't call from here because they might be able to trace it: I'm not ready for the Blacks to walk through this door just yet. Also, if I called from the kitchen, someone might overhear me, and that would be awful. I gather up the few coins that were left from my old stash and walk fast, along the alley and down the hill to where I know there is a pay phone. When I get to the bottom, I call from the phone next to the Super Sucos. If they trace my call to here, they still won't find me.

I take a deep breath and, before I can think about it a moment longer, dial the number for the Blacks' Copacabana hotel, from the piece of paper Christian wrote it on. My fingers tremble as I do it. I am breathing rapidly, but I don't let myself put the phone down. I force myself to keep it against my ear.

When someone answers, I talk quickly.

"Could I speak to Mr. and Mrs. Black, please, in room 1108?" I say it in Portuguese, because that's only polite.

"Sure," says the man at reception, in English. Then another phone is ringing, and someone picks it up and says "Hello?" and it is actually Graham Black, my adoptive father.

My dad.

His voice is not urgent. He does not expect it to be me—not at all. It's six thirty, but he doesn't sound as if I woke him up. I wonder what life is like for them now. They stay in their room and wait. They're not surprised by the phone ringing. They don't even expect it to be me.

"Hi, Dad," I say. "Sorry. I'm fine. I'm sorry. You should go home. I'll call you there, I promise. I need to get a new passport. I need some stuff for that. Tell Mum I'm sorry and . . ."

I click the phone down before he can react. I am trembling all over. I walk back up the hill quickly, not looking back.

The four-year-olds always make me feel good, and today Ana comes straight up to me and clings on to my legs until I crouch down and pick her up. She is heavy enough to disguise my still-shaking arms.

She giggles and strokes my fuzzy head. "Hello, Teacher Jo-Paula," she says.

"Hello, Ana."

Ana is my little savior. She will never know what she has done. She has never so much as questioned my name: she calls me Jo-Paula, and the other volunteers smile indulgently when she does it. No one has asked why she calls me that. It is the most innocuous thing, and it is a secret that would unravel everything. Even though I have had several names since I was Ella, Paula was the shortest-lived and most transformational of them.

"You have small hair," she says now, touching it with the open palm of her hand.

"It's growing," I say, and I stroke her silky bob. Then I put her down and throw myself into singing nursery rhymes with the little children.

I kissed Christian again. He made a mammoth effort to find me, and now I am going to have to e-mail to thank him for the money. All of this makes me smile through the afternoon.

. . .

If I am going to be Jo, I will need to build a life for myself. A real one. Now that I know that the waiter is OK and I'm not going to be arrested, everything is different.

Now I'm beginning to feel like the person I always wished I could be: I am different and bigger and living an actual life that I literally went out and made for myself. I am going to grow into Jo. Jo will not be a Black or a Hinchcliffe or a Carr. She won't be Ella, and she won't be Bella. I called her Marsh, off the top of my head, when I arrived here. Jo Marsh is who I will remain.

I look at Jasmine across the room, and I am filled with gratitude to be standing where I am right now. She is gathering up the leftover stickers from the children's activity this morning, and I go to help her. I need to be open with Jasmine—not in the sense of telling her my full story, but in the sense of talking to her and laughing with her and not being so guarded anymore.

"Where are you from, Jasmine?" I say. She looks at me, and I realize that it came out all wrong. I laugh. "I don't mean 'where are you from?' in the racist kind of way. I mean, you said your parents live in Dublin, but is that where you grew up?"

She grins. "You should say, 'No, but where are you from *originally*?' with a little tilt of your head. Yeah, I grew up in the West of Ireland. I was born in Hong Kong, and my dad died when I was little. He was Chinese. So Mum moved back to Ireland when I was tiny, and I was the outsider, looking like this while being Irish. I never lived above a Chinese restaurant, so that was hard for some people to understand, and not only that but I'm literally bad at maths and I can't play the piano. Baffling. So. She and my stepdad moved to Dublin a few years ago. It's good there. How about you? Where are you from? *Originally?*"

It's funny: Jasmine is my best friend now, and without her kindness I would never have stepped through the door of this place. I sleep on her bedroom floor every night, yet we've never even had this conversation. I suppose that shows how far I have shied away from talking about anything personal. For three weeks, I've done everything I can to avoid the *how about you?*

"London," I say. It isn't very imaginative, but at least it's huge, and a place I know.

"Oh, that must be cool," she says.

"It's OK," I say. "I mean, I haven't been there for ages but it's home, I guess. In a way. Not like this is home, though."

"Oh, it's the best here, isn't it? I'm just loving it."

"Me too," I say, and I mean it. I knew I would love Rio, and even though none of it has been anything in any way like I imagined, I do. I know there are things out there that I will have to face soon enough, but for now I can strive to be happy, just as it says in the poem.

CHAPTER SEVENTEEN

ON FRIDAY BEN turns up just before we're leaving for the club, to say happy birthday to Jasmine. Then he turns to me.

"Have you got a moment?" he says quietly, and he leads me into the kitchen. One of the girls is making coffee, but she takes a look at us and leaves. My stomach lurches. He has discovered that I'm here under a fake identity, and he's about to kick me out. I know it. He fixes me with his all-seeing look. I wait for him to tell me how disappointed he is to discover that everything about me was a lie.

"Congratulations, Jo," he says instead. "We've received the money, and you're a fully paid-up member of the team. I'll find you a bedroom, or you and Jasmine can move into one of the doubles if you like. You two seem to have hit it off."

"Wait, but . . . I haven't given you any money."

"You haven't personally. I assume you arranged it from home, like you said. Our admin staff said they got a call from someone saying they were paying your contribution, and when they had the details, they transferred it straight over."

Christian. That's the first thing I think. Christian has paid for me to be here.

1
DAY

The Blacks. That's the second thing. If he's told them where I am, they could have done it.

Ben is still talking. "Are you going out with everyone tonight?"

"Yes."

"Good. I hope you all have a good time."

"Thank you. Was it . . ." I try to compose my thoughts. "Was it a man who paid? An American?"

Ben smiles. "Your friend who came here the other day? He caused quite a stir, I've heard. No. It was a woman, actually. Your mum."

We pile out into the street together, the seven of us who are going to celebrate Jasmine's birthday. I try to make sense of what has happened. Christian has told the Blacks that I'm here and that I owe the charity some money. They have called to pay it. That's their way of saying that it's all OK. I'm here legitimately now. If they know I'm here, they could have come to get me, and they didn't. They have sent me a message, and I love them for it.

I walk faster, to catch up with Jasmine. She is the longest-serving volunteer at the English school; everyone but her has arrived since I did as the previous set of volunteers moved on to go home, or elsewhere, for Christmas. The girls are dressed in little sundresses and tiny cardigans, with swooshy hair and shiny shoes. I have cobbled together the best outfit I could manage, which involves the denim shorts I wear every day and the halter-neck top I bought in Rio when I was Ella, that I meant to throw away but never did. I have borrowed a silk scarf from Sasha and tied it around my head. Jasmine lent me her makeup, so for the first time in an extremely long time I'm wearing eyeliner, mascara and lipstick. It feels odd, painting on a face. I stepped a long way away from being like everyone else, and now I am stepping back into it, just for a night. I worry that a bald head and a made-up face makes me look ridiculous, but it's the best I can do, really. I'm used to feeling like the odd one on nights out, and the good thing is that now I don't care.

"Oh my God, Jo," says Sasha, when she sees me. "You look amazing. You really do. I mean, you always look amazing, but tonight you are just . . . wow."

Amy, who has gotten over her distaste of the favela thanks to actually living here, nods.

"Yeah. You do look cool."

"No one's as cool as Jo," says Jasmine, putting her arm around me. I look at the ground. I don't know what to say, so I don't say anything at all.

The large woman is sitting at the café opposite our alley, on the main road. She is always around the neighborhood, sitting and drinking coffee. I like seeing the same people every day. Now that my Portuguese is better, I might try to strike up a conversation with her.

When I smile at her, she smiles and looks away. I walk down the hill with the others, all of us heading to the bus stop.

The venue turns out to be much grander than I expected, and everyone is showing their passports at the door. When I get to the front of the line, the woman looks at me and says, "ID?"

"We need ID?"

"It's the law in Brazil," Jasmine says next to me. "Any club, anything like that, you have to show ID at the bar. I did say everyone should bring passports."

"Yes. You did."

Jasmine said that, but I ignored it for the obvious reason. "I'm really sorry," I say to the woman at the door, "but I haven't got it. I forgot. Sorry."

She looks at me through narrowed eyes. "You can't go in without ID."

"Oh, please? I'm with them. They've all got theirs."

This is like being at home in Kent, talking my way into being served alcohol. It usually worked then, one way or another, and I hope it will work now. The woman makes the silence stretch out a long time, then sighs, tells me she'll let me in this once, and tells me to bring my passport next time. I promise I will. I pay the entrance charge, which takes up a scary chunk of my precious money, and she takes a photo of me. I don't like that, but it seems to be happening to everyone.

Then we are in. This is a real old-fashioned samba hall that looks as if it has been here for a hundred years. It is glitzy and glamorous, with chandeliers and polished floors and high ceilings. A man in a tuxedo leads us up a grand staircase and shows us to a table. The downstairs is a dance floor, and we can look down to it over some railings. There is at least one other dance floor in a room nearby.

"Please," he says, handing us menus. "Please, choose a drink."

I look at the glossy menu. This is a different world—a different universe—and for this night only I'm going to enjoy it. I was expecting a venue like Antonio's, where I met up with my darling Christian and his friends: a busy informal bar filled with locals. This is a tourist place, and everything about it is shiny and impeccable. This is the kind of place the Blacks would have brought me to.

It's not a place most of my Rocinha neighbors would have access to. It is strange to be here. I feel like an imposter, but when I look around the table, I see that no one else does.

I thought the others didn't have money, and yet it seems that they have lots of it. I suppose, if I really think about it, that these are gap-year students from Europe and America, and they have paid thousands to join the project, so they probably have spending money on top of that. Of course they have spare cash with them for treats. Most of them are going traveling later. They are in a completely different situation from me. This night is a huge treat for me and a return to normality for them.

It will not occur to anyone that I'm any different from them. Jasmine is the only person who knows that I slept on the doorstep. They all consider my funny hair and my lack of wardrobe to be stylistic or ethical choices. I am a part of the school, and I am good at art. They have no idea.

I was always so careful about the way I dressed and presented myself. Right up until I cut my hair to avoid hurting Tessa and Bella got me to dye it purple, I did everything I could to blend in. I hated attention because it was always bad. There is an English girl here, Lauren, who reminds me a tiny bit of Ella Black, though Lauren seems more straightforward. I often see her watching everyone else, making an effort to do things the way they do them, anxious above all to fit in. She sometimes seems awestruck by me: she thinks I'm older than she is, when I'm actually younger. When Lauren looks at me, I feel as if Ella Black is gazing at Jo, amazed by what she was able to become.

I scan the menu. The waiter, in his white tuxedo, is standing grinning at us, his electronic notebook in hand with a little pen poised above it. Jasmine, as the birthday girl, orders first, and picks a passion-fruit caipirinha at a cost of considerably more than I was imagining I would spend on this entire evening. Lauren orders the same. So does Sasha.

It is my turn.

"The same, please," I say, in Portuguese. By the time he's finished, everyone has ordered a passion-fruit caipirinha.

The drinks arrive, and we all toast to Jasmine's birthday.

Jasmine took me in and gave me food and a shower and her bed, and I will always love her for that. I hope she has the best birthday ever.

"Thank you, everyone," she says. "And thanks to everyone for coming out with me. Four months I've been in Rio, and this is the first time I've done something like this."

Jasmine looks happy. She has put her hair up in a bun for the evening and tried her hardest to look like a grown-up. This is her nineteenth birthday, so she very much *is* a grown-up, but she seems to me to be someone who will look better when she's older than she does now. Her dress suits her: she has a tiny little waist, and the dress she is wearing has a big full skirt and works perfectly. I had no idea she had anything like that packed away in our bedroom. I know that she's spending another month at the project and then moving on to a different project in Ecuador, and I will miss her hugely when she goes.

I realize that I am assuming I will still be at the school in a month, and that takes me back to my project fees being paid, and that makes me giddy.

"Happy birthday, Jasmine," I say as our glasses clink together. "You deserve all the happiness in the world."

"Oh—thank you, Jo! So do you."

The passion-fruit caipirinhas are wonderful. I take a sip and am instantly back in the street in Lapa, dancing with the love of my life.

The fruitiness is different, and it's more sophisticated, but it is the same drink.

We are not far from Lapa here. Christian is back in Florida now.

Hours later I finish my third cocktail and look for someone to dance with. I don't feel drunk because I've been dancing more than drinking, and the music and the people and the heat and the joy will keep me going forever. The club, which was a stately tourist place when we arrived, has become a nightclub with wild Brazilian dance music and sweaty people on the dance floor. Hundreds and hundreds of people are here. I have been dancing and dancing and dancing, letting out everything without stopping to think. I've lost the others, but I don't care.

There are some Brazilians here too, and they are spectacular dancers. I stand at the edge of the dance floor, my empty glass in my hand, and watch their legs and feet, their hips, their arms, the poise of their bodies. It makes me forget everything, and the music goes right through me. It is so loud that even if I did want to talk to someone, I wouldn't be able to.

A man comes over and extends his hand, inviting me to dance. He is handsome, black, and stylishly dressed. I take his hand.

I remember dancing with Christian somewhere down the road from here, and following other people's feet, and having the best night of my life.

Now I dance carefully with my new partner. I try to mimic the samba moves with my feet, but it doesn't really matter what I do. He dances in front of me, not touching, and he clearly wants nothing from me but a dance. After a while he tries to talk, but I can't hear what he's saying, so I tell him that by mime, and we just dance. The song changes, and we keep dancing. When I am sweaty and exhausted, I thank him, and he gives me a little bow, and I wander away.

I step out onto the balcony for some fresh air. From up here, I can see that people are lining up down the street to get into this place. I watch them standing out there in the tropical heat. There are bars all the way down this road, and they have tables outside, and there is a pink flowery vine growing up the building opposite. My head is spinning with the music and the dancing and the drinks, and the sweat is hot along my hairline.

Someone is next to me. It is a woman, an older woman I saw earlier on the dance floor doing wonderful dancing, and she says, in Portuguese, that she's hot. I wipe my forehead too, and I agree. We talk a little bit about nothing in particular. She asks where I am from, and I say London. We stand side by side for a while, staring out at the street, at the hundreds of people wanting to come in.

Then the woman has left, and Jasmine is beside me.

"You all right, Jo?" she says.

"I'm having a wonderful night," I tell her. "How about you?"

"Yeah," she says. "Yeah, it's great, isn't it? Wanna get another drink?"

"Sure."

We sit down with Lauren and a boy named Ted at a table back at the top of the grand staircase, and I am drinking from a bottle of beer. The music is pounding, but it's quiet enough, out here, to talk.

"So you've had a good night?" Lauren asks Jasmine.

"The best," she says, holding her glass up too. "I've had the best night. I have. The very best one."

"You deserve it," I say. "You know, we should find the bus back at some point. They do go all night, don't they? Or do we have to wait around for the first one in the morning? I'm working at ten."

Jasmine looks at me. "You'd be all right to wait it out, if we had to, wouldn't you?" she says. "It wouldn't bother you at all."

"Of course. It'd be fine."

Jasmine starts to speak again, then stops. She puts her drink onto the table and leans toward me.

"You're such an enigma, Jo," she says. I can smell the sweet alcohol on her breath. "I've known you for weeks, but you've hardly said anything. Any time I tried to ask you about your life, you change the subject, and because I saw what you were like when you arrived, I thought you'd been really ill, and I've never wanted to push you."

"I know. I'm sorry."

"You shout out in your sleep sometimes."

"Do I?"

"It breaks my heart. And then—there's a woman who called the other day looking for someone working here. She didn't say Jo, but I'm thinking it was you she was after. Because you're the only one who's, you know. A bit mysterious."

I put down my drink.

My mother paid my fees. And a woman was looking for me. I don't want her to turn up. It is mean of me, but I don't want to see the Blacks. Though apparently I'm happy to take their money.

WE CAN HAVE THEIR MONEY WITHOUT SEEING THEM.

That's not fair.

NOTHING IS FAIR.

"Who did she ask for?" I say.

"Ella. Or Chrissy. I think she's called a couple of times, but I've only spoken to her that once. The others said something about it."

"What did you say?"

"I said no. I said there's no one here by the name of Ella or Chrissy."

Jasmine, my friend, has pulled the rug out from under me. But she didn't give me away, and that is the thing that matters right now.

"You're amazing," I say. "Thank you, Jasmine. It's complicated. Tonight is about you. When we're in our bedroom tomorrow, I'll tell you about myself."

I don't know what I'm going to tell her: some part of the truth, I suppose. A version of it. Not all of it. She looks so happy that I feel guilty about being such a bad friend, but I feel nervous, too. I try to stand up, but my legs are weak and wobbly, and I have to sit quickly down again.

Someone paid my fees. A woman has been phoning me. Ever since Christian found me, I haven't really been hidden.

I close my eyes. The drumbeat reverberates through my body. Jasmine is saying things, but I don't know what they are.

I don't have to hide from the Blacks any longer. I am eighteen. I can live in Rio and teach English if I like. I am doing fine.

The police would not take me back to my parents as if I were an abducted toddler, because I am old enough to live my own life, so I don't need to hide from them either.

I'm not in trouble with the police. Christian said I'm not.

It's not the Blacks or the police I'm hiding from.

It is not them at all.

I turn back to Jasmine. "What was her voice like?"

She is frowning, because she was in the middle of saying

something else, and I have no idea what it was. It might, for all I know, have been an explanation of exactly what the woman's voice was like.

"Oh," she says. "Well. She was talking English, and she had an English kind of voice."

"Was it an English voice like this? *Have you seen a girl called Ella?*" I do my best impression of Fiona Black, with her Queen-of-England accent. Instantly, I regret saying my real name. My real-ish name.

"No. That's what you sound like. It was more like this: *Have you seen a girl called Ella?* No. That's not quite right. It was an English accent for sure but not like yours."

I swallow. I have no idea what my birth mother's voice sounds like, but I do know she is English. I know she is from Birmingham, and Jasmine's attempt at replicating the accent sounded a bit like it might be a Midlands kind of thing. One thing is for sure: if she didn't sound like me, then she wasn't Fiona Black.

And all of a sudden, I begin to panic.

How could someone who did the things she did, and then spent half her life in prison, be able to track me down in the same way that Christian did?

I cannot imagine it, but that doesn't mean it's not possible. I do know that she wanted to see me. My parents whisked me out here to keep me away from her, and I love them now for the madness of that plan. I have no idea if my disappearance got any coverage in Britain, but if her lawyer was able to write to the Blacks, could it have been possible for her to find out that I was in Brazil?

She could be looking for me. The woman who led five innocent people to be tortured and murdered could be calling the right number and asking for the right person.

Lauren is leaning forward. Lauren has been listening in from the other side of Jasmine.

"Oh, yes," she said. "I meant to tell you about that. I spoke to this woman on the phone. She said she was looking for Ella or Chrissy. After you had that gorgeous boy turn up asking for Chrissy but actually meaning you, I thought it might be you, so I asked if she meant Jo."

I stare.

"When was this?"

Lauren pulls a piece of her hair into her mouth and chews it. "About a week ago. Sorry, I meant to tell you about it. Anyway, she said she probably did mean Jo, actually. She was nice."

"Please tell me that didn't happen."

"I was trying to be helpful."

"It wasn't helpful."

"Sorry. I didn't know."

I am on my feet, filled with Bella. All of me is Bella. For a long time I've been Ella-Bella. And now I hate Lauren. I hate her more than anyone right at this moment. I cannot lose control here in public, but I cannot look at her either.

"You have no idea," I tell her. "You have no idea at all what you've done. None. Oh, fucking hell, Lauren."

I want to say more, but I can't because everything that has kept me strong has funneled itself into anger and I am white hot and my ears are ringing and my eyes are going and I have nothing left. I can't do this anymore. The monster is going to find me. The monster is part of me. The monster is coming.

I turn and run. I run down the stairs, past the other dance floor, and follow the sign to the exit. I have to pay for my drinks before I can go. Then I am out on the street by the line of people, and I don't know where to go or what to do but I know I can't stay at the Favela English School any longer. I'll need to move before she gets here.

My head is ringing. My vision is going. My mother is coming, and even my demon has no idea what to do.

She grabs me by the arm and pulls me to a table and pushes me down so I'm sitting in a chair. She reaches across and holds me and pats my hair. I know what I am really hiding from now. I should have known I couldn't shut it out. We are out on the sidewalk, a few yards from the people who are still lining up to get into the samba club.

Jasmine and Lauren have actually heard Amanda Hinchcliffe's voice on the phone. That is impossible. I grew inside her, and she called them and they spoke to her, about me.

That

is

contact.

It's contact between my birth mother and her lost baby.

I cannot control myself.

I don't think I will ever be able to control myself again.

"It's OK, Jo."

The person stroking my hair comes into focus, and I see that Jasmine is here. She followed me, and she is looking out for me, but I can't let her because Bella might hurt her. Jasmine's long hair, loose from her bun, tickles my face as she leans over. I lean away. I have to hurt myself so I won't hurt her.

"It's OK, Jo," she says again. "Don't worry. Whatever it is, we'll make it all right. I promise."

"You can't. I have to go. I think she's found me." I can barely speak through my sobs. My plastic chair is wobbling back and forth, one of its legs shorter than the others.

"Who's found you?"

"That woman."

She doesn't ask any more, and I don't say anything. Jasmine hands me a pile of tiny squares of tissue that they have in dispensers on café tables, and I try to compose myself a bit, watching the tissue disintegrate into papier-mâché on my fingers.

"Sorry," I say. "It's your birthday. You should be in there, having fun."

She rubs my back. Her hand is reassuring.

"As if I'm going to let you run away out into the night in this state. Honestly, Jo. I'm so sorry that we upset you. Lauren and me. I didn't mean to, and I know Lauren didn't either."

"It's not you," I say. "It's me." I stop and laugh at the triteness of the phrase. Nothing is coming out right. "Oh, Jasmine. I'm so scared. I'm so so scared." I take another tissue from her and wipe it carefully along the underneath of my eye.

"Who is she?"

A waiter is standing beside us. I don't want a drink, but Jasmine asks for two caipirinhas and then he goes. I dab at my eyes a bit more and try to take control of myself, but it's difficult because I keep hearing Lauren's clipped voice saying, *I was trying to be helpful.*

I need to get away quickly because she knows where I am. I cannot let her walk in. I cannot I cannot I cannot. I can never see that woman.

Never.

Never.

Never.

Never.

N

e

v

e

r.

The drinks arrive. I don't want it but I take a sip anyway. It tastes like rocket fuel, and I know I'm going to be sick. I stand up and look around. It is a hot night and we are outside and there are too many people. I turn and run into the building and look around for the bathroom and see a sign pointing up the stairs. There is an empty stall, and it smells and the flusher isn't working and it's blocked with paper, but I lean over it and am noisily, hugely sick.

My soul, my future, my happiness all pour out of me, down the toilet.

Jasmine's hands rub my back. I didn't know she was following me.

"There you go," she says. "It's OK, Jo."

I cannot speak or look around. I just feel her hands and hear her taking care of me. The place stinks even more now, and I want water and I want to be in bed and I want to sleep and to be safe and I don't know what I want.

After a while I stand up. She squeezes my hand. "Come on," she says. "I'll pay for those drinks, and then we'd better go."

We walk together down the street, past the line of people waiting to go dancing in the heady Rio night. It doesn't take long, and then we are in proper Lapa, in the same places I went to with Christian. I am wobbly.

"I need to go away," I say. "From here. Right away."

"Do you? Where to?"

I shrug. "North, I think. North Brazil."

"You can come to Ecuador with me if you like."

I manage a smile. "Thank you. I'd need to get a new passport. But she'd still find me."

"Who is she?" Jasmine asks again.

My. Mother. I can't say those words.

"A monster," I say instead. "A monster who is coming after me."

CHAPTER EIGHTEEN

I AM UP early in spite of my hangover. I watch Jasmine sleeping, and I envy her calm face and the way she breathes so evenly. I owe her a massive explanation after last night. I think I'm going to tell her everything. I creep out of the room to make myself a coffee and to plan my escape. Everyone knows I'm Ella now. Amanda Hinchcliffe knows I'm here.

I take a Brazil guidebook and sit on a tiny chair in the classroom and wait for the aspirin I took to kick in. I try to shut it all away, but the fact remains: my birth mother, who went to prison for seventeen years, knows where I am. She paid for me to be here, and she's been calling for me, and I have to go. I need to pack up my few things and leave this place right now.

But she'll follow. If I don't turn and face her, she'll follow me. I am hidden here but she still found me.

I open the book at random. Salvador sounds like an interesting city. I could go there and find some work and . . .

I sigh. I cannot really turn up in a strange Brazilian city or go to Ecuador with Jasmine, with a limited grasp of the language, without a plan. I can't run away forever, and I don't have much money left.

12
HOURS
UNTIL
SHE
DIES

Things don't actually work like that. If I'm running away from here, then the place to go is to Florida, and love.

So I'll need a passport.

Ben comes into the room and says, "Morning, Jo! You're up earlier than you should be, surely?"

"Do you know anyone in Salvador?" I say.

"Salvador?" He sits on the table beside me. "Are you on the move?"

"Not sure. I might be."

"Just when your mum's paid all that money?" He sees me flinch and shakes his head. "Sure—I'll see if I can do anything. I don't know anyone up there doing what we do here, but I'll do some research. I'd happily give you a reference. You should think about getting TEFL certification, you know."

"Thank you."

I won't really go to Salvador, but now Ben might tell anyone who asks that I was thinking about it.

Because it's Saturday, there's just a class of teenagers to teach at ten, and then I'm free, and after I've had a proper conversation with Jasmine, that is when I'll leave.

Lauren teaches with me, but we ignore each other as best we can, and the moment the students have left, she goes out. Jasmine's not up yet. I will be embarrassed to see her, but I know I have to tell her a version of my full story now.

The school's computer is in the back room. I have not done this since Paqueta, but I take a deep breath and type the name of my birth mother into the search engine.

Amanda

Hinchcliffe.

I hate those words. I cannot bear writing them, and I hate the words that come up. I also hate the pictures. I need, however, to have a closer look at them. I need to have an idea of what she might look like, in case she comes in here to find me.

I am looking for pictures of her on her release from prison, but no matter how many pages of Google images I look through, they are all old ones. In the end I read some articles instead and discover that she has been "given a new identity" because public feeling about her crimes is too intense for her to be able to live safely.

There are no photographs of what she looks like now, so I have to look at her when she was seventeen. She was younger than I am now when she was arrested, and eighteen when she went to prison. When she was my age, she was heavily pregnant. Now that I'm that age, I am living under an assumed name in Brazil. That's definitely a thing that criminals do: perhaps, no matter how hard I try to get away, we will always be alike.

That thought is enough to propel me into fury.

I am like my mother. I smashed a bird apart with a hammer not so long ago. I slashed a man across his face.

I am nothing like my mother.

I am not I am not I am not.

YOU ARE.

I don't want to be.

I stare at the photos. When I did this before, I was looking for signs of myself in her face. This time I am looking for signs of anyone I have ever met since I've lived in Brazil, or even before the Blacks whisked me away here.

I stare at the grainy pictures, and it is difficult to tell anything, really. She could have made the calls and paid the money from anywhere. If she were here, she would have come to find me by now.

I read old articles about her life before she went to prison. She was the eldest of three children, with a younger brother and sister and an abusive father. She met Billy Carr (but I skip over him and everything about him and I always will) when she was fifteen. Together they did the bad things.

If I let myself think about the things they did, I will never think of anything else. If I think about the fact that I was there—embryonic and innocent, but me, and on their side—then I will never be able to live a life.

"Oh," says a voice behind me, and it's Jasmine. "That's that woman, isn't it?"

"What's that?" I say. Jasmine has caught me looking at my birth mother. She knows who she is. "That woman." That woman from the news. That woman who did the killing.

"That woman. That's an old picture, but isn't it the woman from, you know, the café?"

Jasmine is pointing vaguely to the outside world, in the direction of the Estrada de Gávea. I turn and look at her, at Jasmine, at my friend. Her face is open, and she's smiling a little bit. She's not working today, so she is dressed in a black dress and strappy sandals.

I hear the class next door singing the ABC song.

Jasmine pulls up a chair and sits down beside me.

"What are you looking at this for?" she says, coming closer. "Oh, God, is she from *prison*?"

"Wait, what do you mean, the woman from the café?" I don't

understand what she's saying. I hear my voice sounding light and casual, which is odd.

"Oh, you know. She stopped me in the street a few weeks ago and asked where the language school is. She's always around the place. Big woman."

I stare at Amanda Hinchcliffe's face.

I think of the large woman.

I stare at her face.

I think of the woman.

I stare.

It doesn't make any sense, but the thing that Jasmine saw instantly is there: they are the same person. She has put on weight. I guess prisoners probably don't actually spend their time doing push-ups in their cells and walking quickly around a yard. She has the same face now as she had back then, and parts of it are my face. I never noticed it even though Jasmine did.

I scroll back, mentally, through the times I've seen that woman. She was there when I was homeless. She was there when I met Ana and came here for the first time. She is always around, sitting in cafés drinking coffee, watching, half smiling. I thought she was a local. I was going to strike up a conversation with her in Portuguese.

"Fucking hell," I say, and Jasmine looks toward the classroom, but they won't have heard me because they're chanting the colors. "Jasmine. Look. I promised I'd tell you the truth, and I will."

Jasmine is rubbing my shoulders, and just for a second I lean back and let it happen. Then I tell her everything, and I don't leave anything out.

I tell her my name is Ella Black, and that a month ago I had purple hair, and then I tell her all the things that are harder to say than those things are. I tell her that I was unhappy at home, that my only friends were Lily and my gay boyfriend, Jack. I tell her a bit about Bella. People start to come in and use the office, so we move upstairs to our bedroom, and I talk about the mysterious dash to Rio and show her the photograph of Christian and me, dancing in the street. I tell her that I found out I was adopted, and attacked my mother, and then found out who I was adopted from. I tell her that I slept on the streets and a man grabbed me by the ankle and I stole a bag from the beach.

I tell her that the monster is my mother.

As I speak, I try to stay calm, because Jasmine is there, listening to every word I say, biting her lip and not shrieking or looking horrified that she's shared a room with me for all this time and lent me her things and made me coffee when I most needed it. I know that Bella is in me, but she doesn't need to take me over yet. Bella is saving herself for later. I know that.

"So," says Jasmine, and she is so gorgeously calm about it all that I want to hug her. "What do you want to do?"

I take some deep breaths.

FIND THE WOMAN.

Later.

WE HAVE TO FIND HER.

I know we do.

OK. LET'S DO IT.

I can't fly into a rage and attack the woman, because that would make me as bad as she is. However, I'm going to find her.

"I'm going to go and look for her," I say.

"I'll come with you."

. . .

For once she isn't at the coffee shop. She isn't at the other café either. We walk down the hill, but we don't see her. That woman is the only person who has always been around: she is the first "local" person I recognized. And now she's not here.

"We'll find her," says Jasmine. She walks over to the nearest motorbike taxi and starts talking in her basic Portuguese, miming someone larger than herself, asking where she is. The guy shrugs and asks his friend. I sit at a table in the Super Sucos, overwhelmed. This happened quickly, and I cannot get my head around it. Perhaps this woman is not, in fact, Amanda Hinchcliffe. How could she have known I was here when no one else did? Surely she's not allowed to get out of prison and go straight to Brazil. I can't begin to make any sense of it.

The motorbike taxi guys are talking about her. They do, at least, seem to know who Jasmine is looking for. One of the waitresses from Super Sucos gets involved in the discussion. I don't tune in closely. I would only understand half of it anyway. I know enough to know that Jasmine hasn't told them why we're looking for that woman.

"We need to go up past the welder and turn left," she says, when she comes back to me. I stand up, and we do. We walk up the hill to the welder and turn left and walk for a little bit. After a while we see an elderly woman sitting on her doorstep with a baby on her knee. Jasmine asks her whether she's seen a woman who speaks English and is quite big anywhere around here. The woman nods and points and explains something too quickly for us to understand, but in the end I manage to catch a few words. We do our best to follow her instructions, all the way to a tiny alley with a sign that reads "Pensão."

I am standing in front of the place where this woman might actually be. I stare at it.

"Give it a shot?" says Jasmine. "*Pensão* means guesthouse. So we could go in and ask. If you want to."

I open my mouth to reply, but nothing comes out, so I take a deep breath and nod, and then I force some breath out of my lungs and say, "I want to."

Jasmine takes my hand and squeezes it. I squeeze back.

"Thank you," I whisper.

"She might not be here," says Jasmine. "But she might. It's worth a try. I think you have to see her, don't you?"

"Yes."

My legs tremble as we walk up the path. I can't knock on the door, so Jasmine does it, and there's a woman standing there who is not the woman we're looking for. This woman asks if we want a room and Jasmine says yes, and I don't know why she does that but I follow them in. The landlady is talking, showing us stuff. She takes us into a room with two beds in it and points to things, and although she's talking slowly because we're foreign and although I can understand what she's saying, I don't focus. I slip away, out the door, and look around.

There is a bathroom. It's small and clean and white. I push another door and walk into a kitchen, which is empty, with a pot bubbling on the stove. The door next to it is a bedroom, perfectly tidy with the sheets pulled tightly over the bed.

Then I push the door next to it.

And I stop, and I stare. The ringing in my head is so intense that I can't do anything except stand there. My vision is blotchy around the edges when all I want is to focus.

. . .

You don't need to do this. You don't need to take control. We can do this together.

GO IN.

Yes.

JOINING FORCES?

Yes.

WE'LL SORT THIS OUT.

Together.

The other rooms here were immaculate. This one is quite messy.

That is not the thing.

There are clothes spilling out of a suitcase.

That is not the thing.

There is a glass of water beside the bed, a book of meditations, a bead necklace, a tiny teddy bear.

Those are not the things.

The walls. The walls are the thing.

The person who lives in this room has covered the walls, which are wallpapered in green and white. She has covered them with pictures.

She has covered the walls with

pictures

of

me.

I stand, swaying, and stare at the largest photo on the wall opposite me. It is a photograph of me when I was Ella Black. I know when it was taken. I am wearing my school uniform, and I am smiling at a camera and holding a little cup.

I won that cup for cross-country, and a girl named Margot, who came in second, was furious with me. The photo was on my school's website: I have never had an actual copy of it. Amanda Hinchcliffe has printed my photo from the school website. I am trying to remember whether my name was on it. I think it was: it was from a "news" section, because my victory in the cross-country made the news.

I am trying to remember, because this feels important. Did this picture say "Ella Black" underneath it? I cannot be sure. If it said "Ella Black," she could have googled me and found it, but if it didn't, she could only have found it by knowing my school and what I looked like, and monitoring the website for sightings of me.

This whole room is evidence. The person who lives here is obsessed with me in all my incarnations. Ms. Hinchcliffe was so desperate to see me that the Blacks moved across the world to get me away from her. This is Amanda Hinchcliffe's room.

She lives here. She is not here now, but she lives here. She followed me. She found me when almost no one else could. She has never spoken to me, but she could have. She could have done anything to me she wanted. Anything at all.

There are pictures of me everywhere. Some are posed (me in a school photo; me smiling into the camera on Copacabana, in the picture that I last saw in the newspaper at that other guesthouse), but more of them are not. I see myself getting out of Fiona Black's car in my school uniform, walking down the street with Lily, and hand in hand with Jack, my lovely fake boyfriend.

There I am in Rio, but still Ella, with purple hair. I am sitting sketching on the beach while the Blacks are fuzzy in the background, talking to each other. I am sitting at a bar looking bored, with the two of them on either side of me.

There is no picture here of me joining the zombie parade, or on Paqueta. But there is one photograph of me homeless. I am on the beach that I now know as São Conrado, sleeping. That must have been around the time that my money was stolen.

She stole my money. She might have stolen my money.

No.

With a startling clarity, I realize she gave me those cheese balls. She was my benefactor.

I feel sick.

There are a couple of photos of me in my Favela English School uniform, and that is all. After that, I suppose, she knew where I was, and then she didn't need to stalk me and take photographs anymore because she could just look at me in real life.

She does not get to do this.

She doesn't get to be my mother.

You don't get to do this.

You don't get to be my mother.

I am saying the words under my breath, and then I am in the room, tearing the pictures down, ripping them apart and throwing the pieces all over her stupid bed. I tear every picture of myself off the wall. I don't care that the woman whose house this is is shouting at me to stop, or that Jasmine is standing there not really knowing what to do. I can't stop, and it's the whole of me because Bella has joined forces with me, and I don't try to stop myself, because I don't want to. I shake the hands off when they touch me. Every picture of me has to be off this wall because I don't belong to her. She doesn't get to lie in her bed and look at my face and pretend I'm her baby.

In the corner of the room, by the table, is a really bad drawing of a baby. She didn't have a photo of me, so she drew me, her lost baby. That makes me pause for a second, giving Jasmine enough time to grab my arm and lead me out of the room. The woman who owns the place is yelling at me.

WE NEED TO STAY. WE HAVE TO DESTROY EVERYTHING.
We can't.
WE SHOULD. TO SHOW HER WE DON'T BELONG TO HER.
But I feel too sad.
I KNOW.
ME TOO.

Someone took those pictures, and I never noticed them. She had someone on the outside taking my photograph, and I never had any idea. No wonder the Blacks had all that security. I wonder whether they saw people taking my photo, whether they suspected this might be happening.

I long for my real parents, the ones who took care of me my whole life.

I am lost.

I

am

lost.

Jasmine is talking to the landlady, explaining that I am the girl in the photographs, and the landlady says she already knew that because there aren't many baldish white girls around the place. She is talking fast, but I'm not listening.

The door opens.

She is there.

CHAPTER NINETEEN

I SEE BITS of myself in her face. This is my birth mother.

"Jo," she says.

"Ella," I say.

We stare at each other. I don't know what to do. Bella is coursing around me, raging, and I have an internal argument while I'm staring.

LET'S JUST SMASH HER UP.

We can't.

WE CAN.

We can't.

WHY?

Because then we'd be just like her.

That stops it: even Bella doesn't want to lunge at her now. I don't want to turn her inward and hurt myself, either.

Jasmine takes my hand and squeezes it hard. I let her do that. I am staring into Amanda Hinchcliffe's eyes, and she is smiling at me.

"But you're Jo," she says, and her voice is soft and different from the way I thought it would be. "You're my Jolene."

I cannot say a word. I am not her Jolene.

"My baby," she says.

I am not her baby. I was, though. Once.

I walk out of the door and down the alley and away from her.

Bella knows she can't attack this woman, but as soon as we are out the door, bad things start to happen. It's not like I can't control myself, because I can, these days. I have had to incorporate my Bella into my being, just to get through. I've found a way to use her strength, I think, for survival. That's why I've felt like a whole person, for the first time in my life.

But I cannot cope with this. Neither part of me can deal with seeing my birth mother. I walk along the alley, away from the guesthouse, away from that woman, who isn't coming after me, away from my wonderful Jasmine, away from the poor landlady. I don't know where I'm going. I know I can't hurt anyone, or I would be like her. I know I can't kill myself because I tried that before and I couldn't do it. I know I can't run off and live off my wits, because I did that and it wasn't fun. I can't go back to the Blacks either. Not now, not like this.

When I get to a bigger road, I walk upward, up to the top of the hill. This is where the drug dealers live. I keep walking to the very top. It's not sunny today. There are clouds in the sky. No one would expect me to be here. I hope they won't look for me here. I can see rain forest on the other hills, and I can see a distant Christ the Redeemer, with his back to me.

I sit down at the edge of a stony path and just stare out at Rio. It's wonderful, beautiful, alive. It's everything I imagined it to be and a million things more. I take a sharp stone in my hand and draw shapes in the sand. Drawing calms me down. It always has. That's why I do it.

But I can't go back to my old self.

I don't know what to do.

CHAPTER TWENTY

I THOUGHT THE large woman was a local person who watched the world go by. I used to think that one day I would talk to her, now that I could speak some Portuguese. I didn't think she would speak English, because she looked like someone who had been in the favela, drinking coffee, part of the scenery, for her whole life.

I never thought for a moment that she could possibly be Amanda Hinchcliffe. She looks nothing like the teenager in the newspaper clippings, to my eye. She looks nothing like the mother in my head. She is not actually gigantically fat, but she looks much older than thirty-six. Her eyes are sad, and her face is jowly, and she wears shapeless clothes that make her look much bigger than she is. She looks like a woman who has had a hard life. Not a murderer, not a released prisoner, not my mum.

We sit opposite each other in the Super Sucos. The air is hot and heavy: there will be a storm later. Jasmine is nearby, poised. I stare at Amanda Hinchcliffe. She has a mole on the side of her face with a little hair growing out of it. Her hair is short and thick. It's not as short as mine. I look at her nose. I know it's like mine. I check my lines of escape again. I can leave easily. I can get out of this place and vanish back into the favela in no time. I can run faster than she can, particularly uphill.

But first, I have a lot of things I need to know, and I'm never going to get another chance to ask her, because I cannot see her ever again, after today.

"Jo," she says, and her voice catches. I see myself in her eyes. In the weirdest, most disturbing way, meeting her is like coming home. I know that this is where I grew from an embryo into a fetus, into a baby. I know this is the first person I ever saw. I know it.

I know that this is my curse.

They took me from her arms and they gave me to the Blacks, but this woman is my birth mother. I don't know what I feel, apart from the certainty. I can hardly believe that the woman in front of me, the woman I have seen almost every time I have ventured out of the school, just sitting at a table or walking slowly up and down the hill, is the woman who conceived me in between murders.

"Did you name me Jolene?" That is the first thing I need to know.

She smiles. She is just staring at my face and smiling. It's horrible.

"Yes," she says. "Jolene. I liked to listen to Dolly Parton. I always loved Dolly. You know the song? It was old before you were born. It was old before I was born, too. And then you called yourself Jo. It was a sign, my little chick."

"It is not a sign and I am not your chick. You did that, didn't you? You left me food and money on the beach. You wrote 'to Jo' on the bag. That's why I called myself Jo. It's not some mystical sign. I would have picked another name if I'd known."

She is unbothered by that. I hate her. I hate her, but I can't take my eyes off her. This is like a horror film come true. The monster is sitting opposite me and calling me Jolene and I can't look away.

"How did you find me?" That is the other thing I need to know. "How did you do that? You were here when I was sleeping on the beach. You found me easily when no one else did."

"I stopped that man from attacking you," she says. "Do you remember?"

I close my eyes. The man who grabbed me by the ankle. Of course I remember. I nod the tiniest nod. I am not going to thank her. I remember her voice, yelling at him in English. She has been watching me, all this time. Every single moment.

All this time.

Like a cat with a mouse.

Like a cat with a baby bird.

"How did you find me?"

She sighs and finally looks away. She is evasive.

"Do you remember," she says, "when you lost your phone? Then you found it because someone handed it in to the police and they gave it back to you."

I do remember. It was annoying to lose it, then nice that somebody found it for me. I went home and Mum had it, after all. That seems less heartwarming now.

Jack and I always used to know each other's whereabouts by tracking our phones.

"You put a tracker on it?" I ask, but I already know the answer.

"My sister. Yes. She took those pictures of you. She got your phone from your bag. Just fished it out, on the bus. It's easy to do it, if you know what you're doing. She has a friend who knows what he's doing with the technology side of it. We knew they'd take you away from me when I got out. I had to see you, my chickie. I had to. You see . . ."

I don't see anything. "So you knew as soon as I was in Rio."

"Yes we did."

"And you came here."

"I only needed to see you. I'm not going to be around much longer. You see, I'm ill, and—"

I don't want to hear her stories. I am incandescent with rage. Everything about me is boiling over. I'm entirely on Team Bella. This woman has broken the law a million times over and I can send her back to prison and I will. I will. The police will be on my side now.

The blood is pounding through my body. I am hot all the way through, to the core, and Bella wants to reach across and push her to the ground and smash her with a hammer like she smashed that bird.

"You got someone to put software on my phone so you'd always know where I was. If I'd thrown it away in Paqueta, you wouldn't have found me here."

"No, I wouldn't have. And that would have been a shame for you, my chickie, because I did help you out as best I could. I chased off the man. I gave you that food. I paid the money for the English school."

I want to say it would not have been a shame for me, because I never wanted anything from her, but I don't say anything. She sees me hesitating and jumps in.

"Jo. Jo, I've been waiting all your life to talk to you. I'm so sorry, but I had to. I don't know if you'll believe me, but everything I've done has been for you, as best I could. It wasn't much."

"No, it wasn't."

"I didn't like the things we did, me and your dad. I mean, at the time it was all I knew. It was strange." She has a horrible reminiscing look on her face, and I look away. "Anyway, I couldn't let the baby be born when all that was happening. I was pleased when we were caught, for your sake."

I hate her. I hate her so much, I want her to die. I screw up my eyes and will her to stop talking. I look at Jasmine, who asks, with her face, whether I want her to call the police. We have agreed that as soon as I've found out the things I need to know, Jasmine will call them. I shake my head. Not yet.

"You had a good life. I was so proud. My sister. Audrey. She kept an eye on you. It wasn't so hard to find out where you were, not if you know people."

"She took all those photos of me."

"I wanted to look at your face. My baby girl." She reaches out to stroke my face. I lean back so she can't reach.

I am not her baby girl. I am myself, but now I don't even know who that is.

"You were doing well." She looks up. "You had a bloody amazing life. Excuse my language."

"I wasn't happy."

"You were perfect. Jo. My Jo. My Jolene grew up perfect."

"I did not."

"You would have had no life if I'd kept you. You don't understand."

I clench my fists. "I wasn't happy, though. I had a kind of . . ." I stop. "I had weird thoughts." This is the thing I need to know more than any other. "Did you—when you were doing the bad things. Did you feel like you had another self who took you over? Did you have ringing ears?"

316

She looks blank. "No. I was always myself. I did those things."

The relief is so intense that I can barely stay upright. I had no idea that that was what I wanted to ask her, but now I see that it was the only thing I really wanted to know. Bella is just mine. She's not a genetic inheritance.

My birth mother stares. Then she shakes her head and takes a deep breath.

"Let me be in your life," she says. "It wasn't my fault, not all of it. I know I can't really be your mum. Let me be a friend. I only want the best for you."

"No," I say. "Just no. I don't care if you say you're dying or whatever. I don't care. No. No. You don't get to do that. No."

I stand up. I can barely see. I have to get away from her, so I walk out of the café. I do not look back, although I want to. Part of me wants to ask a million more questions, even though I know the answers would be awful. This is too much.

I nod to Jasmine, and she gets her phone out. I can't wait. I just have to get away from Amanda Hinchcliffe, so I run down the hill.

There is no taxi, and I can't get on the bus that's waiting there because she might get on it too and then I would be trapped, so I decide to keep walking. I walk toward the tunnel so I will be able to flag down a cab as soon as one arrives.

When I look around, she is coming after me. Her face is crumpled, and she looks distraught. I think of the women who felt sorry for her, the ones she lured to their deaths, and I keep walking, toward the mouth of the tunnel.

"Jo!" she shouts. "Jo. Just wait a minute."

I don't. I keep going. I need to get away from her.

"Jo." She has nearly caught up, right at the mouth of the tunnel. Cars come out of it fast, then slow down if they're stopping at Rocinha. They whizz by so quickly that I feel the wind in my fuzzy hair. She grabs my arm, and I try to pull away, but I can't because her grip is very strong. "Jo. Listen. You don't have to see me. You can do what you like. I just needed to see you, and I promise I'm ill and I won't be around for much longer. Just . . . just know that I love you. I've thought of you every day. I was your age when I went to prison, and I've been there all your life and it's . . . well, I got out and I came straight to get you. Audrey and I got a different passport—you don't need to know. Just know that I would do anything for you. I'd die for you, Jolene. If you need anything, tell me. I'll get it for you. I'll get you whatever you want. I need to give you eighteen years of birthday and Christmas presents."

"You don't. Please don't."

"I want to. You're a better girl than I ever was. Just—live your life. Live it and do things and be happy. Don't put your trust in a man. Look forward, not back. My Jo. You can do anything."

I cannot stand the greeting-card sentiments. I know she is trying to say things that are important to her, but I cannot listen. I have nowhere to go, and so I run into the tunnel. There is actually a little sidewalk in here, and I run along it at the side of the road, hoping that she will not follow. I will run through here and out the other side, and then I will find a cab and get away.

I am not looking back. The traffic fumes are making me choke. The car headlights dazzle me. The sound of all the engines is amplified and it fills my ears, so even if she was running up behind me shouting, I wouldn't be able to hear her.

I don't know for sure that she's there until she grabs my arm.

"Jo," she says. "I'm sorry. I'm sorry for being me. Just let me hug you. Just one hug."

She attempts to grab me in both her arms. She pulls me toward her. I try to escape from it. This is insane: we are in a tunnel that is clearly marked "No Pedestrians." I see a police car coming the other way slow down opposite us, and then speed up. It's going to do a U-turn and come to rescue me. Another siren sounds from the other direction. I am finally ready for the police.

I pull away. She tries to grab me again. I step backward, desperate to get away from her more than anything else in the world.

It happens fast. There is the long note of a car horn. The screeching of brakes. Her grip on my arm pulling me back, shoving me into the wall of the tunnel so that I hit my head. A thump and a thud and an echoing crash of cars driving into each other.

Then there is just me, and I am standing with my back to the tunnel wall. She is lying in the road, and most of the cars are swerving to avoid the pileup and just continuing on in the other lane.

Then the siren is deafeningly loud, and there are more police.

I sit down and try to breathe.

She did say she would die for me.

Dear Fiona and Graham,

Thank you so much for your e-mail. I was really happy to get it this morning and incredibly pleased to hear from you both sounding kind of upbeat. I'm glad Humphrey is OK. Give him a big kiss from me and tell him that, no matter what he might think, I actually haven't forgotten him. And the same goes for you two. Thank you for the photo of the three of you. I'll print it out when I can.

Life here is good. Who would have thought I'd still be living in Rio? I bet you regret bringing me here.

I know we've been in touch more and more lately, and now I want to say a few things, because I've been thinking about them a lot. You can stop reading now if you want. It might be easier for you. If you want to come back and read it another time, then do that.

I try not to think about the past and my origins and all of that, because honestly if I start thinking about it, then I never stop and I get sucked into all sorts of destructive stuff. But I'd like to get this down, and then maybe we can never talk about it again.

You did an amazing thing nineteen years ago. You adopted a baby from the middle of something unspeakable, and you gave her a home and all the love in the world. You did everything you could possibly have done for me. You gave me a home and nutritious food and a family and an education. You protected me: you protected me like mad because you knew the dangers that had surrounded me. You knew what I'd been part of, before I was born. If it hadn't been for you—well, I don't know what would have happened to me because I would have been adopted by someone else. You did a lot for me, and any other couple might not have been so nice.

So—thank you for that. Sincerely, and with all of myself. I mean it.

I wish you'd told me once I was a little older, though. That will always be the thing, and I will never quite get past it. You knew the day would come when I'd find out, and you must have known that the longer you left it, the worse it would be. An adult needs a birth certificate from time to time. I bet you kind of pushed the issue aside through my childhood thinking *It'll be OK* and *We'll tell her later*. But it was always going to happen, and truly, the longer you left it, the worse it was going to be, and then it was bad, wasn't it? You took me to Rio, and my birth mother tracked me there because her sister had stolen my phone, and then it all blew up and I'm still here.

I know it was difficult when I saw you before you went home. Fiona, I realize that the way this happened has been devastating. I wish I could be your real daughter. I wish I could have said it was all OK, that we could go home and I'd take my exams and we'd go back to normal but with no secrets this time. I do wish that. I hate to think of you at home, pacing about, just waiting for me the way you used to do when I was at school.

But . . . although things can't be the same, maybe they can be different than they are now. It'll be New Year soon, and this could be a year when we see each other. I'm studying online (and I am doing a much better picture of Rio than the one I did for GCSE, that's for sure). I'll decide where to apply to university soon. I do appreciate your offers of financial help. I'll pay you back, I promise. I don't even know which country to study in, let alone anything else. But I'll probably stay in Brazil if I can; Christian is living here now, too. We're getting an apartment together in Rocinha. It's the place where I feel I belong.

And finally—this is the difficult bit.

You hid a huge thing from me, and I hid one from you too. I did everything I could to fit into the world you'd made for me. I've been seeing an English-speaking therapist out here, a friend of Maria's, and talking it through with her has made me understand a bit more. So you know how I studied hard and I had my friend Lily and my boyfriend Jack (he was never my boyfriend, btw) and I did well at school and I was never wild and never difficult? Well, that's not entirely true. I kind of separated myself into two halves, because remember that I did actually know I was adopted, because you used to tell me when I was small, but I shut it out and refused to hear it and you stopped telling me?

And what I think happened is that I resolutely made myself "good" so that you'd keep me, but then my "bad" side had nowhere to go. I separated the bad side out from myself, and kind of fenced it off, and gave it a name. I called it Bella. I know to most people that means "beautiful," but to me it means "Bad Ella." Bella would overwhelm me sometimes. I would shut myself away and give in to her. A couple of times she tried to make me hurt myself, but I could never actually do it: I lashed out instead. I killed creatures that Humphrey brought in. I broke things. I smashed things to pieces with a hammer. I destroyed my stuff.

It was getting worse. I wanted to lash out, and I was scared that I was actually going to hurt someone else, that people would see the real me and everyone would hate me. It would happen at school and I would fight myself to control it, and I know I would have failed, in the end.

And then it happened. I lashed out at you, Fiona, and then I hurt the man in the café. I will feel terrible about that for the rest of my life. The fact that you forgave me at once without question is a testament to the kind of people you are. It really is. For what it's worth, I am so, so sorry.

Then when I was alone in Rio, I used Bella's strength to get me through. She and I worked together. I know this is a lot, and it all feels very complicated, even to me, but finding out the truth about myself has helped me pull the two sides of myself together. I feel like myself now. I've never felt that before.

So—I do think of you in Kent, and I do miss you, and I would like to see you. I'm not ready to come back just yet, but could we meet next year, maybe?

Lots of love,

Ella xx

Fiona read the e-mail alone without telling Graham it had come. She could hardly breathe as she sat there, absorbing the words.

Nineteen years earlier, she'd sat in this same spot, trying to concentrate. She realized she had drawn a weird, rambling picture without meaning to: she was just sitting, waiting, and her doodle had taken on a life of its own. It had covered a whole sheet of paper. It was lines and flowers and then trees and birds and cats and waves and beaches. She was drawing everything that wasn't a baby thing. It was a strange sprawling mess that covered the paper she was supposed to keep by the phone so she could make notes if the call ever came.

Everything was riding on this. She felt certain it was their last chance. She was thirty-five, and that wasn't old. Everyone said that. You're still young, they said, as if eight miscarriages counted for nothing. She had given up on that now. It wouldn't work. Her body didn't work. She was not going to have her own baby. That was beyond any doubt.

A dark voice inside her told her it was all her fault, wanted to make her go out and do terrible things to make everyone see how messed up she was. She ignored that voice as best she could, but it had been difficult over the years. Sometimes she had to shut herself away and let it all out.

But that was over now. She was going to give a home to a baby who needed one. Or a child; everyone knew that you hardly ever got a baby. She and Graham had been through so much together, and she was constantly crippled by the thought that he could leave her and have a family with someone else, with someone whose body did work properly, someone who did not have secret horrible thoughts. But he hadn't done that, and he said he never would, and she knew he was telling the truth. They were solid. That was one thing Fiona didn't worry about.

Today, though, there had been talk of a baby. That was why she was sitting by the phone. That was why she was drawing and staring and waiting. That was why she had cleaned the house from top to bottom and done everything else she could think of until she had run out of jobs. That was why she was just gazing at the phone, waiting for something that might never happen.

If they got this child, she would look after him or her forever. She would feed them nutritious food and make sure they had everything they needed. She and Graham would send their child to a good school and make sure they were always warm, never hungry, always safe. She would do everything for this baby. He or she would always be happy, and nothing bad would ever happen.

The phone rang.